CW00819444

QUEEN BEE

NINA MANNING

Boldwood

First published in Great Britain in 2022 by Boldwood Books Ltd.

Copyright © Nina Manning, 2022

Cover Design by Head Design Ltd

Cover Photography: Shutterstock

The moral right of Nina Manning to be identified as the author of this work has been asserted in accordance with the Copyright, Designs and Patents Act 1988.

A CIP catalogue record for this book is available from the British Library.

Paperback ISBN 978-1-80162-212-7

Large Print ISBN 978-1-80162-213-4

Hardback ISBN 978-1-80162-211-0

Ebook ISBN 978-1-80162-215-8

Kindle ISBN 978-1-80162-214-1

Audio CD ISBN 978-1-80162-206-6

MP3 CD ISBN 978-1-80162-207-3

Digital audio download ISBN 978-1-80162-210-3

Boldwood Books Ltd
23 Bowerdean Street
London SW6 3TN
www.boldwoodbooks.com

For Savannah, the Queen Bee of our family.

1

10 MAY 2019 – 8.15 A.M. – GLOUCESTER POLICE STATION

Interview with Natasha Redwood, deputy head of Helesbury Primary School

I had my suspicions from the start. In my job, I interact with hundreds of people every day, you see. Something never sat quite right with me, but I couldn't ever put my finger on it. It was a gut instinct – you know that feeling? There was this void opening up between Evie and Miranda when they had previously been best friends, inseparable, for over a year. Then along comes Verity, and suddenly, Evie is a different person. So yes, if you're asking were there any clues, then, yes, of course, in hindsight – oh, the joy of hindsight! I can look back now and realise that everything that didn't add up at the time, that I pushed aside, were glaringly obvious clues. I should have said something sooner. Maybe then things would have ended differently. But you don't, do you? You ignore the clues – you always ignore them. Even when they are screaming at you in the face.

2

BEFORE

The woman walked along the beach, the wind whipping her hair across her face. She hadn't wanted to come out that morning, but when Bernie, her eight-year-old West Highland terrier, had come and sat next to her feet, looking up at her with his little watery eyes, she couldn't bear it any longer. Once in the bracing air, she hadn't felt glad that she was out in the way that people often did; she thought only of the cosy warm embers of the fire lingering in the hearth and the tin of cookies she had baked with the grandchildren two days before, now perfectly chewy and begging to be dipped into a cup of hot chocolate. But she kept pushing forward, hat pulled firmly over her ears, scarf wrapped tightly around her neck and hands stuffed firmly in her pockets.

She watched as Bernie raced ahead, sniffing in between the small wooden boats moored away on the shore near the brambles. She never understood who owned these boats – most of them looked so old and decrepit. The row of boats came to an end and then a strip of brightly coloured beach huts came into view. The woman had been intending to turn around and head back to the main path that would lead her back home to the warm fire and chocolate, but Bernie had scampered off ahead and was already at the second beach hut, sniffing and cocking his leg. The huts ran for another hundred yards or so. Only a little further – she would turn around at the end of them and head home.

She trudged reluctantly towards Bernie, who had now thankfully stopped, giving her time to catch up with him, the wind coaxing her along from behind this time. Bernie was sniffing near one particular beach hut and so the woman presumed he would take another pee and move on, but he jumped up onto the small wooden veranda – his ears pricked up, as though he were now waiting for someone to walk right out. The woman arrived next to him and noticed that this hut was one of the shabbier ones on the block. The paint had probably been a bright, bold blue once, but had now been bleached an insipid turquoise and was peeling off in strips, revealing the austere wood behind it. It was mid-January, and none of the huts along this stretch would open until at least mid-March, when the owners began getting them back into shape again for the spring and summer season. But something about this particular hut had enticed Bernie over. He wasn't any kind of working hunting dog, but occasionally something would grab his attention.

The woman stopped next to Bernie as he cocked his head from side to side the way he would when someone was talking to him in that high-pitched way people sometimes spoke to animals.

'What is it then, boy?' The woman's breath was a little short and ragged from her exertion in the winter elements. She stuffed her hands further into her pockets, the bitter unrelenting wind thrust itself at her back, and she stumbled forward, taking the four steps to join Bernie on the veranda, who was in no hurry to move. These beach huts were worth a few quid more than the ones down at the tourist beach; people paid for the luxury to be off the beaten track and away from the masses – not forgetting the extra twelve square foot and extra-large window they got for their pound. The front of the beach hut was a glass bi-folding door with a net curtain running across it – perhaps to reduce some of the light bleaching the interiors, but more likely to stop passers-by stopping and staring in.

'Come on now, Bernie. Whatever is it?' The woman crouched at her dog's side.

He cocked his head once more, left then right, as though he were following a conversation at a frequency beyond his mistress's hearing.

'We really need to be getting back now.' She patted his head and thought of the last log she had put on the fire before she left the house; it would be burnt down by now. She braced herself to stand – she wasn't putting up with this nonsense any more – but as she went to turn, she saw a flicker of something move in the corner of the window at the same time as Bernie let out a little bark. She stayed looking at the front of the beach hut; the bi-folding doors were on a latch, but there was no lock. This time, she dropped again to her knees. Then, just as though she had summoned it, the net curtain twitched. Then it moved a centimetre. And then a small hand pulled the curtain to one side, revealing the face of a child, pale faced, perhaps five or six years old. Their hair was cut jaggedly short so that it was impossible to tell if they were a boy or a girl. The woman gasped, stood and staggered backwards.

'Is your mummy or daddy there?' the woman said loudly to the window, looking around the empty beach for a sign of anyone who could claim this child as theirs. The child shook their head.

'Are you all alone?' The woman tried again.

The child nodded.

The woman grappled in her pocket for her phone and without hesitation dialled 999.

3

Dinner at mine, seven thirty? X

I pressed send on the text and waited for the reply. Anabel was eating her spaghetti and David was still at work. I had little else on that day, so I had time to wait for the reply to come back from Evie. We had made a loose arrangement to see one another that evening; I'd been having trouble finalising the specs on the recent set of candles I had created, and Evie was so good for bouncing ideas off. She was a busy mum – like we all were – but she always found time for me. Like, always. In the year since we'd met, I could count on one finger the number of times Evie had ever cancelled, and that had been with good reason – her daughter, Juno, had been throwing up all day. At forty-three, I finally felt like I was in a proper friendship – as sad as that may seem. The time and effort I had poured into female relationships in the past, only for them to turn out to be merely masquerading as friendships, was thankfully a distant memory. Pity I'd had to wait until it all blew up in my face before I discovered that. But that was then. This was a new life; this was what real companionship felt like, not one based on superficial hugs and praise.

The last year has been a new beginning for me, and I wanted to cele-

brate one whole year living in the tiny village of Helesbury, and who better
to do that with than my best friend, Evie. I had never before referred to a
grown woman as my best friend. It had always felt a little childish – adults
didn't parade around announcing to the world that they were best friends.
But I knew Evie felt the same way as me. We were both incredibly grateful
to have one another.

Evie's reply came through just as my daughter, Anabel, sucked up her
last piece of spaghetti.

Perfect, Miranda, looking forward to it x

I felt my heart swell with happiness.

'Well done, sweetheart,' I said to Anabel as she took her empty plate to
the dishwasher. Anabel had always been a good eater. From the day she
had taken her first bite of solid food just over eight years ago, I had known
she was going to be one of those kids who didn't make a fuss with her food,
and I'm not ashamed to admit there had been jealousy from other mothers
who struggled to get anything remotely healthy inside their kids, whereas
Anabel was wolfing down every fruit and veg available. I remained modest
though and tried to share any tips when asked how the hell I got a one-
year-old to eat quinoa and edamame beans – but the truth was, I was just
lucky. Lucky to have met and married David just over ten years ago, and
lucky to have our one and only daughter. Three was the magic number as
far as I was concerned.

* * *

I turned out the light in Anabel's room and blew her a final kiss just before
seven thirty, and then heard the familiar light knock on the front door. I
arrived downstairs moments later and looked at my beautiful friend, her
cheeks flushed from the walk over here in the late March wind. She pulled
off her beanie hat and her bobbed blonde hair was ruffled, yet she still
managed to look chic. We greeted one another with our usual kiss and a
hug. She smelt faintly of vanilla or coconut – I was never sure which and

had never asked her what product it was, as though asking may suddenly alter its presence in some way.

She un-swaddled herself from her oversized scarf and draped it over the banister. 'I'm so desperate for summer now.' Evie laughed in that hoarse throaty way she always did, which I found so endearing. 'I am so sick of these layers.'

I chastised David for leaving his coat flung on the banister every day when he arrived home from work, but Evie doing it felt comforting, like she was familiar enough with me and being in my home to leave her belongings where they found themselves.

We walked through into the kitchen. 'Well, I've created a little piece of the Mediterranean here tonight – a little prelude to the summer months to come.' I held my arms out to emphasise my efforts.

'Oh wow!' Evie gushed at the array of colours and textures laid out on the table. Chorizo, artichoke, yellow peppers and sun-dried tomato hummus. 'This is so beautiful. Thank you.'

She handed me a bottle of wine, still chilled, and I took down two glasses from the cupboard. 'No, Evie. Thank you.' I popped the cork and poured. 'You've been such a great friend to me this last year. I don't think I would have managed it without you.'

'Oh, you would have.' Evie took a glass and we clinked them together lightly. 'You're a very strong person. Very inspiring too.' She looked at me knowingly and I felt a flutter in my stomach. Strong was not how some would have described me before I moved here. But no one knew that side of me in Helesbury. Here, I was someone Evie looked up to. I couldn't quite believe how lucky I had been, and I knew that it had to be luck. We live in a world where anyone could find anything out about anyone at a touch of a few buttons, and yet here I was enjoying an almost entirely new life in the countryside, no one any wiser to my past. It felt like I had been reborn; as though I had been given a fresh chance with a new friend. And this time I was going to hold on to her.

'You've achieved so much in such a short space of time,' Evie continued with her praise. 'The move, getting Anabel settled, getting your business going. I mean, you launched the first village book club – which was exactly what was needed here by the way. I would have done it myself a long time ago, but I have been far too busy. Everyone loves you even more now. You're quite the queen bee. And I mean that in a good way – every tribe needs its queen.'

I felt my cheeks redden. She was only being nice and trying to flatter me, but the truth was I had realised the moment that I moved here that Evie was the most popular woman in the village, adored by all. Had I really taken her spot in such a short space of time? I had certainly no intention of moving into Evie's spot; in my eyes, she was still the most adored woman in the village.

'I'm really looking forward to book club this week.' I smiled. 'I've got so many suggestions for titles for the next few months.'

'Of course you do – and you always give great recommendations. I'm really looking forward to Thursday, too.' Evie's phone pinged from the table where she'd put it when she walked in. She picked it up and swiped the screen to open it as she continued. 'Honestly. An absolute breath of fresh air, as I said exactly what...' Evie was looking at her phone as her voice trailed away.

'Well, don't stop praising me now – I was just getting used to the compliments.' I laughed but stopped abruptly when I could see Evie wasn't laughing. 'Evie?'

Evie glanced up, but she was looking straight through me.

'Is everything okay?' I asked.

She shook her head as though dragging herself from a daydream. 'Yes, all absolutely fine. A client I've neglected, that's all.' She shoved her phone into her handbag.

I quickly searched Evie's face for the truth I was sure she was trying to hide from me. What had she seen that had caused that glimmer of concern? And more importantly, should I be worried? These days a world of information was at your fingertips through a smartphone. Had Evie seen something? Something about me?

'Anyway, here's to wonderful you and this gorgeous house. And to one year in Helesbury!'

I was thrust back into the moment by Evie's usual optimism. She held her glass out again, and I clinked it and felt the warmth in her voice. 'Cheers,' we both said in unison.

As I sipped the cool drink, I allowed myself to feel that I deserved this happiness. The past was in the past. I was here with my fabulous new friend, revelling in my new life. Things could only get better.

4

I was late for book club, which this evening was being hosted by the lovely Hatty. But I would not allow the lateness to absorb me. Back in London, no one would have batted an eyelid if I'd turned up half an hour or even an hour late – things seemed to get going a lot later there – whereas here, it was just going to be me and five other women in a kitchen in a small village on the edge of the Cotswolds. I couldn't just slip in unnoticed. It wasn't our first meeting, but I still felt I wanted – no, needed – to make a good impression. I felt as though I was on probation; one slip-up and things could come crashing down on me again. It terrified me because I knew how easily it could happen.

David had to drag me to Helesbury kicking and screaming but now he'd have a hard time getting me to leave. I'd settled in much quicker than anticipated – as though it was always meant to be – especially when I met my Evie. My sweet Evie. We'd met at the school gates, our daughters – both aged eight, going on eighteen – in the same class. Evie hadn't been living here for long when I arrived, but she had already secured her popular and well-respected status. She made me realise what friends were again.

Hatty had three boys at the local primary, whom she was raising with impeccable manners, but she was also on the PTA, volunteered once a week for the Samaritans and ran a small online hamper business. The woman was a legend. Except when it was her turn to choose books for the book club, but the less said about that, the better.

Hatty and her husband lived in the old post office, the actual post office having been incorporated into the local shop. It was a mere four-minute walk from my house, so I got to wear heels and feel a little bit glam, because that's how I like to feel. I still liked to think I had 'it', whatever *it* is. After I had Anabel, I lost all my confidence. And just as I was starting to feel more like my old self, everything fell apart and I was right back down there again. No confidence, no friends. All my own doing. And I was still repenting for those mistakes.

Being late would make me look bad, I knew it would. And the thought of people thinking badly of me made my hands go damp and my heart pound. I tried some deep breaths to calm myself down, but they didn't work, and I could feel the panic increasing even more. I'd managed to get booked in for a last-minute hair appointment at the hairdressers in Gloucester, and even though I knew it meant I might possibly be late, I wanted to enjoy that salon-fresh feeling.

The stylist had done a great job though, and my dark hair was now perfectly blow-dried and set into big, beautiful curls. I knew everyone would comment, and I'd be centre stage for a few moments. I occasionally missed the glamour of my life when we lived in Chelsea, and a new cut reminded me that I could look my best, but I didn't need to fall victim to that lifestyle, the one that had brought me here in the first place.

As my heels clicked along the road, I thought about the other women who would be there this evening. Olivia, the manager of the local library. A giant of a woman in her fifties, with grey bobbed hair, whom you wouldn't wish to cross on a dark night. Huge hands, just like a man, yet painted so delicately with red varnish. Then there's Natasha, or Tash to all her friends, who was the deputy head teacher at the primary school. Small and mouse-like – wouldn't say boo to a goose until she had to tell thirty-six seven-year-olds to sit the hell down! Then Beth, sweet little Beth. Twenty-three, a student finishing her degree yet still living at home with her parents. I was very proud of our little club; we were women of different ages and from different backgrounds coming together over a common love.

Of course, Evie and I saw each other outside of the club too, and quite regularly; we were forever popping in and out of one another's houses at the weekend. She had truly shown me what it meant to trust someone. And it had taken me a lot to trust people again.

I tried to walk as I would if I were on a busy London road, but the heels were not meant for rough, bumpy paths. I clip clopped past the church and the village hall, and then past the pub as people were beginning to dribble in for their prelude to the weekend. A few more months and we could sit out in our gardens with Pimm's in the evenings. I knew everyone would be there at Hatty's already, because it really is the highlight of the month, and I felt a swell of pride that it was me who had brought this ray of sunshine into their lives – I mean what were these women doing before I came along? I laughed with David sometimes. Then I would catch myself. I wasn't that shallow person any more. I had changed. I had been determined I would cement relationships that meant something; that weren't just for show.

I arrived at Hatty's and went to the back door as she instructs everyone to do. She has a more relaxed attitude towards visitors than me; I prefer everyone to come through the front – I didn't spend eight thousand pounds on the decoration in the hallway for people to trip over riding boots and for the scent of musty leather to get stuck in their nostrils as they trudged their way inside. I know I am trying my best to fit in, but I have certain standards I simply won't let slip.

As I opened the back door, I was welcomed by the raucous noise of ladies who have had a week of responsibilities and are now ready to let them fall by the wayside. Again, I felt a swell of pride; *I* brought us all together. As Evie told me, I was the queen bee. But I wonder if the others saw me that way too?

'Hello?' I called as I stepped over an array of school bags, shoes and what looked like a papier-mâché lobster. I didn't get a response, and instead heard a loud roar of laughter echo through from the kitchen. It jolted my body, then a ripple of annoyance ran through me; my arrival has not been heard or noticed. The annoyance grew stronger still as I almost tripped over a small plastic toy truck as I tottered down the hallway towards what Hatty referred to as the 'hub of the house'. I was annoyed that I was late for my own book club because it sounded as if everyone was already having a great time without me.

Hatty's kitchen had a certain cosy country-cottage feel about it, which, despite the mess, was always warm and welcoming. It boasted a huge red Aga against the far wall, old white and red tiles surrounded it. There was a huge white ceramic Belfast sink to the left and a large oak table in the centre with eight or nine chairs around it; drawings, bills and other papers were piled high and pushed right to the edge of the table so they teetered precariously to make room for six place settings.

I stood in the doorway and took everyone in. Beth and Tash were already seated, each with a glass of wine in hand, and Evie and Hatty were standing at the Aga. But it was the presence of another person who clearly wasn't Olivia, laughing with Evie and Hatty, glass of wine in hand, that surprised me. The laugh, which even as I came in through the back door, I knew I did not recognise. It sounded alien, hollow. My body tightened up. I stood in the doorway, the bottle of Chardonnay I had brought dripping condensation down my wrist and under the gold bracelet that David had given me for our wedding anniversary last month, and took her in. This woman, this stranger. She was unassuming; not the sort of person I would find myself drawn to or even raise my head towards if she passed me by, but somehow – there in that vast kitchen – I felt a presence about her that I couldn't put my finger on. She was a slight woman with mousy-brown shoulder-length hair cut straight at the bottom. It was sleek and straight, but naturally so. She was wearing a brown V-neck sweater and blue skinny jeans, and she was leaning in towards Evie, my Evie, who was laughing at something she had just said. Then she glanced up at me and nudged Evie.

'Miranda,' Evie said, looking up. Was it my imagination or was there a flicker of guilt across Evie's face, as though she were a small child caught with her hand in the sweetie cupboard? I smiled my best smile, but it felt awkward and forced. The other women all looked up and a ripple of hellos sounded around the room. But the atmosphere felt thick and heavy, weighted with the presence of this new person, and the entrance that would have normally seen everyone greeting me with compliments on my hair – which was the one I had been hoping for – was not to be.

'Here she is,' Hatty says blithely, turning from the Aga where there was a pot of something bubbling away. She wiped her hands on her apron, her cheeks pink from the heat of the kitchen and her red curly hair damp around her temple.

I walked round and gave Hatty a light air kiss as the others fell back into conversation. 'Lovely to see you, Hats – this all smells absolutely delicious.' I slid out of my heavy woollen jacket and placed it over the back of a chair just out of the way in the corner of the kitchen, where it wouldn't get splashed with grease.

'Wow! Look at you!' Hatty said loud enough for everyone to turn towards me. 'You put us all to shame. Look at your hair, it's so clean and bouncy!'

There were nods of approval and a big smile from Evie. 'It looks gorgeous, Miranda,' she said, and I felt some comfort from the acknowledgement of my efforts.

Evie stepped towards me and we embraced. My back was up; I knew I was stiff as I held her in my arms, and an act that would usually last several seconds was over before it had begun. I pulled my lips together and widened my eyes, ready for the introduction I sensed was coming.

'Miranda, can I introduce you to Verity.' I inched forward and put my hand out.

Verity reciprocated, placing a small, soft hand in mine. 'Hi.' She struggled to retain eye contact and stepped back towards the warmth and security of Evie's side too quickly.

'Hello.' I took a sidestep and handed the bottle of wine to Hatty, who took it with her usual flourish of gratitude. 'Pour me a large one, Hats,' I said and winked at her. She sniggered and pulled out a large wine glass from a cupboard next to the Aga. 'So, how on earth have you found yourself in this kitchen in a tiny village on the edge of Gloucestershire on a Thursday evening, Verity?' I asked as I turned back to face them.

'Verity has just moved here,' Evie offered.

'Wonderful,' I said, hoping some sincerity had found its way to my voice. But I felt cheated, hurt. I knew it was churlish, but because I'd founded the book club, I felt some ownership over the members. Why hadn't Evie mentioned there was someone new coming tonight? She was supposed to be my best friend, wasn't she? We were only just discussing book club the other day. Surely the mention of a new guest to the club I had launched would have found its way into the conversation? I was stunned, but I tried to act anything other than that.

'Yes, she just moved this week,' Evie continued.

'Fabulous.' I looked blankly at Evie and then moved my eyes to Verity, hoping I would get some response from her, as it felt as though Evie was speaking nervously on her behalf. Almost as though she felt guilty for bringing someone new tonight without even mentioning it to me. *Which she should be*, I thought. The book club didn't need more members.

I began to feel a slight panic rise within me, a fight-or-flight instinct. I had begun to feel safe amongst these women; here with a little empire that I myself had built, and now suddenly it was all thrown off kilter. Perhaps I was overreacting, and later on, when I would be lying in my huge super-king-sized bed, David sat down in the study working until midnight as he did every Thursday, I would regret the way I had handled this first-time interaction with Verity – a friend of a friend. But for now, I couldn't stop the feeling of betrayal that was flooding my body. I leant over and took the bottle of Chardonnay from the kitchen side – where Hatty had left it far too close to the Aga without a scrap of a wine cooler in sight – and topped up Verity's empty glass.

'Better drink it whilst it's cold.' I hoped this gesture would make up for my inability to embrace the situation.

Verity held her glass out and I filled it almost to the top. Hatty was a lovely host, but she lacked the details, like wine coolers, napkin rings; the sort of stuff that was second nature to me. David called me 'the hostess with the mostess', and it was true, I enjoyed looking after people. When I was a child, my parents had entertained almost every weekend. I had watched how my mother lay the table, slowly and meticulously, followed her around the kitchen as she prepped hors d'oeuvres and stirred martinis. Then she would slip out of her apron, give her hair a quick fix and greet their guests. I would sit on the corner step on the staircase, just hidden by the banister, and peek out at the most perfect view of the dining room and the hallway. Occasionally, my mother would clip-clop back through into the kitchen to bring through more wine. I was convinced I was stealthy enough not to be spotted, but when I was older, she told me she knew I was there, but she had never minded. The most important thing I had learnt from my mother was how to play the gracious host, even when the guests were less than amiable. Or when you absolutely would rather do anything but. It was exhausting, always putting on a face, pretending to others that all was well when on the inside, it often wasn't. But it was innate. It was something I simply had to do. I had seen how my mother and father hosted as a way to assure others of their happiness and stability. And I had carried on the tradition. It had been such a relief not to have had to appease anyone after we moved; all those pent-up emotions trying to burst at the seam whilst I socialised with a smile plastered across my face, hadn't been felt for over twelve months. But here I was, those same fears, emotions resurrected as I stood next to Verity. I had felt so comfortable with Hatty, Evie, Beth, Tash and Olivia. Now it all felt wrong and fake again.

I raised my glass to the newcomer. 'Cheers to you, Verity. It's lovely to see a new fresh face in the village,' I lied. 'Are you here for work or pleasure?'

I watched as Evie's mouth opened to speak, and I felt another jolt of annoyance. Was she really going to speak for Verity again? I edged myself closer to Verity, blocking Evie out of my side view.

'I am... writing a book. I'll be staying for a... while.' Verity spoke softly. I could hear a myriad of tones in her accent, but couldn't place where she was from.

'Oh, wow, so you're a writer. How fabulous. A writer in the village!' I looked around at Hatty and Evie.

'I know, isn't it exciting?' Hatty said. 'I told her she'll have to do a little talk in the village hall.'

I felt heat rising through my body at the prospect of this stranger holding the spotlight, taking it away from me. Not that I had anything to offer that was grander, but it felt as though there was suddenly a sense of competition, that I would need to up my game. What had Evie called me? *The queen bee*. To think I had laughed it off at the time. Perhaps I needed to assert myself in that role.

I took a long gulp of my wine. 'So, what sort of book are you writing?' My voice was high and stretched.

'Historical fiction,' Verity said delicately.

'How thrilling,' I said, feigning a smile and interest; historical fiction was not my idea of fun reading. I preferred a good thriller or romcom.

'I don't suppose you've read *So Lucky*, have you? It's my book choice from last month. We're discussing it tonight.'

'I don't get much time to read...' Verity trailed off. She looked over at Evie as she was speaking. I followed her gaze; Evie's expression was taught. '...Which is why I'm here. No better way to expand one's reading horizon than by joining a book club.'

I looked between the two women: one I had known for just over a year, but I considered our friendship to be a pretty solid one, and one woman I had just met this evening whom I knew nothing about. I had so many questions for her. I had felt a distinct energy when I walked through the back door and now my doubts were already being confirmed. There was a faltering in the way she had answered. I was adept at sensing these things with two socialites for parents and seeing so many parties, meeting so many artists and professors, I had observed how atmospheres changed and shifted when certain people spoke. How my mother would lift the back of her hand to her chin and brush it lightly there when she felt uncomfortable at something someone was saying, or when a man moved too close to her and broke the boundaries, causing her to shift away – always looking to my father, who was always caught up in deep conversation about his next big project. Then I would remember how I would go to my mother's bedside in the morning and be hit by a wall of stale alcohol. I would sit next to her and brush her hair as she lay in until midday. Those days had felt so glamorous to me as a child, but as I grew, I quickly saw beyond the theatre, and what lay beneath was as ugly as a bowl of bruised fruit.

Since we'd met, I had seen so many wonderful qualities in Evie, but what was becoming abundantly clear to me now was that no matter how much I tried to trust people, and let them into my life a little, they would always let me down.

'Well, it's a stonker of a book and everyone here is going to absolutely rave about it, aren't you, girls?' I said to the room.

There was a collective murmur; I tried to depict who of the four women had agreed with me.

'Well, I for one thought it was bloody brilliant,' came the voice of Olivia from the doorway. She entered the room, kissed our host first, then came to me. 'Honestly, Miranda, it was hilarious – I nearly wet myself at one point – and my tittering aggravated Angus no end. Oh, hello, who's this?' Olivia still acted as sprightly as a teenager and looked like one, this evening's outfit being pale blue denim jeans, Converse trainers and a rainbow T-shirt. Only her grey bobbed hair gave her age away. Olivia had, for a second, been my saviour, the way she had shown such an interest in the book, but now, she was just as intrigued with the mystery guest as I was.

I moved round to the table in front of Beth and Tash and sat down opposite them.

'You all right?' Tash asked casually.

'Super.' I felt my gut tighten as I spoke the word. 'Anabel loved your assembly on kindness the other day – she talked about it over dinner and again at bedtime.' Moving the attention to Tash was the only way to distract myself from what was turning into an unexpected evening.

'Oh, that's lovely to hear, Miranda.' Tash smiled. The red wine had stained her teeth. I knew she found the job as deputy head stressful at times, and she had confessed to me back when we first met that red wine was her one vice.

I tried to join in with their chat, but my gaze kept returning to Evie and now Olivia standing at the Aga with Verity.

Thoughts spiralled through my mind. Had I done the right thing by letting myself become close with another woman again? Was I setting myself up for another colossal failure? I wasn't sure my mind could take it if something went wrong, if I was forced into a situation to try and protect myself. The one thing I had promised myself was that I would not allow it to happen again.

5

BEFORE

The woman stepped back as the female police officer took the child – a girl – by the hand. The male police officer also moved away as the girl smiled, exited the hut and seemed to welcome the embrace of a stranger. The policewoman thanked the woman and asked her name.

'Diana. I live just on the other side of the cliffs. Do you think she's okay? Has she been abandoned?'

'It's hard to tell,' the policewoman said. 'But she shouldn't be here all alone at her age, that's for sure. We'll take her to the station, get her a nice warm drink and then social services will take it from there.'

'Oh,' said Diana. 'Such a terrible shame. What kind of parents could leave a child locked in a beach hut?'

The policewoman drew the child closer to her and placed a reassuring arm around her. 'Who knows? There are all sorts out there. Some things you wouldn't even believe.'

Diana shuddered. 'I'm sure.'

'Thank you for calling us. Who knows what might have happened if you hadn't spotted her?'

'I have Bernie to thank. He sensed someone was in there.'

The policewoman bent down and patted the little terrier on the head. 'What a clever dog.'

'Yes, yes, he is.' Diana wasn't looking at Bernie, but at the child, who was staring at the beach hut. The police officer held her arm securely over the child's shoulder, the other hand stroking Bernie behind the ears.

'Can you make sure you give your details to my colleague,' she said as she stood up again, 'so if we need to contact you for anything, we can get in touch?'

'I will. Thank you.' Diana took one more look at the child. The policeman, who'd been to their car, was back with a blanket, and it was now being wrapped around the child.

With a final nod to Diana, the police officers began escorting the little girl to the car. The child walked willingly, not a flicker of concern or fear on her face.

6

Interview with Hatty Whilloby

Did I like her straight away? Of course, I did. I'm that sort of person, wear my heart on my sleeve, always looking for the good in people. She was so pretty and down to earth. I thought she was exactly what this village needed. But I sensed right from the start – literally the second Miranda walked through my back door on that evening – that she had her heckles up. I felt the tension all night. Bless her, poor Miranda tried to conceal her jealously, but she just couldn't manage it. She and Evie had become good friends really quickly – I mean, we all warmed to Miranda so much when she moved here from Chelsea.

I'm a mum, a wife, I'm part of the PTA; I have a lot on. There is no way I would have had the time or the inclination to do what Miranda was doing. Of course, now we know, I can see it all for what it is. But no, I wouldn't have thought it, not in a million years – and believe me, I've seen a lot in my time – that something so shocking was going on right under our noses. I just wish we hadn't sat on the sidelines and watched it all happen. I wish I could turn back the clock and have been a better friend. But that's the joy of hindsight, isn't it?

7

I had barely eaten any of the dinner at Hatty's last night that she had so lovingly prepared. It had been a thick, hearty meal: a beef stew with creamy mash and green beans. I ate lots of green beans, but only a little meat and a mouthful of mash, because every time I tried to swallow, it felt as though the food was stuck in the back of my throat because as I ate, my gaze kept falling on Verity.

She said very little throughout the meal, and when she did speak, she used just a few words. I was on edge as I sat there in Hatty's kitchen. Everything before had felt so settled, yet within the space of a day, it had become messy. If this Verity was to become a permanent fixture in the village, would I be willing to share Evie with her? I kept imagining scenarios of confrontation with Evie about my true feelings for Verity. I was pre-empting the future. I didn't want to feel that way, I just needed to know that everything was going to be as it was between Evie and me, that nothing would change. I had never been very good at competing; I was a very sore loser.

Was it so selfish of me to just want Evie to myself? Things always get so complicated when women's friendship groups begin to grow. Meetings would start off with just two, then slowly but surely, someone would introduce a friend to the group. All perfectly innocent, of course. 'Oh, I'm bringing my friend, Sally, on Saturday. You don't mind, do you?' Then before you know it, Sally's brought her yoga chum along too, then she's brought her sister. Soon enough, what was once a small, secure and civilised gathering is now overflowing with women who have very little in common.

I felt I had done so well up until now, making friends with Evie and the other girls. Everything felt right and simple. I knew that my past mistakes wouldn't be exposed with these girls; I was safe. So why did I feel so on edge around Verity? As though she might be the one to suddenly upset the applecart. I had tried to envisage Evie, Verity and I as a threesome, but even that didn't sit right with me. Had I sensed something about Verity that I didn't like? I was too afraid to admit it to myself. If there was any hint of a negative thought, I needed to push it away before it carried me away. This world I had built here for David, Anabel and me was because of what I had made happen before. I'd already had my second chance. There certainly wouldn't be a third one.

So, instead of relaxing at book club last night with the small select few, I found I kept watching Evie to see how she responded to Verity, to see if her eyes lit up with interest at anything she said – which was very little. I tried to hang around at the end to subtly quiz Evie, but she said she had to dash off for the babysitter. Verity had already left half an hour before her, having said she was tired and needed an early night.

I couldn't even enjoy the fact that, in the end – as it turned out – everyone loved my book choice and raved about it. I was too exasperated by this new woman in Hatty's kitchen. Suddenly, seven, which I had once considered lucky, now seemed such an ugly number.

* * *

After a terrible night's sleep, I found it difficult to get going the next day. I had woken with a headache and groaned at what sort of day I knew lay ahead. Anabel and I hurried through the school gates just as the bell sounded – which is the closest I have ever come to getting Anabel to school late – and I cursed Verity's untimely appearance last night, holding her entirely responsible for the pounding raging through my temples.

I bent down and pulled Anabel into an embrace, to make up for how short I had been with her in the last thirty minutes; I had all but yanked her hair into two bunches and not the usual elaborate plaited affair I prided myself on achieving every day. I released her from my embrace, gave one bunch a light tug and kissed her button nose.

'I love you, Anabella boo.' At just eight, she was on the cusp of being aware of what her peers thought of her, and so she looked around to check no one had seen before she kissed me plaintively on the lips. I watched her wander slowly to the next gate, where her teacher was waiting to greet her. I always called her Miss Honey, as she reminded me of the character from *Matilda*, but her name was actually Miss Mead. Anabel took one last glance back before she walked into school. I stood for a moment, my hand shading the sun from my eyes. The warmth on my face was soothing, and I wanted to stay there for a while, allowing it to do its healing work and cure me of this headache. But my mind had already begun to flood with the jobs I needed to complete before the weekend so David and I could relax. Sabrina, my cleaner, was just arriving as we were racing out of the house, and I took a moment to feel the relief from the knowledge that if nothing else got done today, I will at least have a tidy house.

The candle business I started last year was going from strength to strength. More retailers were taking bulk orders, and today I had two conference calls: one with the supplier of the essences and one with a distributer. Nothing really happened on a Friday, and it was unusual for me to be so busy – I was usually well and truly wound down by Thursday evening, but not today. Today, my stomach was in knots; I felt out of sorts, little pelts of negative energy forced their way in, and I was using every bit of strength I had to fight them off. It was an old familiar feeling I thought I had seen the back of; I always thought moving here would mean I wouldn't have to feel like that again. I would never have to become that person again. I looked off to the right of the playground where a couple of groups of mothers were still gathered, taking a few minutes to catch up on the local gossip.

It was then that I spotted her. Verity. She was wearing a running vest and shorts. She had appeared to have been a slight woman last night, but she was now revealing firm, toned legs and muscly arms. She was standing next to Evie and Hatty. I immediately began walking over, my heart began to pound. Would I be able to pull off the same act as I had last night and engage in casual conversation with Verity?

'Morning,' I said in the happiest voice I could muster.

All three women turned and chorused their hellos.

'I see you've found out where we all gather on a weekday morning,' I said to Verity, trying to maintain a tone of humour. She looked at me blankly, then raised her head in acknowledgement of my poor attempt at a joke. Evie and I leant in for a quick hug.

'Oh, yes, "Mothers' Club".' Verity did quotation marks with her hands. Was she trying to be smart? So why was she here, making herself part of a clan she clearly thought was some sort of joke? I felt the anger burn in the pit of my stomach. Had Evie noted Verity's remark?

'But you don't have kids?' This had been established last night, but the words were out of my mouth before I could stop them. Evie glanced at me. *Why else would she be here at the school gates?* I wanted to add, but her expression was twisted and anxious, as though I had clearly stepped over some invisible line.

'No. No,' Verity said and looked down at her trainers. Had I touched on a sore subject? Thinking again, when the topic had been mentioned last night, it had been brushed over quickly, by Evie if I remember rightly. Messy divorce? Fertility issues? I had definitely made Verity feel awkward, and I definitely felt bad for that; having kids wasn't for everyone. I mean, I only had one myself and surprised myself daily that I had achieved that! I had left it very late into my thirties and had got used to a life of just David and I. I found it hard when a screaming ball of pink and purple slipped into our world and turned it upside down.

'It's Verity's first day writing her book. I bumped into her on the corner. We got to chatting and... well, found ourselves here,' Evie said hurriedly.

'We always said a coffee shop is what this village needs,' I said to Verity. 'I mean, there are enough of us who would use it. All this standing around on corners, so uncouth.' I did the last bit in the voice that made me sound posher than I was, and Evie laughed. And I suddenly felt that pull between us, that magnetic force that had brought us together in the first place.

'Fancy popping in for one?' I said just to Evie. Verity, in her running get-up was ready for a marathon by the looks of things, and I didn't feel bad for not extending the invitation to her.

'Love to.' Evie smiled, and a swell of happiness erupted. There was something about being in Evie's company that made me feel she would always have my back, no matter what. Evie was the saviour that I needed after the misdemeanour that had cost me so many friends and nearly my marriage. She showed me how a friendship could be easy, that you didn't need 150k followers on Instagram to feel special. Just one good friend was all you needed. I would have been happy with it only ever being Evie and I. But now Verity was here, and the thought of two becoming three unnerved me.

'I just need to do a quick HIIT workout. See you at ten?' I said and began to make my exit towards the gate. Verity was just behind me, and as she walked past me, her arm brushed against my running top. She moved her head ever so slightly to look at me and I saw something hollow and fractured in her expression. Was that why Evie was drawn to her? Why she had befriended her so easily? Did she see something in her that needed fixing? That had been me once, the new girl with the insecurities. Evie had managed to banish them and brought the real me out. Did she need a new project to work on now I had come out of myself? It was Evie who had mentioned the queen-bee thing. I certainly didn't consider myself to be worthy of such a title – I still felt like an outsider. Especially with everything that I knew I was keeping from them.

As we all went our separate ways, I watched Evie walk away, and then I clocked Verity again. She was now running away along the street. I watched her for a few more seconds until she turned the corner, then I jogged home.

* * *

I was just getting out of the shower when the bell went. Evie was five minutes early.

Sabrina was just walking past my bedroom with the hoover in hand.

'Sabrina, could you possibly get the door and see Evie to the kitchen?' I pulled the towel around me tighter.

'No problem, Mrs Wallace.'

I had told Sabrina many times not to call me Mrs Wallace, but she either kept forgetting or it was just in her nature to address her employers so formally. I dressed hurriedly and heard Evie being shown into the kitchen and kindly making small talk with Sabrina. Evie was one of those women who genuinely meant what she said. Kindness was her forte; the genuine stuff, not the false hopes of 'Oh, we must get together'. No, Evie was straight up from the start, invited me over for coffee, introduced me to everyone in the village and made me feel welcome. I tried not to think how it was Verity who was receiving that attention now. Back in London, I had been made to feel welcome in the same way, except all that kindness and attention had been swiftly retracted once the truth came to light. I was an imperfect being. I made a mistake. But that had meant nothing to my 'friends'. Now, Verity's presence was making me feel so uncertain about my friendship with Evie that I suddenly felt the need to try harder with her. Something I hadn't felt I needed to do before.

I had talked to Evie about the difficulties with running my new business, how reluctant I had been to move to the country and how I had always wished I was not an only child but had repeated the same fate for Anabel. I asked Evie how she felt about only having Juno, and she waved it off as though she had never really considered having any more. We could have gone further, but I sensed Evie was holding back. She was a single mum, and she had never talked to me about Juno's father. I had been on the cusp of revealing so much more to her more than once – maybe if I had offered up the truth about my past, she might have reciprocated – but had stopped myself in case she rejected me. I had lost so many friendships before, it would be too much to lose even one again.

I headed downstairs in jeans, a T-shirt and an oversized cardigan.

'Hi, you.' I went straight to the kitchen table where Evie was sitting with her phone in her hand. I couldn't help but notice she was on WhatsApp and that she clicked the screen to black just as I leant in to kiss her. But I had already seen Verity's name across the top. I vowed I would make this time with Evie count, and so I tried to push away the paranoia. People were allowed more than one friend, for goodness' sake.

'So, book club was a success last night. Well done on the book choice – everyone loved it.' Evie's words were like honey to me. It mattered to me what people thought and liking my book choice – as petty as it seemed – was important.

'Yes, yes, really pleased with my ability to wow you all with slutty women's fiction.'

'Is that a new genre?'

'I'm making it a new genre. Coffee?' I asked.

'Love one.' She placed her phone on the table. I eyed it, trying not to imagine Verity on the other end tapping out a reply to Evie's message that had said something along the lines of 'Hope you had a good run'.

'Is Verity settling in, okay?' I asked as my thoughts took me back to her regardless of trying not to.

Evie looked at me. I put two cups under the spout of the coffee machine. It spluttered into action.

'She seems to be settling in just fine.'

'Good, good.' I called over my shoulder. 'And you met her on the street, you say?'

'We were in the library,' Evie said quickly. Was it too quickly? 'I showed her where the historical section was – you know how tiny that library is. Blink and you miss it! – and we got chatting about books. I mentioned the book club, and before I knew it, I had invited her along. I hope you didn't mind, Miranda – I know that book club is your baby. To be honest, I don't think she will be coming again. Apparently, she has quite a lot on with this book, so...' Evie trailed off.

I wanted to ask more questions. To predict the future, I suppose. To ascertain whether Evie was intending to dump me for this new girl. But I couldn't admit that, barely even to myself. I wasn't sure I'd be able to take it. I couldn't take being rejected again.

'Wow, sounds like a perfectly romantic meet-cute,' I said, and Evie wrinkled her nose and shifted in her seat. A hint of a smile played across her face. Was I making her feel uncomfortable? I knew better than to push things, yet there was still that part of me that yearned to pick at the scab a little more. It was a terrible habit and one I wished I didn't have. The problem was, when you moved away somewhere new, you think you are escaping your problems, but really you are just taking them with you. I had hoped so much that I could have been a much better version of myself here, but it seemed that no matter what I did, those demons would always come back to haunt me.

8

I sat alone in the kitchen on Friday afternoon, trying to focus on my candle business tasks at hand, but thoughts of Verity kept swirling through my mind. There was nothing for it. I would have to organise a party in her honour, or she would instantly hate me. I would also need to prove to Evie that I was a good friend. There was always the chance that the perfect light I had tried so hard to paint myself in would quickly fade, and everything I had been keeping from her would suddenly be exposed. I needed to keep people on my side, let them see me as a good neighbour. I knew I was doing it for purely selfish reasons, and it alarmed me momentarily how easily I was able to manipulate the situation in my mind.

I wrote to David's designer and asked him to knock me up an invitation, he told me he had a spare hour and when the simple yet elegant design arrived first thing Monday morning, I sent it straight to the printers in town and asked for thirty invites for later that day. I wasn't quite sure if I could cobble even that many people together in this tiny village, but I was going to give it a try. Monday afternoon, just before I was due to pick Anabel up from school, I hopped into my car and headed to collect the invitations.

As soon as I got into the car, I panicked that I had forgotten my phone, so I started rummaging in my handbag on the passenger seat, my foot barely grazing the accelerator. Traffic flow was not at all heavy through the village, but my senses were still attuned to London traffic, so I didn't hesitate to slam my foot on the brake pedal just before the car came into contact with someone standing in the road.

When my eyes managed to focus on the figure, I saw who I had almost hit. Verity stood unscathed and unflinching in the road, inches from the front of the car, and I realised – as I looked in the direction of her gaze – that I was directly outside Evie's house and Verity was staring right down her pebbled driveway. Evie's was a short drive that led to her quaint cottage with faded sand-coloured bricks, a red slated roof, three windows upstairs and two larger windows on the ground floor that framed a bright blue door; a tiny overhang served as a porch. There were two small shrubs, pruned into cone shapes, in pots on either side of the door. I had always thought it a very pretty-looking cottage, but I wasn't sure I would ever be able to deal with the worry of the upkeep those old places required. I opened the passenger window, leant across and called out to Verity, but she didn't seem to hear. Perhaps she was in shock. That was all I needed, to have almost killed the person I was throwing a party for.

I unbuckled my seat belt and hauled myself out of my Range Rover.

'Verity?' She was wearing running gear again, and I wondered if she was training for a marathon or something. This time, she turned and looked at me but there was a vagueness there, as if she couldn't see me properly. 'Are you okay?' I asked.

'Yes, I'm fine.' Verity snapped, and she put her hands in front of her and began wringing them together. It was an action I had witnessed my mother do a thousand times before one of her parties. But as soon as those guests arrived, she glided through the house; all anxious tics evaporated.

I ignored Verity's sharp tone – perhaps she was in shock from the near collision – but exasperation consumed me. 'Well, I almost ran you over just now.'

Verity looked at me. That vacant expression was back, before it was gone again in an instant. 'Yes, yes, I'm sorry about that. I was... somewhere else completely.'

'Thinking about the book?' I offered.

'Yes, indeed. Not writer's block, the very opposite, in fact. Writer's overload.' Her tone was colder now. I could see she was still somewhere far away, her face angling back towards Evie's cottage.

'Well, if you're sure you're okay.'

'Absolutely.' Verity's voice now came across as though she were dismissing me for being silly. Then she turned to me, her eyes firmly on mine. 'You know, you really shouldn't concern yourself too much with other people's lives.' Then, taking one last look towards Evie's house, she walked slowly from the middle of the road and onto the path, not pausing to look at me. I felt my breath catch in my throat; any words that I should have retaliated with were trapped there too.

I took one long, deep breath and slowly let it out, and then I climbed back into the car. I strapped myself in and Verity slowly made her way along the path a few paces before stopping again, directly outside Evie's house. I drove away slowly and watched her out of the window. She remained standing there, opposite Evie's driveway, not moving.

* * *

I made it back to the school in good time to collect Anabel, who came running out, eager to get to me, and almost tripped over her untied shoelace. I was still mulling over the way Verity had spoken to me, but I was trying not to let it mar the moment with Anabel.

'Darling, slow down.' I bent down to tie her lace.

'Mummy, can Juno come and play after school?'

I looked around to see if I could see Evie anywhere; she was usually bang on time.

'Well, darling, I can't see Juno's mummy here, so we'll just wait, okay?' The two girls skipped off to the monkey bars a few metres away. I motioned to Miss Mead that I was keeping an eye on Juno, and she waved back.

I pulled out my phone and texted Evie.

School's out. Anabel wants to know if Juno can come to ours? I'll do them some dinner.

Evie text back almost immediately.

Of course, I'm literally at the gates now.

I looked up towards the front gates and was surprised that it wasn't Evie I immediately saw, but Verity gliding past. She didn't look into the playground, and Evie walked in a few seconds later. The chances of the two women not seeing each other were very slim. Had Verity held Evie up and made her late? But not once had Evie not been on time to collect Juno.

Evie strode over to me, and I noticed she was wearing her riding boots and jodhpurs.

'Everything okay?' I asked her, the concern obvious in my voice.

'Yes, yes, just held up with the horse. Damn gate stuck – couldn't get it shut.'

I nodded. She was a mere few minutes late. It was nothing to concern myself with. Miss Mead was still hovering by the classroom door that led out onto the playground. Evie waved at her, and she was finally able to go back inside and close up for the day. The playground was practically empty now. Most parents didn't tend to hang around for long at the end of school; their kids usually dragged them away to the local park or back home for snacks and TV.

'Is that fine for Juno to come back to ours then? I can drop her back if you like.' I motioned to the girls to come, and they both skipped over happily.

'No, don't be silly. I'll come and get her.' Evie smiled, but she didn't seem her usual chirpy self. Her brow furrowed as she spoke; she seemed somewhere else entirely. 'To be honest, if you could spare the time, I'd be grateful if you dropped her back, as it will give me a chance to get ahead with some clients. I have two lots of accounting that I promised I would have back last week.' Evie finally said, and I moved closer to her and put my hand on her arm. Of course, she'd mentioned a client she had forgotten about the night we had dinner last week.

'Oh no, that's not like you to get behind – you're usually so efficient.' For a moment I had considered mentioning the run-in with Verity earlier, but I stopped myself just as I realised how unnecessary it would sound. Evie wasn't superhuman. We all had bad days, and Evie was clearly having one of those. I wouldn't make it worse for her. Besides, I was calmer now; I was going to put Verity's abruptness down to a one-off. I had nearly run her over, after all!

Anabel was back at my side, and she thrust her book bag into my hand.

'Juno can come to play,' I said to her.

'Yes!' The girls ran off back to the bars. We both watched after them and smiled.

I turned to Evie. 'Just tell me if you need any more help, with Juno, or anything. It must be so hard being on your own, but you do such a fantastic job.'

She gave me a pained smile. She hated me telling her what a great job she was doing – it must make her feel uncomfortable somehow – but I wanted her to know that she wasn't alone. I only had Anabel to think about, but I couldn't imagine how I would manage everything without David's help. It was those times at the end of the day, when Anabel was tucked up in bed and I could sit down with David and a glass of wine and discuss our days, that made it so much easier – to share the load.

'It's fine. It's my own fault for getting distracted with... with other things.' She stuttered slightly. I wondered if there was something else that was bothering her. Was it perhaps that Verity was distracting her? My stomach twisted at the thought of Verity consuming all of Evie's energy so she'd have little left to offer me.

'Is six okay?' I said, taking Evie's arm in mine.

'Six, it is,' she said. I waved the girls over, and we walked to the gates and down to the bottom of the hill together before Evie bent down to Juno's level and said, 'I'll see you later, sweetie. Be good.'

Juno mocked back, 'Be good,' and Evie pretended to swipe at her.

'I sometimes wonder about this one. The cheek on it!' Evie laughed.

'It's the tween stage. I think we can expect a lot more of that,' I said, although it wasn't something I was looking forward to.

We kissed our goodbyes on the corner, and I walked the girls home, feeling content to have Juno in my care. I was doing a favour for Evie, giving her some time away and Evie would still see me as the good friend I was to her.

9

I settled myself at the kitchen table and began to write out the list of who to invite to Verity's welcoming party. I had already put a margherita pizza in the oven and set the table with a little salad of cucumbers, cherry tomatoes and celery, so I had a few minutes before I'd call the girls in.

The first few invitees were easy: Hatty, Beth, Tash, Olivia, Evie and, of course, Verity. If they all brought their partners, then that would be a good start. Of course, Evie was without a partner, and according to Juno, she never saw her dad. Although I wish I knew more, I had never pushed this point. I respected Evie too much to do that – whilst also being acutely aware there were some things that I was keeping from Evie, too. Evie always gave the excuse she was far too busy for a relationship, and she never seemed to mention wanting to get a boyfriend either. I found this quite strange. She was such an attractive woman, and still only in her mid-thirties – she could easily start again with someone else. I had mentioned this once to her, even offered to launch her on a dating site – because, I told her, I was sure I would have just as much fun as, if not more than, her – but she brushed the idea away, saying she had enough on her plate without bringing in a man to complicate things.

Perhaps this would be my chance to set her up with someone from the village. The new vicar was nice, young and unmarried. What was the rule with dating vicars? I wondered. Were they allowed? I had seen a nice-looking man delivering parcels a few days ago. Perhaps he was single and available for a party in a few weeks. It sounded pathetic when I thought about it, but I just really wanted my friend to find companion-ship. Maybe if she settled with a man, we could have double dates and Verity – with her single status – would be pushed to the sidelines. It felt such a callous thought that I chastised myself the moment it came into my head. But then I reminded myself Verity had behaved uncivilly towards me, and I need not feel bad for wishing she was anywhere but hanging around Evie.

I thought about Verity and how I hadn't seen a ring or heard about any partners. Perhaps this was why Evie was drawn to Verity, because of her single status. Even though Verity was childless, I felt as though this must be where Evie felt the connection, the pull to the new resident in the village. I knew I was overthinking things as usual, but I supposed it was because I had been here once before, in a similar situation, when I presumed everyone was my friend. And things had ended badly for too many people.

Dredging up those kinds of thoughts would only put me back on some self-sabotaging episode, so I poured my energy into the party invites, continuing to add names. Mrs James, who helped Olivia at the library; Steph, who sometimes worked in the shop... My train of thought was inter-rupted by the small voices that were trickling through from the lounge, where Anabel and Juno had planted themselves with a couple of dolls. Anabel was still very much into dolls, which was quite precious. Juno didn't have any dolls and Evie said she had never cared for them. She never grew her hair very long and was always happy to get muddy, whereas Anabel would stand on the sidelines, watching with an intense curiosity. I would cheer her on with words of encouragement – 'It's okay, Bel Bel. It's only mud. That's why we have washing machines!' – but she would continue to resist. In a way, I was glad; the thought of her traipsing all that muck into the house gave me the jitters.

But for now, I was glad to hear Juno taking such an interest in Anabel's dolls. I wondered what Evie would say later when I mentioned it to her. She would probably quip that Juno was 'just not that kind of child'. Whatever that meant.

I stopped writing so I could listen better to the conversation the girls were having.

'She just has a mummy,' Juno said.

'No, a mummy and daddy,' Anabel said sternly, and I wanted to go in and explain to her that it was okay for someone to have only a mummy. The desire to intervene was so strong, but I resisted, more out of curiosity, as I was intrigued to know how Anabel would respond.

'Why not just a mummy? Not everyone has a mummy and daddy.'

There was a slight pause, and I could almost see Anabel's crinkled expression as she considered what her friend had said.

'You don't have a daddy at all?' Anabel asked eventually.

'No. He's not here,' Juno said as a matter of fact.

Another pause. Then Anabel said, 'Oh, that's sad.'

I waited for Juno's reply. Eventually, it came.

'Yes, it is. He is a great man though. Mummy told me.'

My ears pricked up even more at Juno's statement.

Well, this was very interesting. Maybe this was the way to find out a little more about Evie and Juno's past – go straight to the child. There were obviously things that Juno wanted to talk about; I was no child psychologist, but it was clear that little Juno was holding on to something. I wanted to listen for longer because Evie revealed so little about the man she referred to as 'Juno's father'; I hoped with time, she would feel she could tell me more about this chapter of her life, but I knew I would have to be patient. Again, I tried to push away the nagging thought that Verity was also single and that maybe she and Evie had more in common with one another than I ever could. Would the two of them with their single status trump our connection with the girls? If a choice were to be made, would Evie choose Verity over me?

The conversation fizzled out as quickly as it had started, and a few minutes later, the smell of baked pizza brought them both through into the kitchen.

They ate at the table, and my stomach grumbled at the sight of the toasted cheese. The desire to steal their crusts and the leftover slice was almost unbearable. I nibbled on a piece of celery as I thought of the Gusto box David was preparing tonight. A nice healthy noodle dish. I wasn't someone who obsessed over food. I simply enjoyed the element of control it brought. I often felt I had little control over anything else in my world, and so food was where I could have the final say. I threw the remaining pizza slice away.

The girls then went off upstairs and I stacked their plates in the dishwasher and went back to my party list. This event was going to be a good opportunity for me to show off my hostess skills and maybe even bring some life to the seed of the idea that Evie had planted: that I could be the woman in the village that others looked up to. I felt the notion tugging at me harder. If I established my status here in the village, then if the truth ever did come out about what happened in London, at least I would have my reputation here as a defence against my past life disaster. I wouldn't let my thoughts linger on the alternative and how a fall from grace in such a small community could be catastrophic.

Even after everything that had happened, I still missed the socialising we did in London. I had been reluctant to host anything too lavish since we moved in, should people think me too pretentious. I had held back, trying to summon the courage to bring people together at our new house. But this low-key barbeque would be just the ticket. It was important people liked me but didn't think I was trying too hard.

I had just added a few more people to my list when I heard the cries of one of the girls. It was impossible to tell which one at first, when Anabel came running into the kitchen. Anabel's face was a crushed with disappointment; Juno's expression one of boredom when she trailed in behind.

'Darling?' I asked as Anabel climbed into my lap and buried her head into my chest.

'I don't want to play with Juno any more.'

I looked at Juno for some sort of explanation, but she was just standing there with a bemused expression.

'Okay, then will someone tell me what happened and let's see if we can work it out.'

I got nothing from either of them.

'Juno? Honey, can you tell me what happened?'

Juno shrugged.

'Okay, then, Bel, can you tell me?'

'I want Juno to go home,' Anabel whispered into my chest.

'Are you sure we can't work this out?' I was praying one of the girls would open up some more so that I could resolve this feud and wouldn't have to drop Juno back home whilst the two girls were still upset with one another. Evie would surely think me incapable that I couldn't keep them from squabbling for just a few hours. And what would that do to our friendship? Would she turn to Verity and tell her what a terrible parent I was?

'It's fine, Miranda. I don't mind going home. I can walk myself,' Juno said confidently, and it would not have surprised me if she did march out of the door without me. She had so much more gumption than my Bel; she had a much more mature way about her.

'No, no.' I jumped up, almost propelling Anabel across the kitchen. 'We'll go together. I'll just get my jacket.' Anabel stood soberly in the middle of the floor, trying her hardest not to look at Juno.

I grabbed my coat and Juno's book bag and coat, and we headed down the drive together. Juno walked a few paces ahead and Anabel stayed next to me, not speaking. I would have to interrogate her once we were back home. Evie's cottage was only a few minutes away, past the church and the two semi-detached houses that sat there all alone, as though someone had thought about building more but sort of lost the will. Next, the field with the pony who was always looking out for an apple or a carrot – he was greeted only with sour faces from the girls. Then finally, we turned the corner and there was Evie's house.

I had always found the inside of Evie's cottage a comforting place to be, so welcoming with its open fireplace and huge range cooker. Although she rented, the owners had given it to her on a long lease, and I knew she hoped to stay in the village for some time. Maybe she would think about buying a house here at some point so we would remain close. David and I were settled here now, and I realised this sort of support network was exactly what I had been searching for for so long. Here I felt safe. Here I *was* safe.

The door was always unlocked at Evie's (that would never happen in London), and Juno – who was already three paces ahead – flung it open. I heard her run into the lounge and call her greeting as though she hadn't seen Evie in weeks. 'Mummy!'

Her little voice carried through from the lounge into the hallway, where I looked down at a still forlorn Anabel. I closed the front door, Anabel hovering at my side. I gave her a reassuring smile.

'Come on, Bel. Let's just see Juno in and then we can go home and have hot chocolate.'

'With marshmallows?' came Anabel's voice, small and meek.

'Yes, Bel Bel.' I took her hand.

In the lounge, I could hear Evie asking Juno a series of questions: did she have a good time, she was back early, where was Miranda?

'We're here.' I walked towards the lounge, followed closely by Anabel. I stopped in the doorway.

'Oh.' I couldn't stop the interjection slipping from my mouth. Verity was standing in the centre of the room, next to the sofa where Evie was perched. Juno stood between them. Verity was staring at Juno, as though she weren't quite sure how to handle a child. *Christ, Verity, she's only a kid*, I felt like saying to her startled face, but was taken aback as I clocked the two empty coffee cups on the table in front of them.

'Hi, Miranda,' Evie said brightly, ushering her child closer. 'Did they have a good time?'

I ignored Evie and watched as Verity pushed her hands into the back pockets of her jeans, clearly relieved as Juno moved away from her. 'Hi, Verity,' I said bitterly. The interaction from earlier in the day was suddenly fresh again in my mind. I wanted Evie to hear my tone, to know somehow that Verity had insulted me.

Verity glanced at me briefly. 'Hi, Miranda.' Evie was too wrapped up with Juno to notice the coldness in our interaction.

'Anabel told me to go home,' Juno said. 'I don't think we're friends any more.' She collapsed onto the sofa next to Evie. She didn't look at all sad. In fact, her expression was fairly nonchalant. But then they were just kids, I reminded myself. But in a way, I was jealous of her ability to just say it like it was; no filters, no barriers. If only I could just come out and say, 'Hey, Evie, I'm worried this new woman is going to come between our friendship. Any chance you could give me a heads up on that?'

Verity looked as though she were about to say something, but stopped herself.

'Well, I'm sure it's just a little falling out, and maybe you both just need to sleep on it.' Evie looked up at me. 'Nothing serious, I'm sure.'

'No, God no,' I said. 'To be honest, I'm not sure what it was over. Maybe you can prise it out of Juno, and I'll have a go my end.' I laughed.

Evie nodded and gave me a reassuring smile.

I glanced at Verity again. She looked uncomfortable, as though she wasn't sure whether to sit down again. Had she been about to leave when I arrived, or was she staying for a bit longer? And if she was, why? The coffees were drunk. There was no need for her to hang around. I wished she would leave now so I could be alone with Evie. I knew I needed to share the earlier incident with Evie, but not with Verity standing around like a spare part. However, it didn't look like Verity was going to move. I could almost sense her determination to remain exactly where she was, as though she was waiting for me to leave.

I felt Anabel tug at my sleeve. She was probably anxious to get back for her hot chocolate. 'Yes, darling.' I reassured her. I turned to the others. 'Well, I'll be getting back then. It was nice to see you again, Verity.' I felt one last rise of heat in my chest as I spoke those words. How many times was I to see her in the space of just a few days?

Evie jumped up. 'I'll walk you to the door.'

At the door, Evie suddenly pulled me into an embrace and I was surprised by the sudden intimacy.

'Everything okay?' I said as we pulled apart.

'Yes.' She smiled. She looked down at Anabel and rubbed her head. 'Don't worry about Juno. Whatever it is, I'm sure you two will clear it up at school tomorrow.'

Anabel gave a shy shrug, and I took her hand again, suddenly feeling an uncomfortable sensation that it was us against them. Anabel and I. Evie and Juno. And Verity. I felt the memory surface itself, and was reminded of what it was to feel like an outsider, to know everyone was against you.

'Come on, Bel. Let's get you home,' I said, needing to get out of there. 'Bye, Evie. I'll see you in the morning.'

'And text me if you find out anything,' she mouthed quietly and motioned to Anabel, who was halfway through the front door. I nodded.

We walked a few paces down the driveway before I stopped to look back at the house. I saw through the window as Evie returned to the lounge, there was a pained expression on her face. Then she approached the window and drew the curtains without even a wave. The last slither of an image I saw was Verity as she took a seat on the sofa next to Juno. So, she obviously wasn't heading anywhere. This book of hers wasn't going to get written with the amount of time she seemed to spend with Evie. Maybe Evie was being polite and Verity was overstaying her welcome. Perhaps that's what the hug was for when I left just now. Was that my cue to say something?

I decided there and then that I would not be throwing the party in Verity's honour. It would be for me to mark my place in the village. I needed everyone to see I was also a fabulous host. Trying so hard with Verity was pointless; I knew I should just quit now and save myself another potentially painful episode.

I could feel tension in my shoulders and a pain shot through my chest. This was not a good sign. I hadn't felt that sensation for so long.

When we got home, I sent Anabel off to the snug to watch Netflix. When David arrived home just after six thirty, he looked surprised to find me sat at the kitchen table, a bottle of red wine already open in front of me. He slipped out of his suit jacket and took a large wine glass from the cupboard and sat down opposite me. He poured himself half a glass, leant over and kissed me softly on the cheek. I was glad he was there, in front of me. Still, after all these years, after everything I had put him through.

He had been my rock these last ten years. Even when my life fell apart around me, David subtly picked up all the pieces and helped me feel like myself again. So subtly that I had only realised what he had done afterwards. I was so lucky that we had such a solid relationship, one that could withstand such a traumatising event.

'Tell me your day wasn't as disastrous as mine?' he said, gently clinking my glass. He began talking about his day and stopped, waiting for me to chip in.

Eventually, I took three long sips of wine, finished my glass, then I looked at my husband. I wanted to scream, I wanted to cry, but he had seen enough of that last year. This was our new start, our fresh beginning. I didn't want to remind him of how awful I could make situations. So whilst my mouth spoke the words, 'I had a good day,' my mind wanted to tell him that I had a horrible feeling that it was happening all over again.

10

BEFORE

The girl liked to remain quiet during the day. Her mother had told her it was best that way; she was prone to headaches and didn't like to do much when it was light. Staying indoors was what the girl became used to. When her mother was asleep, she would sneak out into the garden and look at the buddleia that grew in next door's garden and draped over into theirs. She would look at the butterflies perched on the large coned purple flowers, inspecting each one in turn for differences in the patterns on their wings.

Eventually, when the sun would begin to dip behind the buildings, she would creep back into the house and gently wake her mother. Then their day would begin. They would go out to a café or walk in the park. It was fun, if a little lonely swinging all by herself.

'But we have this all to ourselves,' her mother would say, pushing her higher on the swings as the city lights came bursting into life, and the girl imagined herself flying off the swing and landing amongst them, like a superhero. That was what her mother told her she was. Every day. A superhero in plain clothing. But she didn't much feel like one. If she was a real superhero, she could make her mother stay awake in the day and make her take her to zoos and the woods like other children's parents did. Or even school. She wanted more than anything to go back to school and be with her friends, she remembered overhearing some grown-ups discussing it once. She could be a superhero at school and no one would ever know. Maybe she would really be able to fly off that swing and land amongst the city as everything else carried on around her. But her mother said they would need to wait until she was a bit more settled. But more than anything, she wished to be a superhero so she could stop the bad things happening, and that would make her mother the happiest. Just like she was before.

11

I avoided Evie the following week. She had texted a couple of times but I didn't rush like I usually did to get back to her. Instead, I had sat on three of her messages and now they were backed up on my phone, their presence nudging at my conscience. I wasn't being petty. I had to. Since I had seen Verity at Evie's when I dropped Juno back home last week, I felt I needed a little bit of space just to get my head together, so I could be a better friend. I was proud of myself. It may perturb Evie, but if it meant that I could stop any erratic behaviour developing, then it was better for everyone.

Anabel and Juno's spat came to nothing, thank goodness. I really wanted them, needed them, to remain friends so as not to threaten mine and Evie's friendship.

Miss Mead had organised a gathering in the classroom for a Mother's Day message from our children. It was very sweet and I had begun to love these little moments. But, this time, I was dreading it. I didn't feel up to socialising, and just wanted to bring Anabel home and curl up under a blanket with her and watch *Cinderella*. But Tash had been insistent at book club the other week. She said the children had been working so hard on the message and lovely cards and so on, and I knew it was my duty as a good mother, no matter how painful it would be.

I arrived in the playground and saw a group of parents gathering next to

Anabel's classroom. I couldn't see Evie. I walked towards the classroom door and Miss Mead was at the door with a beaming smile on her face. How was it possible for someone to smile so inanely all the time?

'Good afternoon, good afternoon, good afternoon,' she repeated as each parent in front of me walked through. Suddenly, I realised I should have told David about this event as I saw a few of the dads stepping through with their wives. But David hated this sort of thing, being stuck in a tiny classroom, forced to sit in those comically tiny chairs. David was a tall, sturdy man. He'd once come along to one of these when it was Anabel's first week at Reception and we were still in Chelsea, and I remember glancing over at him and thinking he looked like Buddy the Elf, and I had to stamp on my own foot to stop myself laughing. Those were some of the fonder memories I carried with me from living in London. I tried not to think about how our time there had ended so badly; I won't allow myself to bring any of that to my new life.

'Are you okay?' Miss Mead said with a laugh as I approached the door. She had obviously seen my involuntary head shake as I cast aside the memories I didn't wish to surface.

'Oh yes, fine, thank you,' I said with so much enthusiasm that I could see beneath Miss Mead's veneer. She wasn't entirely convinced by my response.

'Okay, well, find your child and take a seat next to them,' Miss Mead said.

I squeezed my way through the door and the tiny, congested corridor and began to feel a sweat coming on. Once we had all assembled inside the classroom that should realistically only seat twelve children comfortably but now had eighteen children plus parents, I was seriously wishing for it all to be over. I tucked in next to Anabel, who was looking slightly self-conscious about the whole thing; I regretted my decision to crouch after ten seconds as the numbness set in.

I looked around and made the obligatory smiles and hellos to a few of the parents, but I couldn't see Evie anywhere. Miss Mead took her place at the front of the room and clasped her hands in front of her, that saccharine smile plastered across her face. She didn't say anything but just looked from one side of the room to the next, and it was in fact the children who shushed the parents – picking up their cue from Miss Mead – and eventually the room fell silent. I glanced over at Juno, who didn't look at all perturbed that Evie hadn't shown. If that was me at her age, I would have been shamed into a corner.

But I wondered if it was a side of her mother that Juno knew better than me. Before the last week, I had never known Evie to be late. Why was her time keeping so suddenly all over the place?

'Welcome to Sunflower class on this lovely March afternoon,' Miss Mead began. 'The children have been working so hard to bring you today's performance—'

Miss Mead stopped abruptly as the door flew open and Evie stepped into the room.

'Sorry, so sorry,' Evie said, expertly picking her way across the sea of chairs and feet to get to Juno at the back of the room. I glanced over at her to catch her eye, but she was whispering something to Juno, who just shrugged and put her chin in her hands and carried on looking at Miss Mead. I observed Evie for a few moments more; she looked flushed, her usually straight, sleek bob was pulled back into a small messy ponytail. Had Evie looked this unkempt before? It was hard to tell. She had such a natural look about her most of the time, an effortless grace. Was her appearance becoming a little more dishevelled? What could have happened that would have meant she couldn't make her hair neat or put her usual lip gloss on? Straight away, I wanted to ask if she was okay, if there was anything I could do.

I looked down at my own appearance, and suddenly felt conscious of having made a bit of an effort in loose trousers, white shirt and my black biker jacket, coupled with some Reebok Classics. I still took a certain amount of the metropolitan with me, even though I now resided in a tiny village. But looking at Evie, I felt as though I were standing out too much. Would she think I was trying too hard? Suddenly, I felt a wave of guilt for having not replied to her last few texts. What was I playing at? I shouldn't be pushing someone like Evie away.

The children all got up and sang their little song about mothers and it was very touching. I glanced again over at Evie during their performance, but she had her face firmly fixed towards the front of the classroom. If I could just catch her eye, I could smile at her, let her know we were okay. But it was almost as if, though she was looking at her daughter, she wasn't seeing her there at all.

After the song, there was a choice of sewing a purse – which I felt was a little twee even for country school – or a spot of potato stamping. Anabel chose sewing. I let her take the lead and occasionally helped her get back on track when the wool became tangled. I surreptitiously looked at my watch and saw it was twenty past three. I was desperate to be out of the room, which had begun to envelope me and make me feel uncomfortable like an oversized itchy jumper. I wanted to call over to Evie. Of course, her daughter was on the other side of the classroom, but was that the only reason for keeping her distance from me? Not even a glance in my direction so far. Was it me? Had I messed things up?

Anabel grappled with her purse for the final time just as Miss Mead clapped her hands and asked us all to pack up and for the parents to leave and wait for their children in the playground whilst they were dismissed. I couldn't get out of the classroom fast enough. I kissed Anabel – even though I would see her in less than five minutes – and made my way to the door. I called my thanks to Miss Mead and was just walking past the coat pegs when I felt a hand on my shoulder pulling me back. I turned and Evie was behind me, looking flustered again, as though she had just run after me.

'Sorry I've not seen much of you the last few days.' I knew it wasn't an apology, but a statement – to me – because it was me who had avoided her.

'That's okay.' I smiled. I felt the relief wash over me. We were back on safe territory. I vowed never again to let my emotions over Evie's friendship with Verity affect me. Evie and I were good.

'Glad that's over, aren't you?' I felt myself fall straight back into the easiness of our friendship.

'Err, yes. Look, Miranda, I'm sorry if it seems I'm a bit preoccupied at the moment and we haven't had much time for one another. I wondered if you fancied a wine night? Maybe I could come over this week?'

'Yes, that would be lovely,' I said. All the frustration from the last few days had simply melted away. I suddenly wished that I had answered Evie's texts. It was not as if they were long messages that required a lot of thought about the response, but I could rectify that. You would have thought I would have learnt to treat friendships with better care. I had behaved badly. Again.

I put both of my arms around her and pulled her in for a brief hug. 'Look, how about tomorrow? I'm not doing anything.'

'Yes, tomorrow sounds great,' Evie said as I released her from my grip.

'Oh, Evie!' Tash appeared in the corridor as more parents streamed out of Anabel's classroom and I was forced to move towards the wall. 'Hi, Miranda,' she said, then took Evie's arm. 'Can I have quick word?'

Tash pulled Evie around the corner. Instinctively, I edged further into the wall to avoid the swell of parents passing me and heading through the door and into the playground and I found I was in listening distance of the conversation happening between Evie and Tash.

'I just needed you to check something on Juno's admin file. It's just a discrepancy about her birthdate. We have her down as this on our files, and the form you filled out for the farm trip has this date.' I could clearly hear Tash speaking to Evie.

'Oh. Silly me,' Evie said. 'I've been a bit distracted recently; I must have been thinking of someone else entirely when I filled out that form. The birthdate you have is correct. Sorry, Tash.'

'Oh, don't worry at all, I thought I'd just double-check – no one would have usually noticed but we have that new receptionist, and she is very particular. Checks everything!'

'No, no it's my fault. My mind has been somewhere else these last few weeks.'

At those words, I edged back away from the corner of the wall a few steps and smiled a few goodbyes to the parents who were still passing me. A few seconds later, Evie rejoined me.

'Sorry about that. Suppose we should go and collect the girls.'

I walked behind Evie towards the playground. I wondered if she would mention what she had just discussed with Tash to me, confide in the fact that she was struggling a little bit, that things were getting on top of her. I was, after all, her best friend here in the village. Wasn't I?

'You know, if you ever need any help with anything, you only need to ask,' I said.

Evie didn't speak until we stopped in the playground. Then she looked at me, saying only, 'Thanks.'

I had expected more from her, but perhaps that one word was enough of an acknowledgement that something or many things were bothering her. I knew not to push further. I had learnt my lessons from my past mistakes. I would sit tight and let Evie come to me when she was ready. Perhaps, tomorrow evening after a glass of wine, she might feel she could tell me what was going on. I couldn't risk losing her. I knew all too well that true friendships were worth holding on to.

12

The next evening, I set out a platter of nibbles, some anchovy-stuffed olives, some smoked cheddar – Evie's favourite – and vegetable crisps. I had bought a bottle of crisp Chardonnay, which was chilling in an ice bucket, and I had lit one of my own brand scented candles – lime and basil – and put on some Erykah Badu on low on the Sonos.

David came in and put his arms around my waist from behind as I was putting two side plates and napkins on the kitchen table. This was where we ate most of our meals, even though we also had a huge dining room. But so far since we moved, we hadn't had the guest capacity to fill the twelve seats because I hadn't been able to bring myself to invite that many people into our new and oh-so fragile world.

I stood up and fell into a backwards embrace, David's arms tucked firmly around my waist.

'How are things today?' He spoke into my hair as he kissed my head. Had he sensed something? I thought I had been clever in holding my feelings in and not speaking them out loud to David. But he had seen and experienced the worst side of me when everything came out. He was perceptive enough; perhaps my recent emotions over Evie had been palpable enough for him to feel.

How are things today? I had heard that statement many times after it had all happened, but it was only when we had finally moved away that I was able to say, 'I'm good, I feel good.' I wanted to say that again, but the words stuck in my throat. If I told him how I truly felt, how would he react? This was our fresh start. I had promised him no more dramas. Back then, when things turned sour in London, David was right there and did everything he could for me. And even though it was all my own fault, he never once showed he was angry or upset with me. He just did what was needed to be done dutifully, and then swiftly put in an offer here at Fairvale View. We moved a few months later, but I had never been able to shake away the horror of that period. It still sat quietly between David and me, but I hoped one day I could be done with it for good. Evie and the other women in the village were part of that process; if I could quietly mould myself into the clan, then everything that happened before would be a mere blip.

'I'm good.' I forced out the words, but they were merely a whisper. It felt strange lying to David again, but I knew I couldn't tell him the truth. It would bring a wave of memories cascading down on him, and I wasn't sure he would be able to deal with them again.

* * *

Evie arrived just after eight, looking a lot more presentable in blue slouchy trousers and a pink jumper. Her cheeks were full of colour and her hair was tied back neatly. We went through into the kitchen and she oohed at the nibbles and wine. 'Just what the doctor ordered,' she said.

For a second, I was going to quiz her. Was she seeing a doctor? Should I be worried?

'Who did you get to babysit?' I asked instead, wondering if she might have asked Verity.

'Beth,' Evie said. 'She's saving for her summer holiday to Greece, so she's happy to take on as many shifts as possible.'

'Wow! You'll have to up your social life,' I said as I poured her a glass of Chardonnay.

'I wish.'

I poured myself a glass.

'Here's to us.' I clinked her glass.

'To us,' she said and took a long sip. 'Mmm, that's yummy.'

'So, you've been busy then?'

We sat at the table.

'Yes, I've been getting lots of referrals, so I've just been trying to see if I can fit them all in.' She scoffed. 'Turns out, I can't, so I've had to turn a couple down. But I've kept hold of three of them.'

'And does it... you know, still fascinate you? Dealing with other people's figures.' I asked, leaning forward with my wine clasped in my hand.

Evie laughed. 'I wouldn't say fascinate, but I do enjoy my job. I enjoy that each time I do someone's books, it's definitive. With other forms of work, like art or creating things – like your candles – I suppose sometimes you get stuck in a whirlwind of ideas and you don't know which way to go, but with accounting, there's a sense of safety in figures. I know it sounds drab, and probably won't get me any dates soon.' Evie waved her hands around.

'Oh, I don't know, Evie. I bet there are a lot of guys who would kill for a girlfriend like you. I feel as though maybe you're ready to get out there and start dating.' I knew not everyone needed a man or a woman to complete them, but I could sense there was something missing with Evie. I wanted her to feel secure, like I did with David. 'I know you won't tell me about Juno's father and that's fine.' Evie sighed and went to speak, but I cut in. 'But it's fine, Evie, I get it, you don't want to drag it all up for me, I'm not asking that. I just don't know how long it's been since you dated a guy?'

Evie took a deep breath. 'Ever since I moved here,' she said.

'But that's almost two years, Evie!'

'I know,' she said sadly. 'I know.'

'Do you feel... ready?'

She looked at me and I could see a sadness in her eyes. 'Yes, I do, I think.'

I put my wine glass down and clapped my hands together. 'That's wonderful news.'

Evie gave me a weak smile.

'Isn't it?' I asked.

'It's... Well, it's complicated, that's all.'

I felt my enthusiasm wilt. 'Oh, okay.'

'I mean, I do really want to, you know, meet someone and everything. It's just well, I have Juno, and it's just us, and I have this huge responsibility and I cannot let her down.' Evie's voice broke on the last word.

I stood up and moved to the chair next to hers and bent down to put my arm around her. She cleared her throat and shook her head. 'It's fine, I'm okay.' She patted my hand. I took my cue and sat back down and I waited to see if she would elaborate any more.

'My time will come – I won't try and force something that isn't ready to happen.' She spoke forlornly for a second. 'I mean, I'm not exactly in bachelor paradise, am I?' She laughed, and I had to laugh with her as it was only a few days ago I was trying to think of any eligible men in the village.

'Well, it's funny you should say that, but I was having a bit of a creative moment the other day and I thought what a wonderful idea it would be if I threw a party here. For Verity. A sort of welcome-to-the-village kind of thing.'

I suddenly found myself telling Evie all about my idea, even though I had made a firm decision not to host the party in Verity's honour, but suddenly seeing Evie so down and forlorn, I felt I wanted to work with her. Verity had only just moved here and perhaps I had mistaken her reluctancy to socialise with me as rudeness when she was probably just nervous. If I could show Evie that I was willing to try and befriend Verity – despite her offending me the other day – then Evie would know I was a good friend. And if she ever discovered anything about my past, she would know it was all a mistake and I had reformed.

I waited for Evie's response. She looked a little confused. 'I thought maybe I could invite all those non-existent bachelors!' I added for some comic relief.

'I... I don't know if that is a good idea,' she said.

I looked at her and furrowed my brow. 'Does she... not like parties?'

'I... I don't know, I mean...'

Neither of us spoke for a moment and I felt the familiar dread hit my stomach. How was it possible I could keep getting things so wrong? What was the point in my being forty-three if I still felt like a fifteen-year-old girl inside who was scared of being rejected?

I took a long sip of my wine to fill the silence.

'Do you know what?' Evie said. 'I think it would be fine. I only doubted it because I thought that, well, from what I know of Verity, she is very shy and what with her being a writer, she spends a lot of time on her own. And also I'm not sure how long she's staying here, so I wouldn't want... She might not want anyone to overwhelm her.' She looked at me. 'Do you know what I mean?'

I gulped down my wine again and nodded. It was a bad idea. I was trying too hard. I just needed to find a happy medium. Evie was right – why would Verity want a party throwing in her honour? It was a bit over the top. Stupid Miranda.

'But this is you and this is what you do and so, I think she can only say no, right? And even if she doesn't come, then it will be a lovely party anyway,' Evie said reassuringly.

I looked at her and felt the hope return. 'Well, I did sort of get the invitations printed already,' I mumbled.

Evie snorted a laugh. 'Well, there you go then. The party is on!'

But in my mind, with Evie's sort-of blessing, the party was no longer for Verity. She would be invited, of course. But this would be a celebration for me to mark how far I had come. To create a seal between the past and the present. To show Evie what a great friend I was. If I could be half as popular as Evie was, then she would need me as much as I needed her. We would be a force that was stronger together. This was me, Miranda Wallace, here and now. I could be a mother, a wife, a friend and a socialite. I could do it all.

* * *

I saw Evie to the door at a quarter to eleven. It would take her a few minutes to walk home and then she would only need to pay Beth for three hours.

'It feels so late,' she said.

'I know, and on a school night as well!' I giggled. I'd had three glasses of wine, to Evie's sensible one glass. I would need to drink one large glass of water now and another one before bed. We hugged and kissed goodbye at the door, and I waved her off down the road.

Back in the kitchen, I began picking up all the plates from the table and stacking them in the dishwasher. I went back to collect the wine glasses and my eyes were drawn to the extra phone on the table. Evie had taken it out of her bag just before she left to text Beth that she was on her way home and had obviously forgotten to put it back in before she left.

I reached for Evie's phone and just before I thrust it inside my pocket, I cradled it in my hand for a moment, and considered trying the passcode. But I stopped myself. What was I thinking? This wasn't normal rational behaviour. Besides, I didn't want to know; I wouldn't be able to stand it if I saw one thing relating to me. I would overthink it and then begin analysing it.

I picked up my cardigan that was on the back of the chair and pulled it around me, before grabbing my keys from the hallway and heading out of the door. It was only two minutes since Evie had left, so I would hopefully catch her walking into her house. I strode down my drive and turned right. I walked for fifty yards, then turned left at the field and just in the distance I could see Evie's house. The driveway was illuminated by the security light which was spilling out onto the road light like a little spotlight, guiding me towards it.

As I neared, I could hear raised voices, and I approached the wall next to the driveway expecting to see Beth. I stopped quickly when I saw a man standing on the drive. I pushed myself towards the wall where there was a bush and peered round. I thought I was sufficiently hidden by the shadows and so I settled in to hear what he was saying. I tried to sneak round a tiny bit further to catch a better look at him: slim build, balding head; perhaps in his late forties. He was wearing a brown jacket with jeans and was pacing across the pebbles. I could see the front door was open, but there was no sign of Beth, but then I heard Evie.

'This is not acceptable, Graham. This is not what we agreed,' she hissed.

'I'm sorry, but that's just the way it has to be for now. I didn't promise you anything, did I?'

'No, you didn't promise, but you may as well have done, getting our hopes up. I'm really very unhappy right now.'

The man's voice became lower. 'I understand. I completely understand.'

'I don't think you do.' Evie's voice dropped to match his.

'Look, I have to go – I can't hang around here all night. I'm texting you that number right now.' My heart leapt into my mouth as I looked at my hand, at Evie's phone, which would be pinging any second with a message from this Graham.

I saw him pull his phone out of his pocket and so I turned and ran as fast I could to the corner, fear pelting through my veins as I envisaged falling on the concrete after my three glasses of wine and then having to explain to Evie tomorrow at the school gates what had happened.

I made it round the corner and was just passing the field when Evie's phone pinged in my pocket. My goodness, that was close.

I jogged the last fifty yards home and closed the door behind me. I stood in the hallway and tried to make sense of everything I heard. But none of it did. Evie had been adamant she didn't have a partner and she had been so shady about Juno's father. Was this Juno's father or was he just someone Evie had been dating quietly? If it was either of those, then why didn't Evie feel she could tell me? A cocktail of anger and frustration rose and spilled through my body, fuelled by the alcohol.

I'm not sure how long I had been standing in the hallway, deliberating it all, when the knock came. I looked down. I was still holding Evie's phone. I ran to the kitchen and placed it back on the table where it had been.

Then I strode back to the door, took a few deep breaths to steady my heart. I knew it would be Evie.

'Hello?' I said to the closed door.

'It's me, Miranda. I forgot my phone.' Evie's voice was small.

I opened the door, and Evie looked flushed and harassed on the other side. It was as if she'd sprinted here.

'I thought I'd got rid of you,' I joked, because this is what the Miranda who hadn't just been spying on her friend moments earlier would have said.

Evie hovered in the doorway.

'Come in.' I stood aside to let her in and walked to the kitchen. She followed. 'Where do you think you left it?' I said with my back to her.

'There it is.' She came into the kitchen behind me and dived straight towards her phone on the table, where, as far as she was concerned, it had been since she left.

'God, they're like our right arms, aren't they?' I joked. 'We can't live without them.'

'I just know I'll get a client texting me first thing in the morning wondering where their accounts are.' Evie gave a weak smile and looked at the screen of her phone for a moment. Was she wondering if I had looked at her phone?

'I'd better go – Beth is still there waiting for me.'

I immediately wanted to question that statement, because how was it possible that Beth was there when Evie had been standing outside shouting at the man she called Graham. Surely, she wouldn't have acted that way in front of young Beth. So, was it possible she was lying about Beth babysitting? Could Juno be home alone?

I gave her another quick kiss and walked her to the door.

'Right, I'm locking up now – no more visits tonight, please!' I said jovially.

'I promise.' She began walking down the driveway. 'Night.' She raised her hand without turning back. I closed the door and locked it. Then I stood in the hallway thinking about the one thing I needed to do. But I knew from history and experience that once you start digging around, it can have devastating consequences for so many people. The wise thing would be to just carry on as if everything was normal. But I knew I wouldn't. I couldn't. When I next saw Beth, I would need to subtly find out if she had been babysitting for Evie tonight. And if she hadn't, then that would mean Evie was trying to cover up the presence of the man, Graham, at her house tonight. And then I would need to know why. *And this, Miranda*, I thought to myself, *is how you end up in trouble.*

13

10 MAY 2019 – 10.36 A.M. – GLOUCESTER POLICE STATION

Interview with Olivia Cunningham

I run the library, and I see plenty of people every week. But I was never sure if Evie's story of the two of them meeting in the library stood up. It was Miranda who planted the seed in my mind. She was always in and out of the library all week, picking up art packs for Anabel, dropping off books and taking out new ones. So, I suppose she would have known better than me. I keep my head down, if I'm honest. And libraries aren't the most exciting places in the world, are they?

I mean, don't get me wrong, I love my job, but it's not like working in a pub or a shop where you get to gossip with the punters and find out everyone's business. But yes, when Miranda mentioned that she had never seen Verity in the library, not once, since she had moved to the village, well, I kind of took her word for it. Then I went back over the loans for the last few months, and I could see that indeed, Verity hadn't taken anything out. I just presumed she had joined the main library in the town – it has a much larger section of history and historical fiction. I mean, you shouldn't judge someone over their library loans, should you? [Laughs loudly.] And anyway, it's not my job to pry. She seemed like a shy girl.

Not like Miranda, who is like the queen bee of Helesbury. I mean, some thought she earned that title a little too quickly, but I never felt that way about Miranda. I have always had a great amount of respect for her, so you can imagine how shocked I was when I discovered what she had done. Saying that, there had been hints at an unsavoury past – a mother who had a breakdown when she was a child, apparently. Please don't say I told you that. I'm just relaying what I heard. Like I said, I have a lot of respect for Miranda. I don't care to gossip about others – everyone has their history, after all. But sometimes, you can't help it, can you? This is a small village. And it's a small world. It only takes one conversation for rumours to start. Then before you know it, you've discovered all sorts about a person.

14

The next day, I spotted Evie in the playground, standing in her usual spot surrounded by a gaggle of mums. Hatty was there and a couple of other mums, Sadie and Gail. I knew them, but I wasn't as close with them as I was with Evie or Hatty.

I bent down and kissed Anabel.

'Have a lovely day.'

'I will,' she said.

I admired her plaits as she turned towards school. I had made the extra effort with a fancy new style I had seen on YouTube at the weekend. I caught Anabel's hand just before she walked away. 'Bel Bel, before you go, is everything still okay with you and Juno?' It had been something of nothing and seemingly blown over already, but with the way I was feeling about Evie and I at the moment, I wanted to make sure none of it had subconsciously seeped through into the girls' friendship.

Anabel pulled a face as if to say, *Duh!* 'Yes, Mum, everything is fine. We're best friends!'

'Okay.' I let her go and she ran into the school.

I stood up and approached the group of mums. As if she sensed me coming, Evie turned and smiled, welcoming me to the gathering.

'Oh, here she is!' Hatty laughed as I joined them in their semicircle. 'I've

just been hearing about your little wine night last night, on a school night!
My goodness, you rebel.'

'I know,' I said. 'Regretted it a bit this morning when the alarm went off
at seven.'

'Well, you look amazing. She always does, doesn't she?' Hatty said. 'I
need to get some style tips from you, I think, Miranda. My boys run me
absolutely ragged – I never have a moment to think about what to wear or
what to do with this!' She pulled at her strawberry-blonde frizzy hair.

'There's loads of tips on Instagram – you should look on there,' Gail
piped up.

'Instagram, not my bag, really. I do a bit of Facebook, like to keep the
family happy with pictures of the kids – They like every single one of them.'
Hatty laughed. 'My own private fan club. How about you, Miranda, are you
any good with that social media stuff?' Hatty looked at me and I felt my
hands go sweaty and my mouth seemed to instantly dry up. This wasn't the
first time the social media conversation had come up. I had managed to
swerve the questions each time, or change the subject. I had a very simple
Facebook account, which I kept private and only posted a few family snaps.

'I don't really do much of that either. I'm just so busy with everything
else,' I said quickly, hoping to bypass the subject again.

I felt the eyes of the women on me, silently questioning me. Were they
thinking, *What else?* I had a husband who earned a substantial income,
only one child and I ran a very small business. I rarely volunteered my
services for PTA events, and I had a cleaner who came twice a week. It was
a poor cop-out of an answer, but even to hear the words, *social media*, sent
me into a sweat.

'Wow, hotshot businesswoman like you. I thought you'd be all over that
stuff,' Hatty said, not unkindly, but it still made me want to turn and run
straight out of the gates.

'I don't really need all that. Just my website and Etsy, and well, word of
mouth really.' I knew that if I put my mind to it, I would be able to sell a
hell of a lot more, but to do that, I would really need to be active on social
media. I barely scraped a profit most of the time because I spent so much
time, money and effort on perfecting the ingredients and the packaging. I
kept thinking to myself that one day I needed to just go for it – I knew

exactly how, but there were too many things stopping me. My reluctance to get back onto social media being one of the main reasons. Everyone knew you couldn't run a successful business without being active on all the channels. But I just couldn't bring myself to do it. Not yet. It had been the route to all the damage, and I wasn't ready to revisit that. Not to mention how much of my time it had taken up in the end. Time away from those I loved and who loved me.

'They are gorgeous candles – you do such a lovely job with them,' Hatty said. 'Would you consider having a stall at the summer fete this year?'

I gulped and smiled my way past the panic. Saying yes was not going to come easily, but I had squirmed my way out of too many PTA events since I'd arrived and I could see the desperation in Hatty's eyes. Anabel had another two years at this school – I would need to start showing willing. And I truly wanted to. I just wanted to do it well, not make a mess of things or let anyone down. Helesbury had a well-established community, and I was still a newbie even though Evie was trying to convince me I had made my mark in the village. I still felt I needed to tread very carefully.

'Of course.' I gulped out my reply, and Hatty looked thrilled.

Gail and Sadie waved their goodbyes. To distract from any further talk of me having to showcase my work online, I decided to mention the party. 'I have an announcement.'

Evie and Hatty looked at me.

'I am having a little spring gathering. Evie knows, because we spoke about it last night. It's my way of saying thank you to you all for welcoming me to the village. And to welcome our latest newcomer, Verity.' Her name tasted bitter on my tongue. 'All are welcome, bring hubbies and kids – if it's a nice day they can play in the garden, and we'll have a barbeque and lots of wine!' I felt about in my over-the-shoulder bag for an invite, slipped one out and handed it to Hatty.

'Oh, will you look at that? How could I possibly decline with such a pretty invite? Did you design this?' Hatty turned the piece of paper over in her hand.

'I had some say in it, but a designer friend did it.' I felt a swell of pride rise in my chest.

'It's lovely, isn't it, Evie?' Hatty said.

'Oh yes, I have one for you too.' I pulled one out for Evie.

'Thank you,' she said. 'Oh yes, they are lovely, Miranda.'

'And the forecast for April looks stunning,' Hatty said. 'What a treat! My old man loves a barbeque. And the boys will be on their best behaviour, let me reassure you.'

'It's fine,' I said to Hatty. I knew she kept those boys on a tight lead when they were anywhere socially.

'Should I take one for Verity?' Evie said, and I looked at her suddenly. The conversation from last night was silently hanging between us. The party that I had conjured up for her, which was no longer in her honour. 'I could put it through her door on my way home—'

'It's fine – I'll do the rounds of the village today and post them. It will fill a few hours. I might even get a few cups of tea thrown in!' I said, not waiting for Evie to finish. Would she be put out at not personally delivering Verity's invite? I was curious. I had an itch that needed scratching and getting a little look at Verity's house would satisfy that for today.

I said goodbye and headed out of the school gates. I was looking forward to my long walk around the village, dropping off invites. I would make sure to knock hard on Verity's door. I wouldn't, of course, mention our recent run-in – I would kill her with kindness. I would no doubt be disturbing her from her writing, but hopefully I could get a little bit more of an idea about who she was. If she were to invite me in, that is. It would be extremely rude not to – it's what people in villages did. I also knew I would get to speak to Beth at the shop as she worked there on Fridays. I would subtly ease last night's babysitting into the conversation. If, indeed, she was there. I had it all planned out – it felt almost cunning, and there was a part of my mind that was quietly telling me to stop, to remember what happened last time. I thought back to Verity's words to me, which had almost been like a warning, telling me to keep out of other people's business. I had lingered over her comment and thought long and hard about why she would have said that. But the other part of my mind, and the part that was winning so far, was telling me I needed to know more.

* * *

I found my way to the shop first. The bell above the door pinged as I walked though – a sound that perpetually reminded me I lived in a village, should I dare to try and forget. Beth was standing at the counter with a textbook in front of her. She was in her last year at university in Gloucestershire but saved money by still living at home. I wanted to come straight out and ask her was she babysitting last night, but I knew another way would be better. Beth looked up as I entered the shop and immediately closed her textbook.

'Oh, no need to do that on my account,' I assured her. 'I will be a couple of minutes.' I headed down the aisle. 'And then I have something for you,' I called back towards the counter.

'Ooh, sounds very exciting. Don't leave me hanging too long!'

I glanced back at Beth, who had already opened her textbook again. She was such a studious girl. It made me long for my school days again, made me wish I had studied harder; maybe got myself a business degree.

I picked up a wire basket, meandered the shop for a few minutes, picking out the biscuits that David liked, a bag of kiwis – they were not organic, but we had run out and Anabel was potty about them. Eventually, I found my way to the front of the shop, treated myself to a magazine, and popped the basket onto the counter just as Beth closed her book again. It was a very old-fashioned shop, with one of those tills with 3D buttons that clicked when they were pressed and a register that pinged when it opened. It was comforting in so many ways.

'How are you today, Miranda?' Beth asked as she manually rang my items up.

'I'm good, thanks. How are you getting on with Hatty's book choice?'

'Oh, I love it! It's my favourite genre, I love a time-slip. And it has romance and a mystery. Perfect. I'll be cracking on again tonight. That's my treat to myself if I do my uni reading this morning.'

'You are so diligent, Beth. I don't know how you fit it all in – working, studying, and the babysitting. Are you still getting plenty of offers?' I was surprised at how easily I was able to slide right into the subject.

'Yes, bits and bobs,' Beth said. 'Nine pounds thirty-five, please.'

I handed over a ten-pound note. Was she not going to elaborate? Was I going to have to ask her outright?

But just as I was about to speak, she continued.

'I was babysitting last night, actually, when Evie came to yours.' She handed me my change.

The relief flooded through me. Evie had been telling the truth all along. Beth *had* been babysitting. The only mystery remaining now was who this Graham was and what was he doing at Evie's last night when Beth was clearly still there. The only possible explanation was that he was Juno's father, and Evie had found him on the doorstep before she went inside, and therefore Beth had no idea he was there.

'Well, thank you for stepping in – Evie and I had a lovely catch-up,' I said, pocketing the change, and then I began placing the items in my canvas shopping bag.

'It was nice to get off early though,' Beth continued.

I felt my gut tighten, and I looked up at Beth, my hand still poised halfway in my bag.

'I managed to get a whole three chapters more reading in before bed. I always study well in bed. Don't ask me why.'

Beth rambled on, but I was still only hearing that she hadn't stayed the whole night, which meant she wouldn't have been there when Evie was outside arguing with Graham. But Beth wouldn't have left early, knowing that Juno would be on her own. She must have done a handover.

'Oh?' I said, trying to sound casual. 'That was nice for you.'

'Yes, it was handy that Verity came and took over at about ten. I was glad because I was absolutely shattered, and I knew I had to be here at six.'

'Verity?' I said, trying to keep my tone light, but I was reeling from the shock. Why would Evie book Beth into babysit and then Verity take over at ten o'clock? I tried to cast my memory back to last night, but I had had three glasses of wine and couldn't remember if I saw Evie on her phone for much of the evening. The only time I saw her text was right at the end of the evening, which I had presumed was to let Beth know that she was on her way back. But she was obviously contacting someone else. Had it been Verity? Or Graham?

'Yes, it was helpful – I did say to Evie that I was working this morning, so it was a thoughtful thing to do. And Verity didn't seem to mind.'

'Coming out at ten o'clock at night?' I said flatly, before realising how it sounded as Beth looked at me. 'These writers, hey! Up at all sorts of hours of the night,' I added quickly.

'I totally get it though,' Beth said. 'When my friend had to write her dissertation last year, she was up for about forty-eight hours – she just couldn't sleep. I know I'll be exactly the same when I do mine next year.'

'Well, sounds perfectly hideous. I love my sleep.'

I turned to leave and was about to say cheerio so I could walk the rest of the village and mull it all over when Beth spoke again. 'You said you had something for me,' she said.

'Oh, yes!' I had genuinely forgotten in all the frustration. I was ready to get out of there – the temperature was suddenly quite stifling inside the shop, even though it was still fresh outside.

I hooked my canvas bag in the nook of my arm and slipped my hand into my shoulder bag. I reluctantly pulled out an invitation. Not because I wasn't keen for Beth to come to the party but because, with this newest nugget of information regarding Evie's dishonesty, I was no longer sure I wanted to host the damn thing.

'It's an invitation. To a party I'm hosting in a few weeks. I think we are due a mini heatwave in April, so I definitely picked the right date,' I gabbled, no longer feeling as enthusiastic about it as I had when I arrived.

'Oh, wow, what's the occasion?' Beth took the flyer and examined it.

'Just a...' The whole welcoming Verity to the village idea felt even more ridiculous now. 'A just-because party. I love hosting, and David and I have barely entertained the entire year we've been here, so it's about time I put that big old house to use. Feel free to bring someone.'

'Really?' Beth squeaked, and I presumed she already had someone in mind.

'Yes, fill your boots.'

'You're so kind, Miranda – what a lovely idea,' Beth said, smiling.

'I know, it's one of my many faults,' I said as I waved goodbye. I really had to get out of there.

Out in the street, I sucked in the fresh morning air and tried to calm myself, but I felt a surge of anger when I thought about Evie blatantly lying to me last night. Then I remembered a period during the evening where I was alone at the table for some time. Evie had got up and gone to the toilet.

David stopped by the kitchen for a whisky, and we'd chatted for a few minutes. That was when Evie must have been organising for Verity to come over and relieve Beth.

I knew where I had to go next, so I took a detour down the alley that led to the rec. I came out on the path that framed the green and carried on until I was out on the other side of the village.

Potter's Earth, the cottage that Verity lived in, was one of three fairly new terraced cottages. I had never been inside one, but I knew they had been kitted out well. Potter's Earth was the last one on the right. I went through the tiny white gate and knocked hard on the door. I instantly looked at the window to my right, which I knew, from what I had seen many times walking past, was the living room. The blinds were drawn, but I distinctly saw one of the slats move. I knocked hard again, and then a shadow appeared in the glass of the front door.

I heard a few locks clicking, and then the door slowly opened – not all the way – then Verity positioned herself in the gap.

'Can I help you?' she said, as though she had no idea who I was. She was squinting as though she had been asleep, and my knocking had woken her.

'Verity, good morning!' I said as brightly as I could. 'How's the writing going?' I edged myself to the left so I could try to see past the tiny gap she had left between herself and the door frame, sensing my slight movement, she matched it by moving one inch to her right.

'It's going as well as it can,' she said as though it were such a tedious question. To be fair, I was sure she was asked it all the time.

'Good, good, you must be exhausted. I mean, I know a writer's life can have you up all hours sometimes.' I was thinking of her sat in Evie's house last night when Evie and Graham were having it out in the driveway. She must have known he was there. Verity narrowed her eyes just a fraction at me.

'It can do,' she said drolly.

'Still, it's a real skill, you must love it.'

'I do.' She offered nothing more.

'Well, I just popped by to give you one of these.' I held the invitation out in front of me. 'I have completely lost my mind and decided to invite some people over for a barbeque and drinks party in a few weeks. I thought it would give you a real opportunity to meet everyone in the village properly. I know you met a few of us at the book club, but this village is deceptively large. There are over four hundred people living here, would you believe! All those little houses tucked away in corners.'

'Wow. Four hundred people.' Verity held the invitation loosely in her hand and continued looking at me. She had not inspected the invite the way Hatty and Beth had. I felt the swell of annoyance, but I held my cool. I wasn't going to give Verity the satisfaction that her behaviour was getting to me. I had to make Evie see that I could treat her new friend with grace, even though she spoke to me as though I were nothing.

'Oh, don't panic. I'm not inviting them all, just a handful. And partners. Do you have a partner, Verity?' I asked, knowing it was a totally inappropriate question to ask on someone's doorstep, but I felt inappropriateness left the building when Verity spoke out of turn the other day.

'Not at present,' she said.

'Well, that's fine. Bring yourself. Have a drink and get to know a few people.' I waved my hand around.

Verity looked at me as though she were ready to end the conversation. I supposed she wanted to get back to her writing.

'And are you on a deadline, Verity?'

'Permanently,' she said quickly, and I shuddered at the way she said it – it sounded so ominous.

'Right, okay, well, I'll let you get back to it. I'm not one to keep a craftsman from their work. Enjoy the rest of your day, Verity.'

Verity mumbled something I didn't quite catch and closed the door. As I walked out of the gate, I could hear the clunking sound of several locks being put back in their place.

It was not just that Verity hadn't invited me in, it was the way she seemed to go out of her way to stand in the doorway to ensure I couldn't see past her. I was only just getting used to the village way of life and considering I had come from Chelsea, I felt I had nailed it pretty well. I just knew I needed to give a little more of my time for things like the PTA. But watching Verity behave like some sort of hermit with leprosy, I realised I was doing a damn better job of fitting in than she was. I had never been more intrigued.

I wanted, no needed, to know her story. Why did she choose this village to hide away in a little terraced cottage? And why did Evie feel she needed to give someone so insolent so much of her time?

I had felt fine for the last year. I had managed to slowly begin to let go of all the things that had haunted me for so long. I had finally made a friend in Evie that I felt was worthy of investment. We had struck up a great relationship. And now suddenly, Verity arrived in the village and Evie didn't seem the same. Then, to top it all off, she was lying to me. And in my opinion, people who tell one lie so easily, are capable of telling many more. I knew this first-hand, because I had told far too many myself.

15

BEFORE

The girl's mother took her out to the local café just as the sun was starting to set. She'd taken an envelope of money from the little drawer in the coffee table in the lounge. The girl thought there was quite a lot of money in there, more than she had ever seen in her life. She was glad her mother was feeling a bit better today – she was very good at resting and it was something she'd been doing a lot recently. Someone had advised her it would help, so her mother must have listened. The girl had overheard a conversation at the doorway when a man and a lady came around. 'You must rest,' they told her mother. And so that was what she had done.

The little girl thought her mother was very good for listening to the man and woman, and so she made a mental note to always listen to her mother and do exactly what she told her to do, whenever she told her to do it. The girl could, from time to time, be cheeky, or a 'little madam' as her grandma had once told her.

She missed her grandma and her grandad. She missed all the people she didn't see any more, like friends from her school. She even missed the annoying little boy who had lived opposite to her. That was in the old house. That was what her mother referred to it now and so did she. 'We will never be able to go back there again,' her mother had said, and the girl believed her. She had made her peace with that house, the house that had left her with so many amazing memories. That was what she would hang on to. But for now, she had her mother, who was up and about and happy and had an envelope of money in her handbag.

She could see her mother was a little bit happier now than she had been earlier, before the man and the woman came around. She didn't remember seeing the envelope with the money in it before they had visited, so she presumed that they had brought it with them. The girl liked the man and the woman. They said she could call them B and H. She didn't think they were very good names, but they were easy to remember because they were letters of the alphabet and the girl had been practising writing, because she loved to.

When she was older, she was going to write down everything about this adventure that she and her mother were having, and maybe one day, someone might want to read it. The girl didn't want to ever forget, even though sometimes it wasn't much fun and didn't feel like much of an adventure. The house they were living in was a bit cold at night and her mother didn't really put the lights on in the evening. Instead, she had taken to lighting candles and burning incense, which the girl liked the smell of. Years from now, the burning scent of incense would flood her body with images from this very house and the nostalgia would be so fierce she would hardly be able to think of anything else.

They walked to the local café, and the girl ordered her favourites: a toasted cheese sandwich and hot chocolate with marshmallows.

Her mother began to speak and as she did, she laid her hand across the girl's arm as she ate with her other.

'I am very sorry for everything that has happened. You have been so brave and clever. I'm sorry we had to leave our lovely house, and I am sorry you saw and heard some things that I would rather you hadn't. You were especially brave, staying all alone at the beach hut. I'm sorry I couldn't stay there with you. And I'm sorry it's taken me this long to talk to you about it. I want you to know you can ask me any questions any time you think of them. I won't get mad at you.'

The girl nodded and ate her sandwich. It was her favourite, and she didn't want to stop eating to talk to her mother – it tasted so much better when it was hot. So, she just nodded and smiled a greasy smile. She was glad her mother was happy. She had always been such a happy lady before all the other stuff happened.

Her mother sipped her coffee. 'What do you want to be when you grow up?' she asked with a big grin.

The girl thought for a moment, then she put down the crust of her sandwich and wiped her mouth with a napkin. 'I'd like to be an actor.'

Her mother nodded. 'I think you would be exceptionally good at that, my clever, special girl.'

They finished their drinks, then walked the few blocks back to the house. The girl was never going to call it *their* house. She already knew that they would not be staying there for long. That was why B and H had come today. To tell them it was time to move on again in a few days.

As the girl settled into her bed that night, with her mother reading from the Chronicles of Narnia, she felt a little like the children who had been left at the strange house in the book and wondered if she and her mother would ever find somewhere to call home again.

16

I woke up to the creaking sound of the bedroom door and Anabel's little face peering through.

'Now, Daddy? Shall I go in now?' Anabel whispered.

'Yes, poppet,' David whispered back. The two of them crept in, and I lay still and kept my eyes closed so I could put on my best surprised expression when I opened them. I had always been good at acting – it had been something I had wished I had pursued when I was in secondary school. Who knew where I could have been now if I had? Acting was something I had done a lot of recently. Mainly putting on a brave face for Anabel and David when things had really got on top of me. I got so much joy from Anabel's expression when she saw how happy I was. I always knew when one of these surprises was coming because I usually had to play some part in orchestrating it, like this Mother's Day morning. David had texted me Friday and said there would be a special breakfast.

I heard the sound of the tray hitting the bedside table, and I opened my eyes and stretched. I turned over and looked at Anabel and David standing there with my best stunned and happy expression.

'Darling,' I said in a husky whisper.

'Happy Mother's Day, Mummy.' Anabel leant in and gave me a hug.

I started to sit up, and David put a couple of pillows against the headboard.

'Wow, thank you! This is so lovely. I feel so spoilt.' I flattened the bed sheet, and David placed the tray on my lap. The aroma of the freshly ground coffee was already calling to me.

I looked at David and blew him a kiss. 'Thank you.'

'Mummy, I went out and picked these daffodils this morning,' Anabel broke in. 'There are loads in the village, did you know?'

I laughed. 'I had seen one or two, yes, darling.'

'Shall we go for a walk later? After breakfast?' Anabel said excitedly. 'It's really sunny out.'

'Well, then, we absolutely must go for a walk.' I looked at David and he nodded enthusiastically. He had been working so hard this last week and he had been looking forward to us all spending today together.

I sipped the coffee, which was just how I liked it – strong and milky – and I broke open the croissant. Anabel got onto the bed beside me and lay her head on my shoulder. What did I do to deserve such a lovely little girl? I wondered.

* * *

After we had cleared up after breakfast and I had showered, the three of us headed out into the village. The church bells were ringing joyously, and David took my hand as we approached St James's, a beautiful little building, which was just behind our house.

I was occasionally tempted to step into the church and attend a service, but Conner, the vicar – a man who could only be in his early thirties – liked to talk, and I knew once I showed an interest, I would forever be expected to attend or join in with the Women's Institute. Conner was outside the church, greeting parishioners as they arrived.

David stopped to say good morning as we passed.

'Ah, good morning there, lovely Wallace family. Can I not convince you to step inside this morning for a Mother's Day service? Flowers and chocolates for the mothers!' he said the last part to Anabel, who gasped and looked at me.

'Can we, Mummy, can we? You get to have more flowers, and I can have the chocolate.'

I looked down and laughed. 'Oh, is that so? What if I want the chocolate?' I squeezed her hand, so she knew I was joking.

'I will share it with you, Mummy,' she said, more coyly this time.

'Right, well then.' I looked at David.

'Fine by me – we still have plenty of the day left to walk and do whatever else Mummy wants to do.'

'That settles it.' Conner pressed his hands together gleefully. 'Oh, I am pleased. Do take a seat wherever you like.'

We walked into the tiny church, which had just four pews on either side. David motioned to the right-hand side in the second aisle and so we scooched in. There was a display of bright purple flowers on either side of the lectern. Anabel sat between David and me, excitedly swinging her legs.

'This is us now, is it? Churchgoers,' he whispered. 'This was your plan all along, wasn't it? Get me to the country, get me converted.'

I slapped his leg. 'Oh, stop it.' Then I whispered as Anabel leant forward to retrieve the song sheet from in front of her, 'It's for Anabel.'

'I don't mind.' He looked at me. 'I just want you to be happy.' He gave me that half-sympathetic smile, and I felt myself crumble inside. He was right, because that was all he wanted. And I felt such a terrible wife for having let him down so colossally before. I hated myself again for allowing things to build up over Evie and Verity. I hoped that by hosting the party in a few weeks, I could put it all behind me. People would see me as a balanced individual who had her life together, and I would have buried any negative feelings by then.

'I don't think you have anything to worry about any more, David.' I squeezed his leg and smiled at him. I knew that I would never let what happened before happen again. Not here under the microscope of such a small community.

The church became packed rapidly, and almost all the pews were full by the time Conner shut the doors and made his way to the front of the church. Then I heard the doors open again, and I, like many others, turned to see who was making a late arrival. I was stunned to see Verity hovering in the doorway. She didn't clock me as she scanned the room for a spare seat and eventually slipped into one in the back aisle on the left. She picked up the song sheet and kept her head bent down. Her shoulder-length hair was hanging loose as she dropped her head. David turned to see who I was looking at, and when he couldn't work it out, he looked at me with curious eyes. I shook my head and turned my head back to the front, to the lectern where Conner was clearing his throat and about to begin his sermon.

* * *

The service was lovely, with a few surprising jokes thrown in, which David had laughed wholeheartedly at. I tried to get away quickly so I could see Verity on the way out. I wanted to know why she was here in church, alone. On Mother's Day! But David had dawdled, helping Anabel go back for her song sheet, which she wanted for her keepsake box, then Conner collared David, and I could hear David's booming laugh from the doorway, where I stood scanning the road both ways to see if I could see Verity as the congregation filtered out around me.

When David finally joined me outside, he had that curious look in his eye again.

'Where did you get to so fast?' We fell into step, Anabel a few feet behind us.

'I wanted some fresh air,' I lied.

'You wanted to see something, that's for sure. I saw you rubbernecking all through the service. Who did you spot?'

I sighed. 'That Verity woman.'

'Oh, she's "that Verity woman" now, is she?' David said. 'And what could she possibly have done to annoy you in church?'

'She— She didn't annoy me, actually. I just wanted to catch her eye, to ask her if she was going to accept the invite to the party.'

'Miranda,' David said quietly. I knew what his tone meant. He had only ever said my name in that way on a few occasions. But with Anabel in tow, I knew he couldn't say anything about what had happened before. Besides, we had both agreed never to bring it up again, not even as ammunition in an argument. It would only be spoken about if it really had to be. Which was David's way of saying, *if it ever happens again*. A wave of panic tickled my senses. Was he worried about my state of mind again?

But David didn't speak. He just took my hand, and we walked slowly, making our way through the village. Anabel caught up with us and began chatting about the service as she walked in front. Would we go to church again? Wasn't Conner nice? And then suddenly Anabel stopped and called across the road. David and I stopped just behind her and realised we were just about to pass the three terraced cottages on the opposite side of the road. And there, just outside Potter's Earth, were Verity, Evie and Juno.

'Can I cross over, Mummy, and say hello?' I was dumbfounded again, as I often seemed to be these days whenever I saw Verity and Evie together. Which seemed to be quite often. David told Anabel to look left and right, even though there was no traffic, before she dashed across. On the other side of the road, Evie raised her hand and waved at me. I managed to raise my hand back at her and pulled my mouth into a semi-smile.

'Don't you want to go over? Wish her a happy Mother's Day?' David nudged me.

I crossed the road and David dutifully followed. Anabel and Juno were deep in conversation.

'Good morning,' I said to both Verity and Evie.

'Such a lovely morning it is too,' Evie said. It sounded stiff, and too much like a conversation filler.

'Gorgeous.' I turned to Verity. 'How did you enjoy the service just now?'

Evie looked at Verity. 'You've been to church?' she asked, and I felt a flutter of joy, then instant guilt. Had I been trying to catch Verity out?

Verity nodded. 'Yes.' She cleared her throat and looked anxiously about, not knowing where to rest her gaze.

'It was a lovely service, wasn't it?' I said.

'It was. He is a very nice vicar,' Verity said, shifting her feet and looking anywhere except at me. I knew that some people found social interactions difficult, but Verity's inability to even look at me when I spoke to her was starting to annoy me.

'So, are you very religious?' I asked, and I could feel David shuffle his feet next to me and clear his throat. I knew what he was thinking – it was too personal. But the woman had just been in church. We had been coerced in with chocolates and flowers, which I now carried in my bag, but Verity had rushed in as though she needed no bribe whatsoever.

'Oh no, not really. I like churches, and I felt I wanted to be in one this morning. For research.'

'For the book.' I added to the sentence for her. *This illusive book,* I wanted to add. So far, I had only managed to get within a few feet of Verity, barely extracting any information from her about her life, yet whenever I saw her with Evie, they seemed perfectly at ease. She had babysat Juno, for goodness' sake. Why had she made such a beeline for Evie? If Evie was making time for Verity, I needed to be involved to. Not all the time, but it would be nice to be included occasionally instead of turning up at book club and finding her there, seeing her around the school, finding out she had been babysitting Juno. This was the sort of stuff that enraged me, and usually I was such an even-tempered person.

'You must tell me all about it sometime. I love to read, and I'd love to hear all about your writing process,' I said.

'I suppose it's difficult talking about the writing when you're actually doing it,' Evie said to Verity, who looked at her for a moment as though she were really considering what she had said.

'Yes, yes it can be,' Verity said.

I felt a rage of anger bubble up inside me again; Evie had blatantly answered my question to Verity for her.

'Juno bought Verity flowers – look, Mummy. Daffodils like yours!' Anabel said, and I looked down at Verity's hand and saw a large bunch there. That was exactly the sort of kind thing Evie would do for someone. Here was Verity, clearly childless on Mother's Day, and so she had given flowers to her. I felt a wave of envy, that the two of them were clearly in the early stages of cementing some sort of bond. I felt like a spectator on the sidelines. I could muscle my way into the action; tell them 'Hey, three's not a crowd! It's the magic number' but I preferred relationships to evolve naturally, the way mine had with Evie.

I thought a little more about why Verity could have been at church this morning. Perhaps she had lost her mother and found this day difficult. Perhaps she couldn't have children. Or the worst possibility, maybe she had lost a child. Whatever it was, Evie was far more clued up about Verity's personal circumstances than I was. And here I was, on the outside looking in, picking up scraps of information that had been dropped and neglected.

'They are so pretty. What a big bunch,' I said.

'I went a bit mad and picked loads,' Juno said.

Evie gently placed her hand on her daughter's head and stroked her hair. 'What do you have planned for the rest of the day?' she asked, still with her hand on Juno's head.

I looked at David. 'Well, we're walking around the village, and then, I don't know. David, do you have any other plans?' I quipped, and Evie smiled. She knew that David was a great guy, but I occasionally had to chivvy him along.

'Well, I, erm, I thought maybe a slap-up lunch at the pub,' he said spontaneously.

'On Mother's Day. You'll be lucky. They'll be fully booked, I would imagine,' Evie said.

'Oh, right, well, a roast at home it is. Do we have any meat in, darling?'

'There's a leg of lamb in the fridge.' I smiled knowingly at Evie, and she smiled back. Oh, why couldn't it be just like this all the time? Just the two of us sharing in-jokes. I didn't need loads of friends. I had been there, done that, spent far too many years trying to please too many people. All I wanted, all I had hoped for when I moved to Helesbury was to meet one woman, one mum friend with whom I could feel myself. That had been Evie, just a week or two ago, and now, it was just me, looking in on these two women, seeing this relationship evolving in front of my eyes and wondering if I should push my way in or stay sat on the sidelines. Evie kept me calm – just her presence in this village was enough to make me realise I was enough.

I wanted to ask Verity if she had thought about my invitation to the party, to shine a light on a topic that wasn't so close to her heart on a day like today. But even in my attempt to do good by not focusing on Verity's apparent loss, I would end up looking selfish. So I swallowed the words that were bubbling on my tongue.

'Right, let's get this walk done. We would have been finished ages ago but we keep getting a bit sidetracked, what with popping into church for an hour this morning,' David said, and I was relieved he had read the situation right and was about to take me away from it. I took hold of Anabel's hand and we said our goodbyes and began slowly strolling away.

* * *

We arrived home after our walk ravenous. David busied himself with getting the lamb prepared and into the oven, and I climbed into the window seat and tried to relax with the magazine I had picked up the other day but had yet to barely glance at. My mind was on overdrive, and I had to try and calm down before things started to get out of control again.

My phone flashed and buzzed on the coffee table, and instantly I knew who it would be. I had meant to call my mum first thing, but I'd forgotten. I sighed and put the magazine down. I would have to answer it, today of all days.

'Mum!' I said. 'I was going to call you shortly. We have just got back from a huge walk around the village.'

Fifteen minutes later, I put my mobile phone down on the coffee table and let out a long sigh. I was glad I had spoken to my mother, because it meant I could breathe easy for another week or so. I knew she was lonely since Dad passed, but it was as though she could no longer remember how anything was when I was a child, as though she had conveniently forgotten the endless days spent in her bed when my father was nowhere to be seen. Their relationship had been fraught with tension, and it was only something I had come to realise with time. Seeing her as this beautiful hostess as a young child, I'd been dazzled by the theatre of it all. It was only the next day that I would see the shoddy ruins of the mess left behind once the show was over. But in the same way my father sucked all the energy from my mother, the same was true for me when I was with her or spoke to her on the phone. I had to use every ounce of energy to remain positive and upbeat. I curled up in the window seat, felt the heat of the sun wrapping me up like a blanket as I closed my eyes for just a few seconds.

* * *

I woke suddenly, gasped for air and sat up. I had fallen asleep, and in my dream had seen the face of someone at the window. It had been her. Verity. I felt her presence, and I shuddered. I reached out and touched the windowpane, as though the vision had actually been real.

'What are you doing, love?' David appeared in the doorway to the lounge. I turned and tried to bring myself back to the present – I was still half lingering in the dream. Verity's face was no longer at the window, but it was still there in my mind's eye. What had begun as a sorrowful expression morphed into a steely-eyed stare as though she were trying to rip me apart with her eyes.

'I, I had a horrible... nightmare,' I said to David, feeling foolish for falling asleep and waking in such a panic.

'A nightmare in the middle of the day? It wasn't about my cooking, was it? I'm sorry I haven't laid out the red carpet for you, love, but I am trying my best, I promise you. I just came to tell you another hour and lunch will be served.'

I rested my head against the inside of the window frame and watched David leave the room, feeling spaced out, unable to fathom what day it was and trying to recollect how the morning had unfolded. Falling asleep in the middle of the day was something I did when I was stressed, but luckily David hadn't made the connection and was probably just pleased to see I was relaxing on what was supposed to be my day. But I could feel the tendrils of uncertainty beginning to creep through my mind. That alone should have been enough to send the familiar alarm bells ringing. What was more unsettling was that I knew my feelings about Evie and Verity had instilled a disquiet within me, and it was already too late to stop it all unravelling.

17

Wednesday was market day in the village. It had been just three days since I had chatted to Evie and Verity outside Potter's Earth. I had seen Evie on the school run, but I had not seen anything else of Verity since the awkward moment on Mother's Day.

I had a list and had brought my wicker basket with me. I loved shopping with it – it made me feel so provincial. It was one of the things I had been most excited about when I knew we were moving to this village. I had always imagined myself wrapped in a shawl – or pashmina, in my case – heading to the local market to pick up supplies. And here I was, living my reality. Except it was still the same me who worried about what people thought of me, who wanted to be liked and appreciated, who needed to keep a friend in Evie, who felt threatened by Verity's growing presence. On top of that, I had itchy fingers. My mind was reminding me that I only had to go online, press a few buttons and I could be back in the world of social media. I might be able to find out a bit more about Verity. That was what people did these days when they were discovering new things about someone, go and check out their Facebook profile. See who they spend time with, how much information they share publicly. But somehow, I knew I wouldn't find out that sort of information about Verity online. She was a closed book in person, so I imagined she would have next to no presence online.

The market was situated at the edge of the rec, outside the village hall, and ran from 10 a.m. until 2 p.m. I could probably get a better and wider selection of vegetables from my online Ocado order, but I liked the idea of supporting the local community and eating seasonal produce. I meandered the market and stopped to chat to some of the stallholders, who were always cheery in that market stallholder way. I picked up some local cheese, a head of cauliflower and some carrots.

I was just eyeing up some ginger cordial when I spotted someone coming closer in my peripheral vision. I looked up and saw it was Hatty. She grinned at me.

'I thought that was you,' she said as she came closer.

'Hatty!' I said, thankful it was her. For one panicked moment, I thought it could have been Verity, and after the awkward conversation outside of her house on Mother's Day, I was running out of things I could say to her.

'That ginger cordial is too good! I sometimes have it with a spot of vodka and tonic on a Sunday afternoon,' she quipped. 'I say, you're not busy now, are you?'

'Why, is it vodka o'clock?' I laughed.

'Oh gosh, no – I generally reserve myself for the weekend, or after the boys are in bed. No, I thought we could have a cup of tea, me and you, at mine.'

I thought about what I had planned for the rest of the morning: packaging a few candles and emailing a couple of potential suppliers. That could wait until later.

'I'd love a cup of tea.' I thought about the cosiness of Hatty's kitchen and although it wasn't the sort of place I would host a dinner party, it was exactly the sort of place for a bit of a gossip. I wondered if Hatty would share my thoughts on Verity. I had the time it took us to wander to her house to work out a way to subtly ask her opinion.

Hatty's house was as chaotic, if not more chaotic than I had seen it on book club evening.

'This is what happens when you have three boys – and a man – running around the house at the same time,' Hatty said as we picked our way through PE bags, shoes, hockey sticks and violin cases to the kitchen. 'I won't apologise for the mess either, as I wouldn't have it any other way.'

'Oh no, don't feel you have to on my behalf. I am sure my house would be in the same condition if I had three boys.'

'Somehow, Miranda, I don't think that is entirely true.' Hatty smiled down at me from the Aga. 'I think, in fact I know, you would have a pristine house no matter how many children or what sex they were. Right, now what tea can I interest you in?' Hatty pulled off her thin floral jacket and hung it over the back of a chair.

I had already removed my pashmina and I leant over to the chair next to me where it lay and stroked the material flat. Being in Hatty's house made me enjoy the organisation of my home even more. I had become so accustomed to needing others to see the perfection. Did people still believe in what they saw on the surface? I hoped so.

'I'll have one of those delicious cherry ones, if you have it?' I said, refer-ring to the drink she had served me after dinner at book club the other week.

'Right on.' She filled the kettle and put it on the Aga. 'I've finished the book, I am pleased to say.'

I, ashamedly, had not even started it. 'Wow, Hatty, how do you have the time?'

'I tell them all to bugger off and I just read for an hour a day.'

That would account for half of the chaos, I thought as I stopped myself from taking a surreptitious glance around the kitchen.

'And I know what you're thinking, that I should probably clean my house instead.' Hatty smirked round at me as she prepared the teacups.

'God no!' I said, trying not to cover the lie. 'I should probably take a leaf out of your book – excuse the pun – then I might have finished by now.' The truth was, I had been so distracted by Verity's arrival that I had barely been able to concentrate on anything, let alone to sit and read.

'Well, I'm sure you'll get to it in time. You are very organised like that. I am a bit greedy and like to inhale a book in one.'

I laughed as the kettle began singing its tune.

'That boils fast,' I said.

'Tiny bit of water is the key. Never over fill a kettle – you'll be waiting all day for it.'

We settled down at the table with our teas and chatted about our Mother's Days, and then I found it was my opportunity to bring up Verity.

'I saw her in church that morning,' I said.

'Did you, now?' Hatty seemed surprised. 'Now I would never have had her down as a religious type.'

'Oh.' I was intrigued. 'Why would you say that?'

'Well' – Hatty leant forward as though there might be someone near who could hear us, except her husband was at work and all the children were at school – 'I could just say she looks very unchristian-like, but that would be being presumptuous, wouldn't it? I know we're a small, tight-knit community, so I don't want to sound as though I am gossiping, but then I am usually right about people. My theory is now backed up by the one day I visited her house—'

'You visited her house!' I exclaimed.

'I did – and only by accident, mind. There was no invite. I was walking home from school with the boys and there was a Tesco delivery van outside her house. The chap delivering could only have been a teenager, early twenties at the most. Clearly no idea how to handle produce! He practically threw the bag into the doorway, and I tell you, twelve eggs went everywhere. I saw it all as we approached her house – you know how those pokey little cottages are practically on the path. The lad was a bumbling mess. I approached the door as she was scooping up the bag with the remnants of the eggs, and well, I just boldly stepped over her and asked her where she kept her kitchen roll. She said there was some on the side in the kitchen, so I grabbed a wad and cleaned that eggy mess up in seconds. But it was when I was walking through the kitchen with the roll that I noticed a book on the side with the title *God is not great*. It struck me as odd, because I had never heard of it or seen such a title before. I could only presume it is the sort of book that is read by someone who doesn't go to church?'

'You're right.' I sat back with my tea. 'But then she might have thought the same about me. I've only been to the church once for Mother's Day!'

'Ahh, but you said Anabel was keen, and it was a lovely service. I have been to some wonderful services here before. But if you were the type of person to have a book like that lying around the house, you are advertising yourself as a bit of an atheist, aren't you?'

I nodded. 'I would say so.'

'Which begs the question, why was she at church on Sunday morning?'

'I can only think she had similar ideas to Anabel, that it would make a nice change, and maybe she has lost a mother.'

'Or a child,' Hatty casually added.

I had considered this possibility, and the thought still unnerved me. There was something so sad, hauntingly empty about a mother who had lost a child in whatever circumstance.

'Well, if she did, has, I mean, then it doesn't bear thinking about,' I said. I didn't wish to sound like a gossip either. I wanted to sound more compassionate. 'I mean, if that is the case, then she must be very confused and in a lot of pain.'

'I imagine she is. Maybe that's why she's here, to get away from her demons. Perhaps it was recent,' Hatty said, a stroke of sympathy in her voice.

Trying to paint some sort of picture of who Verity was from these scraps of information could mean that Verity and I had more in common than I would like to admit. I knew better than anyone that running from the past didn't change it. It simply placed an invisible barrier in between the then and the now. But at any point, someone could cross right over and walk amongst the broken pieces of your life that you thought you had left behind.

I began to think and piece it all together. If I had come here to run away from my past, then maybe Verity had come to do the same thing. 'That would make sense,' I said to Hatty.

'What would make sense?' she quizzed.

I realised I was thinking aloud. I hadn't shared any of my concerns or grievances about Verity with anyone. 'Are you saying that you have your doubts about her? New woman to the village and all, and well, let's not pretend we haven't noticed how very fond Evie seems to be of her.' Hatty chuckled.

I let my skin prickle. So others had noticed how much time Verity had been spending with Evie. Did they also notice what a rude obnoxious cow she was, as well? Apparently not from the usual causal tone to Hatty's voice.

'Oh no, I have no issues with Verity at all,' I lied. I didn't want Hatty to see me as someone who found fault in others. As much as I wanted to talk about how rude Verity had been to me on several occasions, I wanted to appear amiable. 'I just like to observe people, and I found it interesting that she was alone in church, and well, now that you have suggested that she might be a grieving mother, then it makes sense that she would want to lock herself away and only come out for little interaction. Perhaps that's why she's so taken with Evie. Perhaps too much company is overwhelming for her.'

'Well, she was very quiet at book club, and I do hope we will see her at the next one – it's so nice to have some fresh blood in the village. And I really want to quiz her some more about her writing. So fascinating.'

I felt a tightening in my gut at the prospect of Verity coming to the book club. I had hoped very much that she would give the next one a miss. We had established our little group, and we were at risk of shifting the dynamics too much by having a seventh member. Well, that's what I would say to Hatty or anyone else should I have felt I had to, but really, the thought of Evie and Verity becoming even closer was what bothered me the most.

'I mean, we are quite a rowdy bunch, aren't we?' Hatty laughed. 'When we get going. I think we may have scared her off.'

'She was awfully quiet,' I added. 'And you're right. We're definitely not quiet.' I reiterated Hatty's point for extra emphasis.

'Well,' hooted Hatty, 'you know what they say! It's the quiet ones you have to watch.' She laughed and walked to the cupboard and retrieved a packet of biscuits. It was only a throwaway comment, but besides the slither of sympathy I had for Verity and whatever tragic personal circumstances had brought her to this village, I knew that for as long as she was here, I would certainly always have one eye on her.

18

10 MAY 2019 – 10.56 A.M. – GLOUCESTERSHIRE POLICE STATION

Interview with Hatty Whilloby (continued)

It was only a few weeks ago I was having a chat over a cup of tea with Miranda about Verity. I try very hard not to judge people and I can't stand idle gossip, but we got to talking about the new arrival to the village and we both came to the same conclusion. Miranda seemed very content with our theory, and I must say it was most plausible. I mean, why does a woman just arrive in a village all alone with barely any backstory, no family, and in a small village like this? So, I did find it odd that she was here, alone. But I had kept my thoughts to myself – like I say, idle gossip is not one of my favourite pastimes. But Miranda seemed to draw it out of me and before I knew what was happening, I was gossiping! I felt bad afterwards and ended up finishing the packet of biscuits that I had brought out to have with the tea. Miranda didn't touch any – such a slim woman that one, don't where she gets the will power.

But, of course, looking back now, I realise that conversation was the catalyst for what came next. When I think about it like that, I shudder, because had I known I was arming Miranda with ammunition, I wouldn't have said a thing about Verity or shared what I had seen in her house.

This is such a small village and for something like that to have happened here, well, it will go down in history, I should imagine. Can it not go on the record that I was one of the people who instigated it with my words to Miranda Wallace? Unless, of course, you think it might paint me in a good light.

You know, I lost a baby after our first child. I have never told anyone this. It was pretty early into the pregnancy, but I was still very much attached. I know how I felt after only a few weeks of bonding with my unborn child, so, of course, it was easy for me to see how a woman like Verity could come across as so sad, coming to a very family-orientated village without a child of her own.

I can also see why Miranda was so keen to get to the bottom of it. Miranda and Evie had been very close, and Verity pretty much just stepped into her shoes. I mean, obviously I was shocked when I heard what had happened that night – I still am. But to be honest, I was surprised about what I found out about Miranda. People say she was on a bit of a rampage that same night, because that woman from her past showed up and stirred up a right hornet's nest. Couldn't have been nice for her. From what I know, that was the reason she went over to Evie's house in the first place, to have it out with Verity. I could never have imagined that the night would pan out the way it did. Shocking. Absolutely shocking. To think we live in a quiet village. Even with a house full of lads, I have always been a deep sleeper. But after this, I am not sure I will ever sleep soundly again.

19

It was the day of the party, and I had been running around like a headless chicken planning the menu and ordering the good champagne from my favourite wine merchant in Chelsea. This was officially the first big event I had hosted here, and I wanted the absolute best for my guests. I had been nervous about what people might make of me; I felt as though I had a heavy cloak wrapped around me, protecting what was beneath – the ugly memories of my past mistakes – and at any moment someone might whip it off and discover what lay beneath. I still carried the weight of the tragedy, but here I knew people only knew this version of me. There was no need to pick and pry. They accepted what they got with me. Of course, in his casual, non-offensive way, David had told me to tread carefully. He suggested I take it slowly, but I felt it had been long enough; people knew I loved to entertain, and I did miss being the hostess.

Everyone had RSVP'd and most had said yes to coming. Even, finally, Verity. The very woman I had been intending to throw the party for in the first place. She hadn't told me directly, of course, Evie passed on the reply for me – I thought it had taken her long enough to get back to me. It was if she had contemplated it right up until the last second. I was no longer sure I wanted to welcome her. I'd barely had any contact with her since I had seen her on Mother's Day. But she was coming, and people would see I wasn't holding any grudges against her, especially Evie. If Evie liked Verity that much, then I needed to show I was willing to welcome her in as well.

I had rushed through an early lunch with David and Anabel, and then Anabel was instructed to go off and play for the afternoon so I could prepare the finishing touches. I had prepped asparagus and goats cheese wrapped in prosciutto, and spring onion bhajis with mint and coriander chutney. I kept the canapés at just two, as there were sirloin steaks, prawn or chicken kebabs and several kinds of salad – courtesy of my Ottolenghi cookbook – for the main courses.

David came into the kitchen as I was polishing the champagne glasses. My mind was swimming with thoughts of the afternoon. From three, everyone would start to arrive. How would I be? It had been such a long time since I had entertained like this. I vividly remembered the last time I had been in a room with people I had considered to be my friends. The shame of it now really, the way they all knew the truth, yet they came anyway... to watch my fall from grace. I still shuddered at the memory. I knew this was a different place, a different time, different people, all of whom I cared for and admired in different ways – but the horrors of the past still haunted me.

David slipped his arm around my waist and kissed my head.

'I'm proud of you,' he murmured into my hair.

I forced a smile. 'Even though I let you down so badly?' The memories were stark in my mind today.

He pulled away and came to my side. 'We don't need to speak of it, Miranda. That's all in the past. This is a fresh start. That's what we discussed, remember?'

'But I do still think about it. And then I feel as though it's written all over me, that everyone secretly knows.'

'No one knows, Miranda. No one in this little village will ever know. You are safe here.'

I appreciated David talking about it with me, as we rarely allowed ourselves to. But today was a big deal, bringing so many people into our space.

I heard the word lingering. *Safe.* Because that was exactly how I did not feel when it had all happened. I felt it was easier for David to put it all behind him – men were good at that – but I was still plagued by all of it. It was still so raw in my mind. But I was trying. I was so grateful for David. For sticking by me through all of it. And by instigating the move to the countryside. Once I arrived here, it was as if I hadn't been breathing right all that time in London. Suddenly, in Helesbury, I felt as though I could take in great big lungfuls of air.

I put down the champagne glass and put my arms around him. He pulled me into him, and I felt the strength of his arms enveloping my whole body.

'What time is everyone coming?' Anabel asked. I pulled out of the embrace as our daughter came through into the kitchen.

'I told you, honey, three o'clock. But people don't tend to come exactly at the time it says on the invitation.'

'Why not? That's silly. I want Juno. I want to play with someone. I'm booooorrred.'

I sucked in a long breath.

David looked at me and then at Anabel.

'You know what, Bel Bel? Why don't you come and help me get the barbeque ready? I need to make sure I have all my tools and plates. Do you think you can help me with that?'

Anabel shrugged her shoulders. 'I s'pose.'

'Good.' David walked to the door, put an arm around Anabel, then quickly turned to look at me before he left the kitchen.

I mouthed, 'Thank you,' and finished the final champagne glass, buffed it up and placed it perfectly in line with the others.

I remember my mother taking several minutes out before guests arrived to sit down and take some deep breaths. It was to ease the adrenaline that had built up as she rushed around, finishing the final touches. Then, when the doorbell went, she would be ready to greet her guests with a radiant, calm smile, not a forced, anxious one. This was one tip I had taken from her, and I did it every time I had guests over, no matter how big or small the gathering. It seemed strange settling myself in the chair minutes before people were due to arrive, the very opposite of what my body was telling me to do, and because it had been such a long time since I had performed this little ritual, it felt even more strange. But I forced myself to stay still, and I took long, slow, deep inhales, holding my breath for a few seconds, before exhaling to really slow my heart rate down.

The doorbell rang at just before three. It was time.

* * *

By four, the house was buzzing and so was I. It had been a long time coming, and I almost wished I hadn't waited so long to get people in my space. It brought me so much joy. Not only because I knew I was so good at it, but it was such a thrill to see the house so full, and to see people mingling and interacting, people that may not usually have spent much time talking with one another. Beth and Conner – who was still donning his white collar, because apparently, he is never off duty – were deep in conversation and had been for the last thirty minutes. He was at least ten years older than her, and I wasn't even sure if vicars were allowed to date, but it was sweet seeing Beth so utterly entranced by him and laughing so delightfully. I looked forward to being able to share some wisdom with Beth if she and Conner decided to make a go of it.

Evie had arrived with Juno, followed a few minutes later by Verity. But I refused to dwell on the coincidence of the timing. This was my party. They were here because I had orchestrated it. Hatty and her husband looked to be having a lovely time chatting and laughing with one another whilst their three boys ran around the garden and made use of the tree house and wooden Wendy house, playing hide-and-seek with the other children.

Seeing the house so full, I panicked that I wouldn't have enough barbeque food. The canapés had gone down a storm and disappeared in five minutes flat. I was just going to go and check on the barbeque situation when David came into the kitchen through the patio doors and announced that the food was ready.

Everyone began to filter outside, and I strolled behind happily. I heard a small voice to my left, the sound of a child saying, 'Because I don't want to,' in that long, drawn-out, whiny way that young kids do, and I instinctively thought it was Anabel. But just outside the kitchen door, I spotted Juno. She had her arms crossed and was scowling. I moved towards the door and then suddenly Verity stepped into the doorway. I looked at her, questioning her with my eyes, trying to ascertain what had happened and why Juno was speaking to her that way. Verity said nothing and simply squeezed past Juno, mumbling, 'Excuse me,' before heading through the patio doors. I walked out into the hallway; Juno was still standing there with a sulky look on her face. I looked along the hall-way, which led to an open back door where guests had been coming in and out of since they arrived, as it also led to the garden. I could not see anyone who looked as if they had just gone through the door, which meant that it was likely that it was Verity with whom Juno had become frustrated.

I bent down and touched Juno's shoulder.

'Are you okay, Juno?' I asked. Then she looked up at me and beamed a smile.

'Oh yes, Miranda. I'd really like a sausage sandwich.'

'Well, shall I take you over to the barbeque and we can find your mum as well? Yes?'

I took her hand and led her into the garden, where the smell of the meats sizzling on the griddle in the warm afternoon air was enticing. Yet, I felt my gut churning in response to the way Juno had reacted to whatever it was that Verity had said to her. Perhaps she had been trying to coax her out to the garden and I was overthinking it – something, I promised myself I would not be doing today. I squeezed Juno's hand to reassure her – about what, I wasn't exactly sure. But I suddenly felt drawn to Juno like a magnet, as I would be to any child who seemed frustrated or upset in the company of an adult.

'What was Verity saying to you just then, Juno? Did she upset you?' I said quickly. I could see Evie was looking at us and waving.

'Hmm, just being annoying,' Juno said, and I choked out a laugh. So I wasn't the only one who had recognised fault in Verity. It was a shame it was only the perception of an eight-year-old child, otherwise she would be good to have on my team.

I found Evie in a huddle with a few of the school mums and Tash.

'I found this little one looking for some food.' I handed Juno over to Evie, who pulled her to her side.

'You okay, poppet?'

'Yeah,' Juno said in that stale way that little kids speak when they are answering for the sake of answering.

'Well, shall we get you a bit of lunch then? How about a sausage?'

'That's what I said. I wanted a sausage!' Juno brightened. Evie took her over to David at the barbeque and I noticed Verity was now over the other side of the garden, alone. I saw this as my opportunity to have a one-on-one with her. I grabbed a bottle of champagne from an ice bucket and two glasses and strode over to her. She was examining the rhododendron bush.

'It's beautiful when it's in full bloom. We were lucky enough to move in when the flowers were just starting to come out.' I held out a champagne glass to Verity.

'I really shouldn't,' she said after a beat, looking at the champagne glass.

I frowned. 'It's a party. You absolutely should,' I said, forcing a smile and trying to conceal the contempt in my voice. This woman had been nothing but hostile towards me.

'I've had only two canapés and I haven't eaten any other food yet.' Verity looked towards the barbeque, where Evie was still standing with Juno.

'I'll make sure David loads you up with a plate right away. Have a drink. I insist.' I shoved the glass further towards her.

Verity looked at the champagne glass for another second or two, her eyes flitting up at me and back to the glass, and then took it from me.

'There we go,' I said, as though I were encouraging a petulant child. I filled it halfway for her. 'Something to wet the whistle.' I raised my eyebrows up and down.

Verity took a drink of the champagne and then dabbed at her mouth with her other hand. 'Very fizzy,' she said drolly, and I found myself take another step towards her as though I was drawn to her like a magnet.

'I have to say, I chose the best for today – I wanted it to be special.' I topped my own champagne glass up and propped the bottle up in the hedgerow. I held my glass out to Verity. 'Cheers.'

She copied the gesture. 'Cheers.' Her eyes met mine for a flicker of a second. Then she was back to looking anywhere but at me.

'You know,' I began, feeling two glasses of champagne doing its work, 'I should let you into a little secret.'

Verity looked up at me, a spark of interest in her eye.

'I actually wanted to host this party in your honour. To welcome you to the village.'

'Oh.' Verity shifted from foot to foot and then kicked at a small tuft of grass with the toe of her sandal. I looked at the grass and wondered how David could have missed such a chunk when he was mowing the lawn earlier.

'Yes, but don't worry, I soon talked myself out of it. I didn't want to overwhelm you. And since you've been anything but gracious towards me since you arrived, I decided to keep it under my hat. I was very keen to have some people around for food and drinks, so it all worked out fine in the end.'

Verity stared hard at me for a second. 'Thank you for thinking of me,' she said, almost robotic-like. I looked across the lawn and I spotted Evie looking our way. She was doing that thing where she was trying to stay engaged in the conversation, but kept sneaking surreptitious looks our way. Did she seem anxious that I had managed to corner Verity and was engaging her in conversation; the first real chat we'd had since she moved here – despite it feeling forced and fake. I could sense Evie was itching to intervene.

'I suppose you must be on some sort of deadline?' I edged a glance over at Evie. I felt as though I were on a sort of deadline myself with this conversation, and I needed to accelerate it to keep Verity engaged. I hoped talking about her passion would do it.

Verity waited a moment before she answered and then took a deep breath. 'Yes, there is a deadline. Sooner than I would have hoped, actually.' Verity seemed unsettled by her own comment.

'Oh, doesn't sound like you're happy about that.' I spoke as politely as I would to a client.

'No, I'm not.' She looked at me and took one gulp of champagne. 'But nothing is ever as you want it to be though, is it?' A glimmer of a grimace appeared across her face.

'No, that is one thing about life – it likes to throw you a few curve balls. But I suppose being tucked away in Potter's Earth, you are able to concentrate?'

'I had hoped I would, but it's proving quite difficult.'

'Are the words just not coming? Is that what they call writer's block?

What does that feel like?' The conversation batted between us like a polite game of tennis.

'There's a mental block, all right. Lots of blocks actually, just things that I had hoped wouldn't be a problem in this project are turning out to be a real pain.'

I double blinked and felt my guard drop. She had to be referring to me. I righted myself. This was my house, I had no need to feel threatened. I would continue the conversation as if we were referring to her writing.

'Well, is there not a way you could – I don't know – jump over any of these stumbling blocks? I mean, you have to do what you have to do to survive, don't you?'

Verity looked thoughtful for a moment. Then she nodded her head.

'I mean, you've been here a while. If you don't feel you are progressing...' I sipped my champagne and looked around the lawn. If I wasn't mistaken, I would say Evie was looking more uncomfortable and almost ready to walk over to us.

Verity was nodding and intermittently sipping her champagne until it was all gone. She looked at her empty glass and shoved it towards me.

'Is there any more of that?'

I bent down and picked up the bottle from the bush and poured her another glass, this time filling past the halfway mark. The bubbles shot to the top and trickled over the rim of the glass.

'Ooh, sorry, not my steadiest pour.'

Verity seemed pleased with the refill and took a long sip, and I felt the atmosphere change. My plan had worked. She was beginning to relax around me. But just as I too was beginning to feel relaxed enough to push the conversation and break down the barrier that Verity had built between us, I heard a 'Hiya!' and a breathless Evie was at our side.

Verity was suddenly very interested in her champagne glass. 'These are lovely glasses, Miranda.' Her tone was lighter and airier than it had been before Evie arrived.

I looked at Evie. 'Not drinking today, Evie?' I looked at her empty hand.

'I've had one glass.' She was speaking quite loudly. 'I find that too many glasses of champagne in the afternoon do not agree with me, especially if I haven't eaten anything.' Evie looked at me with wide eyes and then at Verity and back at me again.

'Oh.' I looked at Verity, who was starting to sway a little. She had downed almost two glasses of champagne in the space of a few minutes. I pulled a grimace at Evie, as a sort of apology.

'To be honest though, Evie, you are a bit of a lightweight.' I laughed. Verity let out an almighty snort, which shocked me. Both Evie and I looked at her.

'Sorry,' Verity said. 'Just that term *lightweight*, always makes me laugh.'

Evie looked at Verity, her face taut and expressionless.

'I think I might go and get some more food. Verity, would you like to come with me?' Evie tried to sound bright.

Verity threw her hands up in the air, the last remaining droplets of champagne flew out of the glass.

'Sure, why not!' she said. It sounded a little childish, as though being here was a bind for her. But then, if she was struggling to get done what she needed to get done, then the last place she would want to be was at a barbeque with families and kids.

'Great.' Evie ushered her past me, and as Verity began to walk away, she quickly turned to me and whispered hurriedly. 'I haven't seen her eat a thing, and she seems quite stressed, wouldn't you say? I think it's the book, it's really getting her down. I'll make sure she eats something.' And she turned to catch up with Verity. Evie grabbed her by the shoulders and ushered her towards the barbeque where Juno was, perched nearby in a patio chair, eating her sausage. As Juno clocked Verity approaching, I was sure I saw her roll her eyes. I smiled to myself as I thought back to her earlier comment when she referred to Verity as annoying.

I watched them all for a few moments, and I wondered who it was that should really be bothering me. When I met Verity at Hatty's for the book club, her presence unnerved me. I was convinced she was the one that was here to try and steal my Evie from me. But watching the way Evie had just swooped in just now and ushered Verity away, it was as though she wasn't too comfortable with me spending time alone with Verity. It all felt strange, and I knew something was off, but I couldn't put my finger on it, because I was sure deep down, I was over thinking it all and I just needed to take some time out from it all and let it be. What will be will be and all that jazz. I didn't move to the countryside for more stress. I came here to get away from it all and to manage my mental health, which had been in complete tatters when I arrived. What if this was all just a trigger? I had invested so many years of my life in Chelsea only to have it all blow up in my face. Evie was the first friend I had been able to trust in a long time and I needed to slow down, not try to rush things. Perhaps I was just letting thoughts of the past become muddled with the present. Yes, that was what I needed to do. I just needed to be more Queen Elsa about this and just *let it go*.

I poured the last of the champagne into my glass and took one long gulp, then headed back over to where Evie and Juno had moved onto the grass. Verity was still next to the barbeque, finally filling up on food. Anabel and Juno began a game of chase, weaving in and out of guests, who all scooped their legs aside to let the girls play. I saw Verity's face had changed colour – she was almost beetroot colour and I edged over to her in case it was the food that was causing her bother, but as I was approaching, I saw her turn to Juno and say something. It looked as though she had just told her off. I walked over quickly and intercepted, worried for Anabel, who would not have taken a dressing down as lightly as Juno had – who was now darting away as though nothing had happened.

'Sweetie,' I said to Anabel, who was looking perturbed that the game had ended so abruptly. 'Why don't you and Juno go and play in your room for half an hour, have a little rest?' Anabel shrugged and followed after Juno. I glanced at Verity and our eyes met – a look passing between us. Then she took a long sip of her champagne, finishing it, then turned and walked into the house.

* * *

As the afternoon morphed into early evening, the day began to lose the slither of heat it had offered us – the sky clouding over was almost like closing the curtains on the party. Verity had left about an hour after the chase incident with Juno. I only witnessed a very quick huddled conversation between her and Evie before she was ushered out of the door. Having managed a very brief conversation with Verity this afternoon, I could see why someone like Evie might feel a pull towards her, a desire to protect her. Verity seemed fractured in some way. I wasn't sure exactly what it was that had caused her to become damaged, but something had, and for some reason Evie felt she needed to guide her, protect her. I supposed it was good for Verity that Evie had invested an interest in her. She was lucky, but I doubted she realised it. Having Evie's attention was like warm sunshine on your skin – when it was on you, you realised how good it felt and how much you missed it when it wasn't there.

Once the final guest had left, I began the task of clearing everything away. I had insisted on paper plates and napkins for ease. I was still slightly fuelled on champagne, so I began to tackle the mess. Evie had stayed behind, as Juno and Anabel were still in the thick of a game of potion making with sticks, petals and water. She had grabbed a black bin liner and was stuffing paper plates and napkins into it. I was straightening up the chairs, collecting champagne glasses.

Finally, we found ourselves in the hallway, and Evie had given a reluctant Juno a five-minute warning. I had pulled a cardigan around me as the evening chill began to settle in, and I hugged my arms around myself.

'Thank you so much for all your help,' I said to Evie.

'No problem.' She leant in and hugged me, and I hugged her back. I could smell the scent of barbeque in her hair. I released her and took a step backwards.

'I just...' I wasn't sure how to broach the topic of Verity dressing down Juno earlier. 'I saw Verity tell Juno off earlier, when they were running around the garden. I just thought you should know, in case Juno says anything to you later. She wasn't doing anything wrong, they were just being kids.'

Evie looked at me for a second.

'Okay, thanks.'

Was that it? Thanks? If someone had just told me that someone had told my kid off, I would have been seething.

'Bit off though, isn't it?' I said.

'What is?'

'Verity, telling Juno off. I mean, I have had it happen to me before, strangers telling off my kid and it really annoys me.'

'I think she'd had a bit to drink. That's why I came over, you know, when you had the champagne bottle and you were topping her up. I don't think she handles her booze too well.' I felt the weight of Evie's words. I had topped Verity's glass up twice. Was that supposed to excuse her behaviour? Evie clearly thought so.

'Did she tell you that? Does she have a problem?' I said curiously.

'Oh no, I don't think so. I think she's just nervous, and maybe she was feeling on edge. Look, I don't really know, Miranda. Can I help you clear anything else up?' A tired frustration was building in Evie's voice.

I suddenly felt deflated. I had expected Evie to pick the issue apart with me, to query Verity's action, but she had brushed it off.

'No, no, you're fine. Thank you so much for your help.'

'No problem, anytime. It was a real success. Well done, you.' She leant in and pecked me lightly on the cheek. Juno arrived at Evie's side. 'Right, let's get you back.'

David joined me at the door, and we all waved goodbye. Anabel scuttled off to watch her show she had been promised in return for her share of the tidying.

I closed the door and David put his arm around my shoulder.

'Now, tell me that wasn't a success.'

I looked up at him and smiled. 'Yes, I think it may well have been,' I said, to keep David sweet. He knew I had been worried about today and to mention the few moments I had experienced with Verity and the awkward moment with Evie before she left would only worry him. I felt sad that Evie couldn't speak to me about all the things that were happening in her life, and it had been awkward mentioning Verity's unreasonable behaviour to her. So, despite the sunny weather and the feedback from contented guests, I could no longer ignore the void opening up between me and my best friend.

David and I walked to the lounge together. Whilst he poured himself a whisky, I picked up my mobile phone. I had been very good at not looking at it during the entire party, but I was sure I had heard it ping a couple of times. I opened up my messages and saw one from my mother and one marketing message. I was struck by a pang of sadness that there was nothing more for me to see. I remembered the days when my phone would be red hot with notifications and the thrill they brought. I ignored the message from my mother for now, and then I felt my fingers itching as I swiped nearer to Google Play, where I could download a social media app within seconds. For all the disaster it brought last time, Instagram had been a source of great comfort to me. I had enjoyed the rush of joy as I had opened a past post to discover it had been liked a further few hundred times whilst I had slept, or I received a message from a fan who had felt inspired by something I had written, or another company had contacted me wishing to collaborate, or I learnt new ways to promote myself through the ever-evolving app. I had been a part of something bigger than just my own grid. It was a community, a family. One that had turned on me in the end – through my own doing – but a family none the less. I was enjoying my quiet life here in Helesbury, but the one thing that made it all worthwhile was knowing I had a close friend I could rely on who would give me that sense of purpose and belonging. Yes, the day had been a success, but Evie was not the same person she was when I met her. There was something unpleasant bubbling between the three of us, which had begun when Verity arrived. And as I felt Evie slipping further away from me, I felt my fingers edging closer to the app store where I was certain I would receive the interest and affirmation I was craving so badly.

20

I decided to sign up for the PTA. I knew it was time that I began making more of an effort in the local community, and besides, I was looking for a distraction. Last night, I had almost downloaded Instagram, the very site that was partly responsible for driving me away from Chelsea and to the comfort of a small village. David had been so tired after the barbeque and he'd had a few beers, so once evening arrived, I had felt the weight of loneliness as he fell asleep. I thought about texting Evie but then I cast my mind back to the way she had received my concerns over Verity's behaviour and the way she had intervened when I was trying to make progress with Verity, and I just couldn't bring myself to do it. I could hear David snoring and my fingers hovered over the app store. Anabel shouted out in her sleep – overtired from a full day's play – and I had dropped my phone on the bed and ran to her bedside. She had saved me from myself. This time. I wasn't sure if I would be tempted again, so to be on the safe side, I began to think of ways to fill my days. Tonight's PTA meeting was beginning at five, and to say I was nervous was an understatement.

Hatty was there to greet me at the gate. I had left Anabel with David, and they were at home making spaghetti bolognaise, which we would all eat together after the meeting was over.

I felt like a little kid needing my mate to meet me at the school gate, but I wasn't going to walk into my first PTA alone.

'Well done and thank you for coming.' Hatty looped her arm through mine, and we headed for the music room where the meeting was happening.

'Well, I said I would. I'm sorry it has taken me a long time to commit, but it's a scary thing, the old PTA, isn't it? I mean, all those mums and dads not agreeing on stuff – it freaks me out a little.'

'Oh, it's not like that at this school. Everyone is usually on the same page, and if they're not, I get them on the same page!' Hatty laughed. 'Thanks for such a lovely party yesterday, by the way.'

'Thanks for asking to me to come to the PTA meeting when I'd had three glasses of champagne.'

'I told you, I'm good at making people do things!' Hatty smacked me on the back.

* * *

The music room was hot and stuffy; someone had opened a couple of windows, but the day had been particularly warm, and this room got all the sun from the end of the day. There were about fifteen people seated on chairs, but it could have been a hundred with how much heat they were all emitting.

Tash opened the proceedings and then it was a case of just waiting my turn. The meeting was finalising the plans for the picnic in the park, which was happening next month I liked how the little school planned such fun events, things that people actually wanted to do.

I was nervous at first and said very little, but before I knew what was happening, I had allowed my hand to rise and I had volunteered to help with bunting and managing the band. I had taken the plunge. I was now a fully-fledged member of the PTA with real responsibilities.

'Now that wasn't so bad, was it?' Hatty said as we walked out of the school together just over an hour later.

'No, it wasn't – you were right, I should have done it sooner.'

We reached the gate and Hatty stopped and frisked herself.

'Oh, damn it, I left my house keys on the table. Let me run back – just wait here.'

Hatty turned and trotted back to the music room. I leant against the gates and took out my phone. I texted David.

Meeting went well, walking home now.

That was his cue to make sure the dinner was ready on the table when I got back. Now the stress of the PTA was over, and I had proved that I could and would have some sort of role in the village, I felt really hungry. It had been a worry for me, putting myself in front of people with no real control over what I was doing, or any idea if my suggestions would be received as realistic. I had been so used to living in an Insta world and marketing to the masses from behind a screen at the touch of a few buttons, but this was a small school with a tiny budget and I needed to find the balance between offering up my skills and knowledge without trying to look too showy. My past dealings with social media were just that, in the past. If I let on what I was capable of, questions would be asked and I still wasn't ready to reveal that side of me.

I pushed my phone back into my coat pocket. The village was quiet at this time of night, save for the odd dog walker. Everyone else was tucked up at home eating their dinner, and the stillness seemed like the perfect opportunity to appreciate where I lived for its tranquillity and beauty. So, I was surprised when a raised voice from somewhere close drew me out of my reverie. I moved forward on the path and poked my head around the corner. I could clearly see Verity standing a few feet away. She was wearing a black headband and black leggings. Her face was pink, as though she had been running. She had small white headphones in her ears, which ran from a phone that she held in her hand, and moved around as she gesticulated her annoyance. I stood very still, straining to hear what she was saying.

'I mean, for God's sake, I have to call you so I can actually get you to listen – whenever I try to speak to you face to face, you stop listening. This is my life too, you know! Everyone is constantly running around worrying about Rachel. They seem to forget I am here as well – I'm the one going absolutely stir-crazy. I just can't see an end to this unless you all start to cooperate with me a little bit. You keep moving the goalposts and I cannot exist under these conditions.'

My phone let out a loud beep – the reply from David. I pushed myself against the railing, but suddenly Verity went quiet. I dared myself one last peek out from behind the corner of the railings, but I saw Verity had turned and was heading away from me in the opposite direction, having heard my phone and sensed a presence.

'Right, that's me sorted, then. Loads of them still in there – I think some of them love it too much. I want to get home to a nice cup of tea, not still be chatting until midnight. You okay, love? Has that meeting taken it right out of you?'

I looked at Hatty and let out a small laugh. 'Yes, I am a bit tired.'

My mind was trying to make sense of everything I had heard Verity say. I was trying to remember the name of the woman she compared herself to, the one who was apparently getting more attention than her. Rebecca, was it? No, Rachel, that was it. Verity had referred to her work yesterday at the barbeque, and so her phone call just then could have been with an editor or an agent. I had no idea that the life of a writer could be so frustrating. I wondered, if it was her job that made her exasperated, why did she continue to do it? Or perhaps she had been talking about her sister or another family member. Verity definitely had some sort of past. This was something I could relate to her about, if only she would let me get close enough to have an open conversation. I knew from personal experience that people don't just up and leave somewhere unless they have a good reason.

I opened the front door to the smell of garlic, tomatoes and bread. Why did someone else's cooking always smell so good? It was exactly the same recipe I had used hundreds of times before and had given a copy to David so he could cook with Anabel tonight, but it just smelt so much better when it was being prepared by someone else and all I had to do was sit down and eat.

'Mummy, you're home!' Anabel ran through into the hallway. She held my hand as we walked through to the kitchen together.

'Yes, I'm back. And something smells delicious. Did you make it, darling?'

'I did. Dad helped a bit, but it was mainly me.'

I let Anabel lead me into the kitchen and seat me at the table.

'You're here, Mummy, head of the table. Daddy is next to you and I am also next to you. We made garlic bread and a tomato salad too.'

I looked at the feast in front of me as David came up from the cellar with a bottle of red wine.

'Wow, are we celebrating?' I asked.

'It's not every day my wife becomes a member of the PTA,' he said, taking out a corkscrew and opening the bottle without a simmer of a smirk. He was obviously very proud. He poured two glasses and a dribble in a glass for Anabel, who hated the smell and the taste still, but was always devastated to be left out. She took after me in that respect.

David and Anabel sat down, and David raised a glass. 'To my beautiful wife and her new role in the village.' He clinked my glass and held my gaze. 'Darling, I am so proud of you,' he added, and I felt a slight tingle rush through my body. It feels good when someone praises you. But the tingle was suddenly replaced by a tightening in my gut. David's praise reminded me of how I had been contemplating getting back onto social media. All for my own selfish reasons. Never minding how it could affect David or Anabel. My lovely family.

I took a long drink of the wine and tried not to let my sudden depletion in appetite show.

* * *

Later, David and I were in the kitchen tidying up. He was putting the plates and cutlery in the dishwasher and I was rearranging it straight after. It was our routine, and he never complained that I was undermining him, and I never told him he was doing a rubbish job.

'I have to go up to London next week for a couple of days, Thursday and Friday,' he said. At fifty-three, he was at the top of his game in the golf-magazine industry, and I couldn't deny how hard he worked. He could absolutely retire in the next few years, but I knew he would keep on working. 'Will you be okay?' he asked quietly, but even now I knew what was disguised in those softly spoken words. He still checked in with me regularly. He had seen how out of hand things had got before, and even though he had been completely dignified throughout the whole ordeal, I knew it had affected him. How could it not?

I put on my best smile and looked at him. 'Of course, I have Anabel, and Evie and Hatty, and well, I have a picnic in the park to organise now!' I laughed.

David leant in and kissed me on the head. 'Good.' He walked out of the kitchen. 'I have a few emails to send. I'll be in my office.'

A wave of sadness engulfed me. David hadn't been away for a night since we had moved here. It was obvious to me now that he had been waiting for the right time to do it, when he knew that I was feeling secure and happy enough for him to pop back to London. I felt guilty that he had been putting my needs before his own business. I presumed after today's milestone of joining the PTA, he saw that as confirmation that I was becoming more settled and would also be busier.

When he was out of the kitchen, I picked up my phone, and before I could stop myself, I had clicked into the app store and typed in *Instagram*. I hit download and then watched the little circle spinning, stopping and starting as it installed. There was a moment just before it fully installed when I almost hit cancel, but then I thought of the two days alone in the house and the space that was opening up between me and Evie, and then it was done. I swiped to my home screen and there it was. I moved it two pages away, so it wasn't the first thing that David might see on my phone. And that very act was the beginning of a new line of deception.

All I could do was hope that I hadn't made a terrible mistake.

21

BEFORE

The girl watched as her mother stood aside and let B and H in through the front door. She followed them into the lounge, where they all sat. On a few occasions, B would take the girl to another room, but the mother said she didn't need to this time; whatever was to be said, she would have to hear it too. The girl didn't understand exactly what was happening, but by the end of the conversation, her mother was crying again. B and H left. The girl noticed there was a large envelope in the hallway after they had gone. She tried to show it to her mother, to say it was all going to be okay because they had money again. Should they go out for cheese toasties and ice cream? But her mother just ignored her and carried on crying into the sofa. The girl sat very still next to her mother and didn't dare move in case she missed the moment when she would sit up and put her arms around her.

That moment came seven CBeebies programmes later. The girl watched them all, but also counted each one. After the seventh one, her mother sat up, gave her a quick cuddle, and told the girl to go and pack her bag. The girl nodded. She was getting used to this now.

The mother promised there would be no more beach huts or social services – it was going to be just them from now on. She promised. The girl smiled and hugged her mother again. She believed her, because that's what you did when the most important person in your life told you something.

Her life was a constant cycle of belief and hope and house moves. Maybe the next house would be the one. Maybe everything was finally going to be okay.

22

Betty Telfer had walked into an influencer event I had attended in Islington one baking-hot Thursday evening, and I had been bowled over. She had an air of superiority that made me feel slightly less worthy, but at the same time, I knew where I stood. She was the alpha female. Always had been in our group. She stood out like a peacock with her bright bobbed red hair and long kaftan-style dresses. That night, the first night, she had toned it down with Doc Martens and a black leather jacket. She was almost fifty, but she always looked ten years younger.

Betty was one of those women who you could rely on for absolutely anything. She was always there, no matter what. She could turn up to the opening of an envelope and make the event feel completely fabulous, usually with a bottle of champagne in her hand. She was well known and well respected in the social media world and had attracted over one million followers, due to her frank and honest posts about her experience of the menopause.

It had been over a year since I'd had any contact with Betty. But just a couple of days after I'd downloaded Instagram again, I'd sent Betty a message. I was craving the buzz I got from a conversation or bit of banter with a friend. Someone who knew me, knew the right thing to say that would make me smile. I knew as soon as I sent that message that it wouldn't be long before she turned up on my doorstep.

'Look at my perfect queen, living the country life. Have you got yourself a small paddock, a couple of geese? Oh, I bet Anabel has one of those gorgeous little miniature ponies,' she babbled as she hugged me and covered me in kisses. 'Where is the little sweetheart?' Betty looked around the hallway as though Anabel would have been there to greet her.

'She's at a sleepover,' I said in a cold tone that Betty immediately picked up on. 'It's half term,' I said warming my words slightly. As soon as Betty messaged me to say she was on her way, I packed Anabel off to Evie's house. I had done so much for Evie recently that it didn't occur to me to feel guilt. Evie was struggling to be a good friend at the moment, so I needed to feel that connection elsewhere. Even if it was with someone I had once tried to block from my life.

'Ah, keeping her away from me, I see. Good thinking. Can't have the whole village talking now, can we? Is that what it is like here? Everyone knows everyone else's business?' Betty walked into the lounge, pulling off her jacket and throwing it over the back of the sofa and handing me her customary bottle of champagne.

I followed her into the lounge and felt my body tense at the sight of Betty's jacket. I thought to myself, if it had been Evie who had done that, I wouldn't have minded, but already Betty being here was beginning to make me feel prickly. It was a rash decision to reinstate my account, then the message to Betty seemed the most obvious way to reconnect myself with the social media world. I had needed a friend, but the friend I really wanted to be here was Evie.

'Umm, it can be. But I, I like it – it's nice.'

'I don't know, how can you cope, after everything that went on. It must be like living under a microscope.' Betty fell into an oversized chair next to the window and looked out of the huge bay window.

'No one knows anything about my past, Betty.'

Betty nodded. 'Good. That's a good place to be. It will make it all the easier for you to start again fresh.'

I breathed in a long breath and slowly let it out. I still wasn't entirely sure, but I had invited Betty here, hadn't I? Which meant that I was willing to hear her out.

'Even though you ditched me and the others, and just ran off without a word!' She looked at me. 'You are forgiven by the way.'

I smiled. I didn't feel a wash of relief at her words. I didn't feel I needed anyone's forgiveness to walk away from the mess that had erupted around me and was causing chaos in my home life.

'I'll just go and pop this, shall I?' I took myself and the champagne to the kitchen, but Betty followed behind me.

'I'll get the grand tour, I hope,' she said as I set the bottle down and took out two flutes.

'Absolutely.'

'Well, this is lovely,' she said, looking around the kitchen.

'Yes, we were lucky the previous owners had some taste. I didn't fancy ripping out an entire kitchen when we had just moved in. There is still some work to be done on a few of the other rooms, but I'll get there in time.'

'And how is David?' Betty said, just as I popped the cork. 'I didn't see another car in the driveway, and if I remember rightly, he drove that lovely Jag. Does he still drive it?'

'Yes, he does.' I poured out two glasses of champagne and handed one to Betty. Trust Betty to comment on the material aspects. It reminded me of the part of myself that I had brought here to Helesbury, a part of me that unless I tried hard to hold on to, would simply slip away, knowing it was redundant here amongst people who valued integrity over possessions.

'And is he driving it somewhere tonight, or did you send him away?' Betty said with a knowing tone in her voice. I turned and we clinked glasses.

'He happened to be away for the night.'

Betty took a long sip of her champagne. 'On the same day, what a coincidence? And a terrible shame. I always had a soft spot for David. He was so very good-looking.'

I narrowed my eyes at Betty. 'He still is good-looking.'

Betty nodded approvingly. 'Oh goody! What a shame not to have seen him.' Betty turned and began walking the length of the kitchen, running her hand over the marble surfaces.

'That is one shiny sink! Do you have a cleaner or have you been following Mrs Hinch?'

'I don't do...' I trailed off.

Betty gave me a knowing look. 'Social media? Well, you're back now, baby. And if I have my way, you'll be staying.' Betty took a civilised sip of her champagne and looked around the kitchen again. 'You must have a cleaner.'

I sat down at the table and gestured for Betty to join me. 'Are we going to talk about cleaners and David all night, or are we going to discuss why you are really here?'

'Because you invited me, darling.' Betty sat down opposite me. 'And it is so good to see you, it has been too long.'

'You invited yourself.' At least that much was true.

'Well, I was surprised to see you back online, I won't lie. After everything that happened, I presumed you had been frightened off for good.'

I shuddered at the memory, trying not to let it engulf me.

'Just tell me one thing, Betty. Have things really calmed down? Would I really be welcomed back?'

'In a heartbeat, darling. The online world is superficial. People quickly forget.'

David's words from over a year ago came floating back to me. *Just go carefully, love.*

It was as though he could foresee it panning out exactly the way it did. But I hadn't listened. I hadn't been careful.

Now, over a year since I left the drama, I was sitting in my new kitchen in my new life with a woman I had tried to forget. And that I was considering doing it all again. It was a real push-and-pull feeling. I was craving something, and I could satisfy it by rejoining Betty and the other influencers. I knew Betty would help me catapult my followers back up to the figure they were before. I sensed her summing up the house, the country life, my candle business. It was all a great marketing angle in her eyes. As we sat up later that night, laughing about it all, she said I was not to worry. She would have my back this time and make sure I didn't go off the rails.

23

Betty's visit brought with it mixed emotions. I needed to go out for a run to clear my head and process my thoughts. I had to convince myself first that what I was doing was the right thing. I knew if I took things slow, built up my profile steadily and didn't become swept up in anything else, things would be okay. I had learnt my lesson the hard way last time.

'I need to get on the' road,' Betty said to me as we finished our coffee in the kitchen the next morning; Betty had understood that she would need to leave early, in case Anabel or David showed up.

Half an hour later, she stood at the open door, dressed and looking as glamorous as she had when she had arrived and not looking the slightest bit hung-over.

'I will message you the minute I get back – last night gave me so much inspiration. I have so many great ideas of how we can launch you back into the Insta world.' Betty gave me two kisses, then slipped into her car.

My eyes were suddenly drawn upwards. Verity was standing on the other side of the road, also in running gear, but she had stopped and was looking directly over at me. I shivered. Perhaps it was the early-morning air, it hadn't quite warmed up yet, but something about the way Verity was now putting the buds from her headphones back in her ears made me think that she had taken them out to listen to our conversation. Betty had never been a quiet talker and always attracted attention wherever we went, from what she wore to the volume of her voice.

I waved Betty off whilst still eyeing Verity on the other side of the road. Then she set off running again, neither of us having greeted one another.

* * *

I welcomed Anabel into my arms as though she had left me for a month and not one night. Evie stepped into the hallway with Juno.

'Can Juno and I play in the garden?' Anabel asked.

I looked at Evie. 'Cuppa?'

'Yes, that would be lovely.' The girls ran outside and Evie followed me through into the kitchen, where I flicked the kettle on. I took down a pot. I had converted myself to making pots of tea since moving here, rather than brewing it in one cup; even for just one person, it tasted so much nicer.

I kept stealing looks at Evie. She looked tired. Her face was a greyish colour even with the little bit of make-up she had applied.

'Did the girls keep you up late last night?' I asked, wondering if this was the cause of her exhaustion.

'They told me they would be staying up all night, but it was probably midnight when they passed out.' She tried to laugh, but it sounded weak and hollow.

'I'll repay the favour for you and have them next week,' I said. 'We've to fill these holidays somehow. Maybe I'll do an Easter egg hunt.'

'If you're sure. Juno would love that.'

'I saw Verity on a run earlier.' I didn't know why I decided to blurt it out. I wasn't sure what Evie would do with it.

'Oh, did you?'

'Yes, she had stopped outside my house.'

'Oh, right. Well, I haven't seen her for a while so...' Evie trailed off. I thought about us all at the party and I found it hard to believe that Verity and Evie had not been in contact since then.

I brought the pot and cups to the table on a tray and looked at Evie's face again. She looked as though she were somewhere far away with her thoughts.

'Here, get a tea down you,' I said. I didn't want to refer to how rough she looked, but Evie seemed to appreciate the gesture and smiled at me.

'Thanks.'

'So, they were good for you, last night?' I asked again.

'Yes, they were, and so sweet as well.' Evie took her cup of tea, warming her hands around the mug.

'I have to say, Evie, you look shattered,' I said.

She suddenly looked sheepish and even touched the side of her face. 'I... do I? Well, I suppose it was rather late by the time I hit the sack. I had a lot on again. I had left it all until the last minute. My own fault, really.'

'Sorry. A sleepover with two eight-year-olds was probably the last thing you needed,' I said, feeling a rush of guilt. I hadn't given a thought to Evie and what she had planned when I asked her at the last minute. I had only been thinking of myself by making sure Anabel was away so I could talk with Betty.

'Oh no, it was fine. Really no problem. I just stayed up too late working.'

Shit. The guilt came harder.

'So, no late-night visitors then?' I asked raising my eyebrows up and down, trying to make light of it. I was, of course, half-joking, or maybe I was referring to the Graham character I'd seen outside Evie's house and who she still hadn't mentioned to me. But Evie didn't have that tired look that came with a slight afterglow from a night of passion. Hers was a face full of worry.

When she didn't say anything, I pressed on. 'Is everything okay, money-wise? I mean, if you're struggling at all, you know you only need to ask,' I said, but the second it was out of my mouth, I regretted it.

Evie laughed and shook her head. 'God, no, Miranda, but thank you.' She looked embarrassed, and I wished I could retract my statement.

'Sorry, I didn't mean to imply anything. It's just you said you were getting behind with your clients and you had a lot of work on. I just wondered if maybe you took on too much work because you were falling behind on payments or something. I wouldn't want you to suffer in silence. I am happy to lend you whatever you need.'

'It's not money!' Evie blurted.

And I fell silent and looked down at my teacup.

'It's... It's Juno's father.'

I nodded. And waited for her to continue.

'He is sort of back on the scene. In a roundabout sort of way. I can't explain it, but it's just getting me a bit down, that's all.' The words rushed from Evie.

I nodded. So, the Graham guy must be Juno's father. It all made sense. If he was turning up at all times of the nights, making demands, then that would influence Evie's mental health.

'And was he there at the house last night?'

'Oh God, no – I would never bring anyone to the house that you hadn't met or vetted first when I'm looking after Anabel,' Evie said, and she was so serious that I let out a small laugh.

'It's okay, Evie, it's your house, your life – you don't need to "vet" anyone for me.'

Evie looked sheepish again. 'Sorry... I'm not... I'm obviously not thinking straight. I didn't mean to say *vet*, I just meant that if I were to invite a man to the house – which I haven't – then I wouldn't do it on a night when I had Anabel. I just wouldn't.' Evie spoke sincerely again.

'Okay, it's fine. I trust you, and that means I trust your judgement of others. I'm sure Juno's dad was someone who you thought was a perfectly nice man at first and then, well, things change, don't they? We can't always get it right, can we? And quite often, we are just caught up in lust.'

Evie nodded. 'He had us all fooled, that I can say.' She looked anxiously around the kitchen and hugged her arms around herself.

'Are you okay? Can I get you a thicker cardigan?'

'No, it's fine. I'm just tired. Maybe I'm catching a cold, you know. I will absolutely be going to bed early tonight, that's for sure.'

'Yes, you do that,' I said. 'You need to look after yourself, you know, otherwise you'll be no good to anyone.'

I offered to have Juno for a few hours whilst Evie took herself off home for a nap, but she declined, saying they had plans to go out. 'Don't forget that early night!' I called after her as they walked off down the drive. She turned and smiled and waved.

'Evie is a bit tired,' I said, looking down at Anabel standing next to me in the doorway.

'Maybe she was tired cos of all the talking.'

I closed the door, and we wandered back through to the kitchen.

'What do you mean all the talking?'

'I woke up in the night because my throat was scratchy, and I went to the bathroom and filled up my glass with water. I heard loud voices coming from downstairs. I snuck down a few steps and Evie was in the lounge with someone. They were talking too loud, like they were a bit cross.'

'Who was she talking to?' I stopped in front of Anabel.

'I think.' She screwed her face up. 'It looked like Verity.'

I tried to act cool, as though I wasn't really that interested, but my mind was racing through the last parts of the conversation I'd just had with Evie. Had she said she'd been alone last night? I'd made a joke about late visitors. Evie hadn't replied to that.

'They were probably having a grown-ups' night, drinking wine like us mummies do sometimes.'

Anabel nodded. 'Yeah, maybe.'

'So, was it a big argument they were having?'

Anabel had moved to the fridge, opened it and stood there, waiting for the miracle snack to jump out at her.

'I didn't say they were arguing, Mummy. They were loud. That was what woke me up, I think.'

I nodded. 'Oh right.' Was I just hearing what I wanted to hear?

'I'm hungry. Can I have a cheese toastie? With pickles on the side?'

I began taking all the ingredients out of the fridge to make Anabel's favourite sandwich the way she liked it, with a little bit of Dijon mustard and mayonnaise. I knew I wouldn't get anything more out of her about Verity's late-night visit and to probe her any further would just annoy her, so I dropped the matter and focused on making the sandwich.

But I was perplexed once again. Why did Evie insist on trying to keep her friendship with Verity a secret? Why did she feel she couldn't mention that she had been with her?

I put the sandwich in the toastie maker and made Anabel an iced tea, another of her favourites.

Before I gave Anabel her sandwich, I suddenly found myself inclined to place it on the counter near the windowsill on a wooden chopping board –

to make it look more aesthetically pleasing – and take a photo of it. In the background were some fresh wildflowers in a vase. It looked like something out of the cookery section of *County Living*.

'Mummy, what are you doing?' Anabel's voice came from behind me.

'I was just taking a photo of the vase in the window, to send to Grandma.' I often sent my mother photos of little things we got up to during the day to cheer her up, so it didn't feel like too much of a lie.

'I thought you were taking a photo of my sandwich.' Anabel giggled.

I laughed. 'Now that would be silly.' I put my phone down, as far away as possible from my reach and gave Anabel her snack. Hearing the words spoken from my own daughter's mouth made me realise it was silly. The whole thing was indeed silly. But if Evie and I were never going to be close enough for her to feel she could tell me anything, then this was the next best thing.

After Anabel had left the kitchen, the scent of toasted cheese lingering in the air, I found myself edging towards my phone. I could still hear the echo of Anabel's laugh. Of course, to a child, the idea of photographing your lunch was an oddity. But Anabel was lucky. She was lost in the wonders of childhood and I was treading the murky waters of middle age where making friends and keeping them was not as simple as it once was. I brushed off any concerns about what others might think of me.

As I went to upload it to my account, I briefly looked at the profile picture I had used all those years ago. I had stuck with the same one. Mainly because it was a great photo of me, but also because if anyone had known me back then, they would know I was back. Betty had reassured me that people had moved on and my misdemeanour from back then would almost be forgotten. People would have moved on to the next drama. The photo had been taken just before it all kicked off. I was sat outside a Mediterranean beach restaurant, a cold glass of rosé in hand, my head tilted slightly to the right, insinuating a relaxed, carefree approach to life. David had taken the photo – he had suspected nothing. To him, I was his wife, enjoying the holiday he had worked hard to pay for, our daughter happily in the kids' club so we could enjoy an uninterrupted lunch. But in reality, I was weeks away from almost losing it all. What had been going through my head that day? I knew I had already discovered the source of my grievances, and the torment was building within me, directing me towards the very act that would bring me to my knees, send me cowering for cover and wanting to get as far away from everyone I had ever known to be my friend.

I had been given a second chance here, but I had to be careful. I couldn't allow myself to get emotionally involved again. As much as Betty had tried to convince me that everything was forgotten, I knew that people didn't forgive that easily. I wasn't sure how long I had been sat staring at the profile photo when the small voice filtered through.

'Mummy?'

'Yes, sweetheart.' I put my phone face down on the table and looked up at Anabel. The photo had uploaded to Instagram. My first photo in over a year. *Do not let it happen again, Miranda*, I told myself silently.

'Can I have some ice cream now?'

I stood up and went to the freezer. 'My goodness, someone is hungry today!'

I assembled three scoops of ice cream and sauce and placed it down in front of Anabel.

'Wow, Mummy, three scoops, and sauce, thank you!'

I smiled. Was I keeping her sweet because I knew I would be checking on the likes on my post in a few minutes? I remembered how it would only be a few minutes' break each time before I caved to more screen time because Instagram was designed to be addictive. And I had once been an addict.

I heard Anabel slurping happily away with her ice cream, so my thoughts turned back to my account. I went back in and was surprised and also disheartened to see that there wasn't one like on my post, even though it was a pretty good picture. *But not good enough, Miranda.* Anabel asked if she could take her ice cream into the snug, and I nodded and waved her away. She was tired after her sleepover, and a bit of TV time wouldn't hurt.

I would need to go in with a more business-like approach if I was going to gain any interest in my posts. I thought about the candles I had been making. What had started off as a bit of a therapeutic hobby, could really become something with the help of my grid.

It scared me how I was suddenly back on a platform within minutes.

But if I went about it with a real business approach, sticking to posts related to the products and my life here, I could have the best of both worlds. I could be back in the game, with people to reach out to at a moment's notice, but also keep a low profile if I wanted to.

I would need to change the profile picture immediately. But with something on brand. I could easily knock up a quick logo on a design app. But for now, I gave the account a name. *Cushy*.

* * *

I spent the rest of the afternoon on Instagram, scrolling through my phone for old images I thought I could use in the future, looking at other similar small business accounts and their grids for inspiration. I wasn't sure how long I had been sitting there when I heard the front door close and sat up startled, suddenly panicked that it was Anabel who had gone out of the front door. I dropped the phone on the table, scraped my chair back and practically ran out of the kitchen into the hallway.

'Anabel?' I called breathlessly. David was standing by the door, briefcase in hand, looking at a letter on the small table where we kept the post. He looked at me, puzzled by my anxious behaviour.

'Miranda?' he said. 'Is everything okay. Where's Anabel?'

'Daddy!' came Anabel's voice as she appeared from the snug where she had been the entire time. She nestled into his stomach, and he dropped his briefcase to embrace her. He eyed me over the top of her head, a questioning look on his face.

When Anabel had finished talking about her sleepover with Juno, she went back to her programme. I was leaning against the wall in the hallway and stepped forward to embrace David.

'How are you?' he asked as we walked hand in hand to the kitchen.

'How was the drive?' I said, not wanting to focus too much on myself. The guilt was seeping out of me – I was sure he would be able to sense it.

'I asked first!' David teased. 'I thought you'd want some company whilst I was away – I'm surprised to hear Anabel has been at a sleepover.'

'I know, but Juno was desperate to have Anabel over. It is the holidays, what could I tell her?'

But I felt horrible for lying. Even though the girls were ecstatic for a sleepover, it was I who had instigated it.

'What's for dinner? I'm famished.' I was thankful David's appetite had surpassed his desire to interrogate me further.

I looked at the time – it was after five. How had I managed to while away an entire afternoon? But then I remembered how easy it was to forget who you were and all your responsibilities when you were absorbed in social media.

'I thought I'd order us a takeaway tonight,' I said, although I hadn't even thought about food or remembered that David had said he'd be home for dinner.

'Okay, well, you'll have to drive to get it – you know they don't deliver out here.'

'I'm going to get Thai. It's the closest. You choose the wine. Tell Anabel I'll be back in a little while.'

David was already distracted with opening his post as I stepped outside and got in the car. I reversed out of the drive and drove a few hundred yards when I saw Verity. She was in her running gear again. Good Lord, did this woman run all day?

I stopped the car, opened the window and called out to her.

'Running again?' I said. She stopped and leant down to the window and recognised it was me.

'Oh, Miranda.'

'Well, don't sound so thrilled to see me, will you?' I said in jest, but Verity didn't smile.

'I saw your friend leaving this morning. Betty, wasn't it?'

I felt my heart speed up. 'Do you know her?' I asked lightly.

Verity let out a snort. 'Know her? No, not exactly. But I know who she is.'

'Oh right.' I tried to hide the despair that had ripped through my body. How the hell did Verity know of Betty? I had scoured through Instagram trying to find an account in Verity's name, but hadn't. But she would have to be active on there to know who Betty was. Which would mean she might possibly know who I was. Who I had been.

'It's interesting to see who you keep company with.'

I felt my gut tighten, and I thought I might be sick.

'She's an old friend,' I said coldly, now wishing the ground would open up and swallow Verity. I was quickly developing a severe aversion to this woman.

Verity just pursed her lips. 'Well, it's not really any of my business what you get up to, is it?'

'No. It isn't.' I retaliated sharply.

'I have been wondering about you actually, and what sort of friend you are to Evie.' Verity casually pulled her leg up behind her into a stretch. 'When I met you, I thought you looked quite familiar, but it didn't click at first. Then when I saw Betty coming out of your house, I realised where I had seen you before. You're that woman off Instagram, aren't you?'

I felt the blood run cold through my body and suddenly my head was spinning. I sucked in some air to ground myself. 'We all have a past, don't we, Verity?' I said. I had no idea what part of Verity's past I was referring to, but it seemed to have an effect, as I saw her visibly shudder and she took a few steps away from the car.

'I'm happy to keep out of yours if you keep out of mine.' Verity tried to smile, but her face was tight enough to match her words, and I felt the skin on my arms and shoulders prickle. Had I touched on something?

'Well, this run won't do itself,' she said.

Before I could retaliate again, Verity was off and running.

Once she had rounded the corner, I took long deep breaths in and out and my whole body began to shake as the adrenaline that I had forced to stay at bay, rushed through me. It was clear to me now that Verity was hiding something. I had lived in this village for a year and not once had anyone brought up my past life. They either didn't know or were too polite to say. Verity, on the other hand, hadn't cared. And that spelt trouble.

24

10 MAY 2019 – 11.13 A.M. – GLOUCESTER POLICE STATION

Interview with The Reverend Conner Greaves, vicar of St James's.

I wouldn't say I am very good at picking up on rifts. It is one of my weaknesses actually, even though I grew up with three sisters and a brother. So, I wouldn't have known that Verity and Miranda weren't getting on. I mean, everyone has their little falling outs, but I don't tend to pay too close attention to the ins and outs.

I've been rather distracted with a dear friend. Beth and I have become rather close, confidants if you will, and so it is towards her that my attention has been focused these last few months. She is very young still and I am ten years her senior, so we are simply spending time together as friends.

But someone did come to me directly. My job as a vicar means I have to respect people's privacy, so I'd rather not disclose who that was. Unless of course you insist? I don't want to be charged with withholding information or anything like that. When they spoke to me, it was very close to the night it all happened. I guess things were really coming to a head and had been brewing for some time. But even then, they were vague in the way they spoke to me. They didn't give a lot of details away about what was happening, but I think really, they just needed to let it all out. I mean, I know you see confessions in the movies, and it's all behind a red curtain, but that's more our Roman colleagues' style. Not the way of a small village like this, much more chats over tea and cake. There are a lot of religious people who live here and some even come from outside the village to hear my sermons. But no, I can't give you all the gory details. All I can say is that they came for a chat, to get some stuff off their chest. But I suppose, in hindsight, I should have been concerned when they asked for forgiveness for what they were about to do.

25

I arrived home with the takeaway in hand, feeling just as stressed as when I'd left and bumped into Verity. Well, not so much bumped into her as made the mistake of slowing down and opening the window to say hello. She couldn't exactly be doing a great job of being a friend to Evie, otherwise Evie wouldn't look like the walking dead. That's not the sort of effect friends have on each other. When Evie and I became friends, she brought me back to life. Because she herself was so full of life. She was thoughtful, and of course, her popularity around the village was important too. People love her, trust her. But now, I barely recognise her. She seems permanently distracted, and I think it is all to do with Juno's father. But she won't confide in me, and it is infuriating because she has probably confided in Verity.

By the time I got back home, it was after six thirty.

David was sat alone in the kitchen, half a bottle of wine already drunk.

'You took forever – I was going to start going through the fridge.'

'Sorry.' I put the takeaway in the middle of the table.

'I warmed the plates.' David pointed to the oven.

'You see, this is why I married you.'

'But seriously, what took you so long?' David took the plates out of the oven and brought them to the table.

'I had to wait ages for the food.'

'I thought you'd ordered it in advance?' David said. Of course, that was how it had seemed because I had said we were having a takeaway but, because I had been so distracted by Instagram, I had completely forgotten to cook. So I hadn't ordered and of course the place was packed. I'd had to wait fifteen minutes just to tell them, 'usual please!' and then wait another thirty minutes for it to be cooked.

'Well, I'd forgotten it was Friday and there was a confusion with the orders. Mine ended up getting lost.' How was it that these lies just came tripping off my tongue so easily recently?

'Oh, that's not like them at all. What rotten luck.'

'Where's Anabel?' I asked, eager to take the focus away from my bare-faced lies.

'Exhausted. Took herself off to bed.'

I felt a wave of sadness engulf me. I had been an awful mother today. What I had just said to David was just a little white lie, but why did it feel familiar to the ones I had told all those months before?

We ate our dinner and finished the bottle of wine, but all the while I was thinking how I could break it to David that I had gone back onto Instagram. I wanted him to know, to ease the guilt I was feeling, of course, but also because David deserved to be kept involved. He was a good man who had stood by me.

'I've decided to launch the candle business on social media,' I said casually as I stacked the crockery and plates in the dishwasher. Although my words were softly spoken, my heart was racing. What would David think?

'Oh right.' David was looking at his phone, catching up on a few after dinner emails.

'Yes, I've called it Cushy.' I felt the atmosphere shift. David moved in his seat. He lifted his eyes from his screen for a second as though he were going to look at me, but he brought his attention back to his phone again.

'Cushy. Cushy,' he said a few times, trying out. 'I like it. Cushy Candles.'

'No, just Cushy.'

'Right.'

I began to relax. David was obviously okay with this.

But then he spoke again. 'Should I be worried?'

I moved over to him and slipped my hand in his.

'Please trust me, David. I have it all under control. What happened before was a mistake.'

David sucked his lips in and widened his eyes. 'Well, Miranda, you are your own woman. I cannot and will not tell you what to do.'

I squeezed his hand.

'However, I will not be the one you can come running to if all of it crumbles around you again. I'm all for making mistakes, but you've been here before – social media on a large scale just doesn't agree with you.'

'David, I have it all under control. I promise.'

'It's not for you to promise me anything, Miranda. I appreciate you filling me in, but I'm not for it, nor against it. It's your gig. Now, what's for dessert?'

I stood for a few more seconds holding his hand, then I went to the freezer and took out the vegan Ben and Jerries ice cream. We had been eating it all year and David still had no clue it was dairy free. Sometimes it was too easy to pull the wool over his eyes.

I thought about what I had just said about having it all under control. But there was still the whole Verity situation that was still niggling away at me. Verity had clearly taken a dislike to me, and I felt threatened by her presence and her closeness to Evie. Could she also feel threatened by me? Especially now she knew my past and what I was capable of. I knew I had to make Evie see that Verity was a bad egg, so if for any reason Verity decided to let slip my past mistakes, I would have already done my job of exposing her first.

* * *

The next morning, I was up before anyone. David liked to have a little lie-in on a Saturday, and Anabel was obviously still shattered from her sleepover. I dressed in running gear and set out waffles, fruit and yoghurt, in case Anabel rose whilst I was running. I plugged in my earbuds and hit the Best of the Nineties playlist on my smartphone. Then I set off down the driveway. It was only just gone seven, and I braced myself for bumping into Verity. I had a speech all prepared. I wasn't going to let her rock up in my village and try to intimidate me.

Saying that, I was thankful that the only other person I saw was Conner going into the church and the lady who worked Saturday mornings at the shop. I think her name was Maureen. I wasn't sure. I was back home by twenty-five past seven and found – just as I had suspected, I would – Anabel sat at the table eating the chopped kiwi and pouring maple syrup onto the dry untoasted waffle.

'Let me pop the next one in the toaster for you,' I said, kissing her head. 'Did you sleep well?'

'I slept good. I was so tired. Sorry, I couldn't stay awake when you went to the Thai takeaway.'

'That's okay, sweetie.' I was panting and sweating. I popped a waffle on a low heat in the toaster and went upstairs and turned on the en suite shower. David was still fast asleep, but by the time I got out of the shower, he was sitting up in bed with his glasses on, reading yesterday's paper.

'Good morning,' I said.

'Morning,' he said, and I wondered if I detected a bristle in his voice. Hopefully, I was imagining it.

'What do you fancy doing today, then?' I said as I dressed.

'Oh, I have a bit of work to catch up on, then I said I'd meet Steve at the pub.'

'Steve!' I said. The work bit I could buy, but Steve? Steve was who I would consider the other token 'elder' dad in the village. He was also in his early fifties, but David had never shown much interest in him – it was usually Steve who suggested a beer and David fobbing him off with work commitments. But suddenly, my husband wanted to spend time with him.

'Yes, I thought it time I got to know him better. We've been here a year and you have all your friends, and well, I only have my friends in London.'

'Well, as long as he doesn't expect Anabel to want to play with Bradley. She says he smells of cheese.'

'Well, that's a bit unkind. He's eight years old. Don't all eight-year-old boys smell a bit funky?'

'I don't know, I'm just going on what Anabel has told me.' I roughly towel-dried my hair.

'Well, it's a dad-only thing, so I'm pretty sure Bradley will be at home, rubbing himself in cheese or whatever it is he likes to do.'

I smirked and then I frowned. 'And you're sure you've not thrown yourself into the arms of Steve because you're avoiding me after what we discussed last night?'

'It can barely be classed as a discussion, Miranda. You told me you're back in the Instagram game and that was about the size of it.'

'You make it sound like prostitution, David.' And then, as I said it, David looked at me over his glasses. It *had been* exactly that. I had been selling myself for money back then. This would be different. I would use it purely for the candle business.

'You do know that's yesterday's paper, don't you?' I said, steering us away from the topic even though I had brought it back up again.

David looked at me again over his glasses. 'Yes, I do.' He looked back at the paper. 'I'm catching up on the story I was reading yesterday. That gangster has just been released.'

'Gangster? What gangster?' I pulled on an oversized dress.

'Tate Jones. He's from our neck of the woods, West Brompton.'

'I have no idea who you're referring to,' I said, applying a thin sheen of tinted moisturiser to my cheeks, but it didn't surprise me that David was discussing with me his favourite topic other than golf: crime and criminals.

'Well, people aren't happy about it. He was supposed to go down for life for killing that motorist in a road-rage incident. Got let off. People in high places. That's the thing with these gangsters, they have enough money and enough connections. He'll be off to Spain, living the high life, I suppose.'

'Well, don't go getting any ideas about a career change,' I said.

'No, I'm quite happy with the magazine for now, thank you.'

'Jolly good.' I turned around from the mirror where I was sitting at the dressing table. 'Well, enjoy your afternoon with *Steve*,' I said, over-enunciating his name so I sounded like a five-year-old.

David took a deep breath and blew it out. 'We shall have a perfectly lovely beer in the pub garden, thank you very much.'

I rolled my eyes and headed downstairs, thinking about how I would spend the day with Anabel. I had already decided I would spoil her.

* * *

By mid-morning, Anabel was finally dressed, and I had packed a little picnic. We were loading ourselves into the car when Evie appeared in the driveway.

'Hi,' she said breathlessly, as though she had just run. 'I did try to call. And text actually.'

I stood up from where I had been stooping down into the boot.

'Hey!' I said and went to give her a kiss. She reciprocated quickly. Juno was behind her, looking pretty glum, as though she wanted to be anywhere but here.

Evie's voice dropped to a whisper. 'Something has come up, a family emergency. I don't want to drag Juno along. I wondered—'

'Hey, yes of course, you don't have to ask.'

Evie let out a quick breath. 'Thank you.'

'Is it anything serious?' I asked, hoping it wasn't.

'It's my stepfather. He's had a heart attack. I need to whiz up to Oxford-shire. I'll only be a few hours. I just need to check he's okay. I wouldn't forgive myself if anything happened and I hadn't seen him.'

'Of course.' Evie had filled me in on her family situation. Her mother and father separated when she was little, and her mother remarried straight away. Frank was in his late seventies; she had always referred to him as a 'fit old bugger'. But it just goes to show that you never know if things are about to go wrong.

'I'm so sorry, Evie,' I said, taking her arm and squeezing it. 'I'll have her for as long as you need me to, just let me know.' I looked past her at Juno. 'We're just off to the petting zoo and then to get ice cream and a picnic!' I said loudly so that Juno could hear. I watched as her face morphed from moody to intrigued then almost happy.

'Thank you,' Evie said.

'No problem. I'm more than happy to help.' I thought about Verity and all the callous ways she had spoken to me. But here I was. I was the one that

Evie had literally come, running to this morning to help her out. I knew deep down that I would always be the one that Evie came to for the practical help, for the things to do with the school or the girls, because this is what we had in common, this is what connected us in the first place, but I wanted us to be much more than that to one another. I wanted to be the one she felt she could confide in so that nothing that Verity said or did would ever be able to come between us.

26

BEFORE

The new house smelt of boiled cabbage. That was what her mother had said as they walked around the five small rooms. It was even smaller than the house they had been in before. And the garden was tiny.

'They just don't care,' her mother said. 'They have no idea, they expect us to live like animals.'

The girl thought for a moment what kind of animals her mother might be referring to and began to imagine herself as a lion, pacing around a tiny cage in a zoo. Then she imagined herself as a monkey swinging from the lampshades. The girl did think that the house smelt bad, but she had never had any experience with boiled cabbage before. She knew that was what Charlie's mum in *Charlie and the Chocolate Factory* made for her family because they were poor. But the girl didn't think she and her mother were poor because there were always big envelopes stuffed full of banknotes, and they always had good things to eat, nice clothes to wear and there was always chocolate and ice cream. But this house *was* a little shabby. The girl wondered why her mother couldn't just save up all the big envelopes of money and put them both in a nice house that her mother liked. She would sacrifice all the chocolate and new clothes to see her mother happy. The girl thought about the people who lived here before them and how they were probably poor and had to eat boiled-cabbage soup. At least they were having fish and chips tonight; that she knew because on the drive here they had passed a chip shop and her mother had said, 'That's dinner sorted.'

Her mother was doing that thing with her hands again, where she looked as though she were drying them, but without a towel. The girl left her mother doing her funny hand thing and went to what was now her room and put her rucksack on the bed. She took out her favourite red teddy and rested it against the pillows. The bed had been made up with a pink duvet with yellow spots on it. It was quite nice. There was no wardrobe and just a small chest of drawers. The girl's mother had packed all their clothes into one big suitcase and a few bin liners. She was sure her mother would put her clothes in there tomorrow. Or maybe the next day. She never did it straight away; it was as if she was waiting to see if they would stay first before she unpacked. She knew her mother hated this house. She hated them all. Not just the smells like boiled cabbage, but the way she didn't get to see her friends any more. Her mother's friends had always been at the house, the proper house, the house that the girl knew to be her actual home. And she hoped that one day they would be able to go back there, and she would see all her friends again and her mother would see all her friends again. The girl liked it when her mother had visitors – it made her very happy. She was a good host and would always have lots of lovely food and there was always music. That was what she remembered the most about the happier times – the music. Because that was what made her mother the happiest – playing her music loudly and singing along. The girl wished she could see her mother singing and dancing again. She knew why her mother was sad. She missed the girl's dad. The girl missed her dad a little bit, but not as much as her mother missed him. The girl hadn't known him very well. He didn't always live with them and was away a lot. His job meant that he had to work a lot, and that included Christmas and holidays, all the times when families should be together. The girl's mother loved singing and dancing, but she had always sang the longest and loudest when the girl's father had been there. And he would join in too and pick her up and spin her around until she was dizzy. There had only been happy times when he was there. She had never once seen her mother sad when her father had been home, but she was never angry or cross when he went away either. And now she was the saddest she had ever been without him. The girl's mother told her that they would never see him again, and for the first time, the girl realised, her mother was angry with her father for not being there.

27

We had walked around the petting zoo five times; the girls were in their element, chatting and laughing at the alpaca's goofy teeth. It had been a godsend that they had each other. It meant that Anabel had a friend, and I was able to get on with a little bit of Instagramming. Already, overnight, my followers had gone up.

I had been taking sneaky photos of the girls from behind as they walked around the farm. I regretted the outfit I had chosen. I had been distracted by David's aloofness in bed as I had dressed and now the heavy dress was trapping the heat of the day, which had turned out to be warm. Usually, I checked the temperature for the entire day before I headed out. I was dreaming of a light pair of shorts.

Eventually, I convinced the girls to stop for a picnic, and I managed to get another few photos of them as they sat on the gingham picnic blanket, surrounded by sausage rolls and eating melon slices. It was the perfect Instagram photo, and just the sort of brand image I was going for with Cushy. I had uploaded one or two more photos since the cheese sandwich. I was going to take it nice and slow. Not make a big deal out of it. I was incredibly happy with the selection of country photos I had taken today, and later, when the girls were distracted, I would upload another image with content. Country life was so in.

Half an hour later, I pulled into the ice-cream parlour, which was a bit of an outside affair, with the cows grazing in a field just beyond. It was a local dairy farmer who made the ice cream, and I thought it would be the perfect local and small business to tag and promote for a future post, perhaps even collaborate with. But I wasn't quite there yet. I was taking things slowly, and I had to remind myself of that.

The girls chose their flavours, and we all got settled on a bench and the girls tucked in. I took out my phone and began editing and adding a little bit of filter and then I uploaded the image. It was a shot of the girls on the rug that showed mostly Anabel in the foreground and a little bit of Juno in the background. She was ever so slightly out of focus, as the main focus was on the rug and the food at the front next to Anabel.

I concentrated hard on the content, making sure I wrote something that was engaging and relevant and would make people squishy with envy at wanting to be sat on that very picnic rug, tucking into some home-made sausage rolls on a hot spring afternoon in the Cotswolds.

I wasn't sure how long I had been working on the post, but it must have been long enough for the girls to finish their ice creams and wander off. I realised it had gone noticeably quiet, and then I heard a scream so loud and tainted with the very essence of me that I knew it had come from Anabel.

I jumped up from the bench and scanned the area. I could just see Anabel a little way off next to the high wall, beyond which was the cow field. I ran as fast as I could and grabbed hold of Anabel, who was pointing at the wall. I couldn't see over it, but I couldn't see Juno either, and a sickening feeling came over me that she must be on the other side of it. There were a few loose bricks on the grass, which served as a sort of step up, and so using my arms as well, I was able to get myself onto the wall. Sure enough, five feet below me, was Juno, sat in a cowpat. I looked up and saw a herd of curious cows with their calves in tow, getting precariously closer.

'Juno, take my hand,' I said, leaning over the wall, and she slowly stood up. She wasn't crying, but she looked shocked. She took my hand and I grasped hers with both of mine. I heaved, and she tried to get her footing on the wall, but it was no good. She couldn't manage it. I looked at the fast-approaching cows – who would be looking to protect their young – and let go of Juno's hand. I swung my legs round, so they were facing the field and jumped down, narrowly missing the cowpat that Juno had just been in. I cupped my hands together and leant my shoulder against the wall.

'Put your foot in there and push yourself up.'

This time, Juno managed it and she pulled herself up onto the wall. I looked around and found a few nooks in the wall. I expertly navigated my feet and hands into them and pulled myself to the top.

Juno was already on the other side of the wall on the grass and she and Anabel were laughing. At least that was something. We were quite far away from the other diners, and I only saw one family looking over and taking an interest, otherwise we had managed to get away with no one paying too much attention. However, my shoulder was grazed from where it had rubbed up against the wall as I had given Juno a leg up, my white plimsols were damp and had a few splashes of mud or cowpat on them. But Juno had come off worst. Her entire back end was covered in cowpat. And she smelt very bad.

'Come on, we need to get home.' I marched off towards the car and the girls followed behind, sniggering.

I needed to get them into the car as quickly as possible. I needed to get away from the prying eyes. It felt as though they were all judging and making their minds up. I felt as though a hundred eyes were upon me, yet when we reached the car and I looked around, no one was watching us. But still the shame grew, which morphed into panic. I had neglected not only my own daughter but someone else's as well. Suddenly, I was thrust back in time to when something similar had happened with Anabel. At a birthday party. She had been climbing over piles of stacked chairs in a leisure centre, where one of her friends was having her sixth birthday party, and I – well, I had been engrossed in my phone. Busy with Instagram. Anabel came off lightly – a bruise on her knee and cheek – but it could have been worse. I had put it down to bad luck – it could have happened to anyone – but I knew these things happened when I wasn't paying attention. And they may have been eight years old, but they still needed supervision. I decided to put the cowpat incident down to a one-off. I didn't need the guilt. It had been a while since I had been properly engaged in social media. I just needed to get over the novelty again and then I could multitask, the way I had seen so many other mums managing to do. The way I used to. It wasn't exactly difficult – it was just taking photos and uploading them with relevant content. I wasn't going to allow myself to feel so much shame. If I did, it would wrap me up and swallow me.

* * *

Anabel and I cocooned Juno as she stripped her shorts off, and I put them in a plastic carrier bag in the boot. She slid into the car seat in her underwear and Anabel hopped in the other side. I drove us home as quickly and as safely as possible, as we all tried to ignore the pungent smell of cow poo.

The girls told me what happened on the way home. Juno was walking along the edge of the wall when she slipped and fell. She had grazed her knee quite badly. I gripped the steering wheel too tightly all the way home as I imagined the scenario playing out a different way had I been paying attention. I would certainly have told Juno to get down had I seen what she had been up to. But Anabel said that Juno had jumped up so quickly that even she had not realised she had climbed up on the wall. Which gave me some relief. Juno was renowned for her spontaneity, the very antithesis of Anabel.

We arrived home just before three. I hadn't heard anything from Evie all afternoon. I ushered the girls into the house, sent Anabel upstairs with Juno to get her into the shower, and I put her clothes in the sink in the utility room and rinsed them off before shoving them into the washing machine. Then I quickly bashed out a text to Evie.

All well here. Juno fell in a cowpat, which the girls thought was hilarious. Hope you're okay. I can have her overnight if you need me to.

I put some cold juice out on the table for the girls and went to check on them.

Outside the door to the main bathroom, I was about to knock when I heard them whispering. I knew it was wrong to listen, because they were just little girls and it was all harmless chatter, but something about the hushed whispers made me pause.

'And you promise you won't tell?' Juno whispered.

'I won't.' Anabel said back in her hushed tone and sounding slightly harassed with it.

'Well, you are a bit of a mummy's girl. You sure you won't tell her?' Juno whispered in a mocking tone. At that point, I wanted to throw the door open and inform Juno that Anabel was not a mummy's girl, but just a normal girl who did what she was told and didn't have the nonchalant attitude of a teenager.

'I said I won't tell, so I won't tell!' Anabel said, a little more angrily. Whatever they were discussing was no doubt harmless. I walked to my bedroom and called loudly from the doorway.

'Girls, are you finished?' I waited a few seconds and then the door to the family bathroom door opened, revealing Juno wrapped in a towel, her hair wet. Anabel appeared by her side.

'Right, let's get you some clothes,' I said, stepping towards them.

'It's okay, Mummy, I can do it.' Anabel walked in front of Juno towards her bedroom.

'Oh, okay,' I said, and feeling rather redundant, I went downstairs to wait for them. I tried not to dwell on whatever it was that Juno had told Anabel. It was just young girl stuff. I knew Anabel kept a diary – if I wanted to, I could read it in a few days' time and I was sure she would have put it in there. But that didn't sit right with me – I would be like a prying bad mother. But what if the thing that Juno had told Anabel was important?

I took my phone out and checked Instagram. The new followers immediately soothed me. I hadn't checked the post since we left the ice-cream parlour. There were more followers and several likes on the picnic post. A thrill rushed through me, as I thought about all those people, looking at and liking the post, and it had only been up for an hour. I knew by the end of the day it would have received more likes. I knew how to upload the right content to get the likes and the follows. Already I could see the account taking off and Cushy becoming a household name.

Betty had sent me a message.

Nice post! I like it. A lot.

I had been worried after Betty's visit that allowing myself to become immersed in the Instagram world would be a bad thing. But Betty had made me realise I did miss it. She was a great social media friend to have – she would be useful in gaining me more followers through her re-posts and general championing of me. It was a strange relationship I had with Betty. We both needed each other: she needed her ego to be massaged, and I needed her to help me gain a following. It was purely professional in that sense. But Betty had a certain likeability and was admired by many. I knew if I wanted to succeed, it was good to know people like her.

The rush of joy at seeing such an increase in followers on the account in such a short space of time made the little chat I had overheard between Anabel and Juno in the bathroom seem insignificant. It was what girls their age did; they talked, they exchanged secrets. I need not be worrying about it.

Eventually, the girls came downstairs, Juno dressed in one of Anabel's dresses, and parked themselves at the table.

'I'll make some pizza for dinner if you like,' I said to them both, and I saw Anabel's eyes light up. Pizza was a once-weekly treat – she couldn't believe she would be getting it *twice*! She looked at Juno with wide eyes.

'Pizza!' she said, and Juno just shrugged. Maybe she was feeling a bit low after the cowpat incident; maybe she was missing her mum. I tried not to think she could be mulling over anything that she and Anabel had been discussing in the bathroom earlier.

My phone alerted me to a message. I hoped it would be Evie. When I looked at my phone, I was relieved to see it was.

On our way back, will be with you in about an hour. Thanks for offering for her to stay over, but I'll collect her and take her home.

'Your mum will be here in an hour. Shall I put that pizza on now? Early dinner.'

'Yes, yes!' Anabel whooped. 'Pizza! Yes.'

I turned to Juno, who was looking decidedly less enthusiastic about pizza for an early dinner. Was Juno close to her step-grandfather? I wondered. I didn't really want to ask. But she seemed so sad. I wouldn't say anything, because I wasn't sure exactly how much she knew; how much

Evie had told her about what was happening. I hoped for Evie's sake that it wasn't going to be the last time she saw her stepfather.

The doorbell rang just after five and Evie stood at the door looking much less flustered than she had when she had left for Oxford.

I pulled her in and hugged her. 'How was it? Was it completely awful? How is he?' I released her from the embrace.

'He's okay. He's going to be okay. Just a scare, hopefully, but a bit of warning for him to slow down, I suppose.'

'Oh good, that's really good. I'm so pleased. Well, come in for a sec. We've had a great day. As I said, Juno fell into a cowpat and got a little scrape on her leg at the same time. She was walking along the wall at the ice-cream parlour and, well, she toppled. It was only a few feet, but—'

'It's fine.' Evie took my hand. 'Thank you so much for having her. I couldn't have managed without you. She is a true wild child – always getting scrapes and cuts. Too fearless sometimes.'

'Oh, okay.' I breathed a sigh of relief. Juno wasn't the type of child to tell her mother that I had been on my phone when the accident had happened. Especially after I had overheard her telling Anabel not to be a grass.

I called for Juno – they were in the snug, watching telly.

'I gave them some pizza. I hope that's okay.'

Evie smiled. 'It's more than okay – you've been a real saint today. Thank you so much.'

'No honestly, anytime. That's what friends are for, right?' I said and cocked my head slightly. She breathed in and nodded.

'You are a great friend, Miranda.' Evie looked towards the door of the snug where the girls had emerged. I felt the warmth of Evie's words hug me like a warm blanket.

'Hey, poppet! Are you ready to go?' Evie said to Juno.

'Yes,' Juno said. She didn't seem particularly thrilled to see Evie. I know if that had been Anabel after six hours without me, she would be throwing herself all over me – especially if she had been dumped in such a rush.

I walked them to the door and Evie and I hugged once more before they left. I closed the door and felt I should have been happy to help a friend out today. But something was niggling at me. It was probably guilt at not paying full attention to Juno today, but it didn't feel like guilt. Perhaps I needed

another hit from my Instagram followers – I was sure there would be lots
more likes now and maybe even a message or two and some comments.
David was still at the pub with Steve and Anabel was happy watching TV. I
could have a sneaky peek, limit myself to fifteen minutes, tops.

I picked up my phone and clicked the side to bring the phone to life. I
tapped in my passcode and then when the screen came to life, I saw it was
still on the last message that Evie had sent me. For some reason, I let my
eyes linger over the words again.

On our way back, will be with you in about an hour. Thanks for offering for her to
stay over, but I'll collect her and take her home.

I hadn't noticed it before, or maybe I had, and it hadn't fully registered.
But that one three-letter-word completely changed the entire context of the
message. Evie had said 'on *our* way back' not 'on *my* way back'.

When she dropped Juno off this morning, she had not mentioned
anyone else going with her, but her text read as though she were not travelling back alone. There was only one person she could have left the village
and travelled to Oxfordshire with, and that was Verity.

I literally felt my blood beginning to boil. There I had been, moments
earlier, standing on my doorstep, telling Evie what a great friend she was
and vice versa. Yet all I really was, was the babysitter. It was Verity she had
taken with her to be by her side when she needed someone. I felt a shudder
of frustration that she hadn't asked me to be there for her. And for the
whole day, I had been feeling on top of the world because Evie had come to
me for help.

Now I just felt angry. Very angry. The same feelings were regurgitating
themselves. Why did I always end up on the outside feeling so rubbish?

I clicked out of the message and went straight onto Instagram.

It was an hour later, I was still scrolling through, when I heard the front
door click, and David was home.

28

10 MAY 2019 – 2.37 P.M. – GLOUCESTER POLICE STATION

Interview with Olivia Cunningham (continued)

I feel a bit like Miss Marple! I guess I just read too many books, but I had begun to sniff it all out. As I said before, it only needs one or two conversations before you begin to piece a few things together. Once Miranda came to me about Verity's lack of visits to the library, considering she was an author, I began to keep my eye on her. I was very inconspicuous, of course, and there isn't much customer confidentiality in a library. But it was true, she hadn't taken any books out. I guessed she just wasn't one of those kinds of authors who need to do a lot of research. Although that didn't coincide with the fact she was writing a historical novel, but I didn't pay too much attention to that. She could have a lot of books at her house, or she could use the internet, or she could simply just have the historical knowledge and was writing the fictional novel around it. I didn't spend too long mulling it over because, quite frankly, I have a life. But Miranda's observation must have sparked an interest, because a couple of weeks ago, I was intrigued when Verity came into the library for the first time. It was a busy afternoon, and I saw her loitering. When I had got the queue down, she slowly approached the desk. I could see she was looking a bit restless – I would even go as far as to say tetchy – as though she really didn't want to be there, and she explained she was there to get online. Well, with the library computers, you can't just click on Google – you need to login with your library card and before you can do that, I have to authorise it. It's quite thrilling really, that level of control the job entails. Other than that, it's mostly just scanning books and re-shelving them. I was quite surprised that a young woman like Verity needed to use public computers for whatever it was she needed to do. Our usual candidates are the elderly, who always need a lot of assistance, or kids who want to play games after school. I would have presumed Verity would have access to anything she wanted via her smartphone I had seen poking out of her back pocket. Oh yes, I told you, I felt like Miss Marple. I set her up and then left her to it. Each person is allocated a thirty-minute slot before it kicks you out. You can log in again if it's quiet. But I would say that Verity was on the computer for less than ten minutes. The computers themselves are lined up against the wall, to give people privacy – if you're just walking around the library, you wouldn't be able to see what people are looking at – unless it's one of our elderly customers who need assistance. So, I had no idea what Verity was browsing, but she looked quite stressed. She kept running her hand through her hair and adjusting herself in her seat.

But yes, it was only ten or so minutes, and then she just upped and left. She didn't say goodbye. By this time, the library was much quieter. It was almost five, our closing time, and I was closing up by myself that afternoon. So, I waited until it was just gone five – I like to give people a few extra minutes, especially if they are returning books or DVDs – then I closed and locked the front door.

I know this sounds bad, but as I said, I was curious, and I didn't really think too much about it at the time. I just went straight to the computer that Verity had been using and logged back on. It's not my usual style, but there was something about the way she was acting that alarmed me.

I went and looked at the history – being a librarian for as long as I have, I am pretty tech savvy – and I pulled up the last article she had been looking at. Initially, it didn't register with me because I just presumed it was part of her research. But when I thought about it later, I went home and did my own bit of research. And that was when I knew there was something more to that girl, that maybe Miranda was right to suspect Verity a little bit. But I swear, not in one million years would I have ever made the association between that article and what happened that night. It was all a bit too far-fetched, even for me. And I love a good thriller with a shocking twist.

29

Once half term was done and dusted, I arranged to meet with Hatty about getting the last bits finalised for the picnic in the park. I was glad of the distraction because I had been avoiding Evie and trying to find things to fill my time, so when Hatty rang and said was I free for a little extra PTA meet-up, just the two of us, I almost bit her hand off. It was just over a week until the picnic in the park. It was the simplest event, but we wanted to make sure that nothing went wrong.

I practically skipped around to Hatty's after I had dropped Anabel at school. When I arrived, she had just taken warm croissants out of the oven and a hot pot of coffee was on the Aga.

'My goodness, if I knew all PTA meets were like this, I would have joined as soon as I got here.'

Hatty laughed and brought two mugs to the table. 'I don't think any amount of sugary carb would have convinced you. I think you have a good heart, but you needed to settle in and make sure you and your family were happy first. That was very admirable, Miranda. Don't beat yourself up about it.'

'Oh.' I looked down because no one had ever said anything like that to me since I had moved here. Obviously, Evie had lots of good things to say to me – at least she did once – but I guess I am just one of those people who needs the reassurance, the adoration from time to time. I really admired people like Hatty – well-rounded individuals who always had a good thing to say about others and who didn't need constant affirmation. Unlike me, who needed it like air.

We bashed out the final few details for the picnic. Hatty's farmer friend from down the road was supplying us with hay bales for seating – which would ultimately end up as a playground for the children – and Hatty was baking a massive batch of scones. A local supplier was providing a few jars of jam.

I had my job: bunting. Make the bunting, buy the bunting, whatever I wanted. I had really liked the idea of making it with Anabel as a little project this week, but I still hadn't got around to it. I didn't have the patience, and I was running out of time. I double-clicked on Amazon on my phone when Hatty was out of the room and received an email seconds later to say the bunting was on its way.

'Gazebo,' Hatty said, polishing off the last of her croissant. 'Do you have one?'

'I do. It was one of the first things we bought when we moved here.'

'Good – you never know, it could pee it down, although the weather report says it's going to be hot. So I guess it could double up as a bit of shade, especially for mums with little ones,' Hatty said, adding to her list.

My goodness, this woman thought of everything. I could barely handle bunting!

'Have you seen much of Verity lately?' she asked quietly, still looking at her list.

'Oh, I...' I was taken aback. Hatty and I had that conversation a while back about why Verity had been at the Mother's Day service, but since then we hadn't mentioned her.

'Well, to be honest. I haven't seen much of her,' I said, but I thought about our confrontation the other day. Then there was the conversation I had overheard outside the school when I had been waiting for Hatty, how angry Verity had sounded. But I hadn't shared it with Hatty at the time. Maybe now was the right time. 'I did hear her on the phone after the PTA meeting. She was running past the school. When you went back in, she had stopped just around the corner from where I'd been stood. She sounded very angry at whoever she was talking to.'

'Oh, you didn't say anything before,' Hatty said.

'No, because you came straight back out and then we just started walking. I wondered if it was anything to add to our theory of what brought her here. She was talking about a woman called Rachel. She sounded annoyed that this woman was getting more attention that she was. I thought,' I said, bringing my theory out in the open, 'that maybe Rachel was her sister, or another author from her publishers.'

'Hmm, interesting, isn't it? Just getting snippets into people's lives. She really doesn't give very much away at all, does she? She's sort of half in, half out, isn't she?'

'What do you mean?'

'Well, it's like she *has* as opposed to wants to be here, and that reluctancy shows. But at the same time, she seems to have struck up an unlikely friendship with the most popular woman in the village. Evie.'

I shrunk backwards at the mention of the burgeoning friendship that had been affecting my own relationship with Evie for months now. 'Yes, I suppose she is.'

'So, she does stick out like a sore thumb in that respect – you can't exist in a village like this and hide yourself away to the extent that she has.'

'No, you're right,' I said, feeling triumphant again that I wasn't the only one who had sensed all this about Verity.

'I don't think she will last much longer, if I'm honest,' Hatty said.

'No?' I said, curious as to where this theory of Hatty's had come from.

'I mean, I've lived here for fifteen years and not in all that time have I met anyone like Verity here.'

I nodded. This was good. If I was feeling braver, I would tell Hatty about how rude Verity had been to me the other day, but that would mean disclosing all the details of my own past, and I wasn't ready for Hatty to see me in that light. Not until I could prove myself to be a worthy member of the community. Then she would be able to see it was all in the past and a big mistake at that.

The conversation petered out as quickly as it had begun. There really wasn't much I could discuss with Hatty without exposing my past. We would both be struggling for anything to really say about Verity, as she was such an enigma. And Evie had not been forthcoming with anything helpful or interesting about her either. In fact, during the barbeque, when there was the faintest chance of me getting to know a little more about Verity, it was Evie who had swooped in and moved her on – under the guise that she hadn't had anything to eat. Who knew if that was a genuine caring act or a tactic to keep me away from Verity because Evie wanted her all to herself? I hated thinking that way about Evie, but I was no longer sure about anything.

I left Hatty's feeling a little less stressed about the situation. It was obvious Verity's presence had piqued the interest of others and not just me, because Hatty's opinion counted for a lot in this village and she must have influenced others besides me with her thoughts.

It was only over a week until the picnic in the park, and if Evie was coming, then she might convince Verity to come and that would be another opportunity for me to observe her in the wild when she was around others, because that was when her behaviour differed. From afar this time, especially so if I were going to talk to Evie. I didn't need Verity dropping me in it and blabbing to her all about my past misdemeanours.

Sabrina had been and cleaned the house whilst I had been out. There was a slight scent of lemon and lavender in the air, and it felt pleasant to come home to a clean house that I hadn't had to do myself. My stomach began to rumble, and I realised it was coming up for midday. I had gladly accepted a croissant from Hatty, but that had been all I'd had today, bar my smoothie first thing.

I put a piece of sourdough bread on to toast and whisked two eggs ready to scramble.

I dropped a knob of butter in a saucepan and carried on whisking my eggs.

Then my phone rang, which startled me. I grabbed it from the side and saw Evie's name on the screen. I felt a swell of happiness. She can't have helped noticing my avoidance of her these last few days, and I felt bad now because I should have checked in with her about Frank. It had been a few days now and I suppose she had felt my absence. I swiped to answer.

'Hiya,' I said. There was a pause on the other end. I waited. This village was renowned for bad reception and quite often someone would call, and the line would stay quiet for a few moments. I anticipated Evie's voice to come crackling through any second.

And it did. But it wasn't her voice as it would be if she were holding the phone to her mouth. It was Evie's voice, but far away. I laughed. 'Oi, you silly sausage!' I shouted into the phone. 'You've called me by mistake.' But I knew she wouldn't hear me. I knew I should just hang up the call and then text her to say she had pocket-called me, and I was almost about to do so when another voice filtered through in the background.

Verity's.

I clung on to the phone and held it tightly to my ear so I could try to hear what they were saying. There was lots of movement, and it was hard to know if Evie had her phone in her pocket or if it was in a handbag. Either way, it sounded as though they were walking and talking. I sat down, barely daring to breathe in case any slight sound I made might give me away.

I listened carefully, trying to pick out one or two words but it was impossible to hear, it was too muffled and there was a constant swish of material against the phone as Evie walked, drowning out her words.

I sat for a few minutes listening to the muffled voices and then suddenly the swishing stopped. They had stopped walking.

'I don't want to inconvenience you,' came Verity's voice, still muffled, but I could just about make it out.

'Well, you are,' Evie said. Her voice was stern and hard. 'And it's adding to the stress I am already under.'

'I'm sorry,' Verity said.

'You've nothing to be sorry about. This isn't your fault. Let me make another phone call, see what I can do.'

'If you could, I would appreciate it,' Verity said.

There was a loud muffle and a bang that made me pull the phone away from my ear. Then Evie's voice, clear and loud, coming through my phone.

'Hello, hello, Miranda?'

Shit, shit, shit. I hung up. Panic seized me. Evie would look at how long she had been on the call and know I had been listening in the whole time. It had been almost five minutes. *Shit, shit, shit.* I stood up and began frantically pacing.

My phone rang again. Evie's name on the screen. *Shit.* I didn't know what to do. If I didn't pick up, she would know I was faking as I had just been active on the call.

I thought quickly and swiped to answer.

'Ah, there you are?' I said brightly.

'Hi,' Evie sounded breathless. 'Sorry, I think I called you by mistake.'

'Yes, you did.' I tried to laugh, but it came out nervous and jittery.

'Did you hear just a load of pocket noise?' She laughed.

'To be honest, I wouldn't know. I tried to call out to you, then the door-bell rang. I've been at the front door with a delivery guy. I left you on the kitchen side.' It was a good enough lie for Evie not to suspect that I had been standing listening in on her for the last few minutes.

'Oh right, okay. No worries. Sorry for the accidental call.'

'Don't worry,' I said. 'How's Frank?'

'Frank?' Evie said, as though she were considering his name for a moment. 'He's fine. Yes, he's doing very well. He should be out of hospital in a few days.'

I felt in that moment that something didn't feel right. The way Evie had questioned her stepfather's name, it was as though she had completely forgotten that he'd had a heart attack and almost died a few days ago.

'Have the hospital staff been looking after him well?' I said flatly. I suddenly felt as though I needed to quiz her more. She had neglected to tell me she had been heading to the hospital with someone else, which I already suspected had been Verity.

'Oh yes, he's a real ladies' man as well, so he's been charming the pants off the nurses.'

'I had a cousin who worked at the John Radcliffe. Is that where he is?' I asked, and there was a beat, a beat too long, before Evie replied.

'Yes. Look, I have to go, but can I pop round later after the school run? I feel I've hardly seen you lately!'

'Sure,' I said sweetly. 'After school, it is. The girls can have a play and we can have a good catch-up.'

'Great. See you then.'

We hung up, and I immediately googled the number for John Radcliffe

Hospital. I spoke to the reception and asked what room Frank Pollard was staying in for a family visit later.

I hung up and squeezed the phone tightly in my hand. As I had suspected. There was and never had been a Frank Pollard staying in the John Radcliffe Hospital.

30

Evie waved enthusiastically at me as I walked through the playground just before three thirty. She was clearly trying hard. Did she feel weird about the phone call earlier? I arrived next to Evie, and she stepped away from the group of mums she had been chatting with. She took out a packet of Lotus Biscoff and shook them at me.

'Your favourite. I was in town today, went to the pound shop. I stocked up, so there will always be loads whenever you come to me as well.'

Oh, good Lord. She really was trying. 'Yummy! Lucky me!'

'Thanks for having me over – it feels like it's been forever. I really need a coffee and a catch-up.'

Do you, Evie? Do you? I thought. *Is there something you need to confess, get off your chest maybe?*

'Well, it will be nice to have you over,' I said. 'Ah, there's the bell.' I was keen to get home. My heart was racing and my palms were getting sweaty. I knew I was feeling stressed out about everything with Evie and Verity, and I just wished that I knew what was going on. But I was terrified to ask, because really, what could it possibly be? Evie was still speaking to me, and as far as she was concerned, we were still good friends. But she didn't know that I knew how much time she had been spending with Verity. Which was entirely her choice, of course, but she hadn't always been honest about it, and well, it just felt off, but I couldn't begin to imagine why. I mean, if Evie had become fed up with me, surely she would just stop making any effort at all? But she was still here. I just wish I had some more info on Verity, something that I could say to Evie to warn her away from her, but I had nothing. Except the way she had spoken to me outside my car when she confronted me about Betty, but I couldn't tell Evie that. It would all sound a little too tit for tat. I would have to bide my time. Perhaps I could get Verity drunk again? Evie had some sort of sixth sense that Verity could turn a little sour after a drink or two. Perhaps she would spill everything out to me after a few glasses of wine.

The girls skipped ahead; their heads stuck together all the way home.

'Thick as thieves, aren't they?' Evie said. 'They are best friends, aren't they?' She continued as they raced through the side gate into the back garden. I opened the front door and let Evie and me through. She slipped her trainers off and followed me through to the kitchen.

'Yes, they are pretty tight,' I said.

'Young friendships are so memorable. I always remember a girl from school. I was so close to her. Sara Chipping, her name was. I hope they remember each other and this precious time,' Evie said thoughtfully.

I looked at her with a furrowed brow. 'You don't think they will still be friends when they are older, then?'

Evie looked at me and shook her head quickly. 'No, that's not what I meant. I'm sure they will. Sometimes things change though, don't they? When they move up to secondary school and college, you know.'

'Well, I have a feeling that those two will stay firm friends for life.'

Evie looked at me. Her eyes were shiny. Were those tears welling? 'I hope so,' she said.

She strode over to the patio doors that opened up to the garden and unlocked the door. The girls would be looking for drinks and snacks soon. When she turned back around, her face was brighter, no shiny eyes. I wanted to ask, did she have plans to move? Was this what this was all about? But I was too terrified to hear the answer. I thought about the conversation I had overheard at the weekend between Anabel and Juno in the bathroom. Juno had told Anabel a secret and told her not to tell me. I felt my gut drop and panic began to swill around in it. I knew Evie had been a little distant recently, but I didn't want to lose her. Maybe this was her way of trying to break the news to me slowly.

I took a deep breath and moved over to the coffee machine. Why was I overthinking everything? Evie was perfectly settled here. She would be a fool to move and take her daughter out of that brilliant school.

I made Evie her coffee how she liked it, and we sat down at the table. Evie took out the Lotus Biscoff and opened them. Even with my stomach churning, I still took one and nibbled on it. They reminded me of every café I had ever been to.

Evie took a deep breath. 'Look, Miranda—'

'Mummy, Juno and I are really hungry. Can we eat those donuts in the bread bin?'

I turned towards Anabel and Juno in the doorway.

Evie rubbed one hand across her face and tried to smile at the girls, but she was clearly put out by the interruption.

I looked at Evie, but she kept her smile up for me as well.

'Is that okay?' I asked. 'Will a greasy jam doughnut ruin Juno's appetite for dinner?'

'There is no end to Juno's appetite – it won't spoil her dinner,' Evie said.

'Okay then,' I said to Anabel. 'And there are smoothies in the fridge. Can you take them outside with you?'

'We will, we're in the Wendy house,' Anabel said and there were a few awkward moments as the girls packed themselves off with the doughnuts and smoothies. Then they were out of earshot again.

'You were saying,' I said, half not wanting to know.

'I wanted to say, I'm really sorry if I have been a bit of a shit friend recently.'

'You haven't been a shit friend.' I got that in quickly. 'Just maybe a little... distant?' I added carefully, not wanting to upset her.

She looked relieved. 'Yes, I've been a little distracted. Anyway, I'm sorry, I really am. I promise I will be better.'

I looked at her, waited to see if there would be any confession. Specifically, to do with the weekend and her fictitious ill stepfather. But she didn't say anything else. She just looked away thoughtfully towards the patio doors, where the squeals of laughter from the girls filtered through.

'Oh, to be that young again,' she said quietly.

I had to agree – eight was the best age. Prepubescent life was still so full of curiosity and excitement without too much mortification.

Evie swung her head back to face to me again. 'Anyway, I vow to be a much better friend from here on in. So, let's toast to that.'

She raised her coffee cup and I raised mine to meet hers. I wanted to ask her about Verity. It was on the tip of my tongue. I wanted to ask her if she had been with her at the weekend. Was she with her earlier when she called me by mistake? I wanted to say, *So, what's the deal with your new bosom buddy? Why is she so weird and why are you so taken with her?* But I just let my mug clink hers and I kept it all inside, where it was beginning to fester and breed into something much bigger and uglier.

* * *

For dinner that night, I put all my fraught energy into cooking a chicken tikka masala with rice and all the trimmings – onion and tomato chutney, minted yoghurt and papadums. Once I had prepped it all, I indulged in a little time on Instagram, checking in on the followers – which had increased again – and answered two messages. I took a photo of the prepped chicken tikka on the chopping board as a flat lay and posted it. I added plenty of literature about cooking a meal for my husband and how Anabel would be partaking in a little too, and how running a business from home was hectic, and I had to make sure I squeezed in time to feed my family a wholesome meal. All the stuff I knew was nonsense content, but people ate it up and felt inspired by it. I had been careful to balance the posts out with candle content too and I had a new batch arriving next week, which I would be using to set up photo shoots. I would check to see how the post was doing after dinner. My treat to myself, it would give me something to look forward to.

David arrived home from work at around seven. He was in high spirits when he walked in the door, and they were only raised further when he saw what we were having for dinner. 'You know the way to a man's heart,' he said as he poured himself a large glass of white wine cold from the fridge.

'Oh, good Lord, you are so sexist. Did you actually just say that?'

'I did, I'm afraid. How was your day? Is Anabel joining us?' He looked at the three table settings.

'She is, she's famished, but she wanted to wait and eat with you.'

'Great. I can't wait to get stuck in.'

I placed platters and bowls in the middle of the table and David called for Anabel. I poured myself a glass of wine and clicked on my phone one last time before I sat down. I could have checked it after I had eaten, but something made me halt at the kitchen side. There was a message from Evie.

Hiya, I've been reliably informed there is an image of Juno up on your Instagram page. I don't use it – as you know – would you mind taking it down? Thanks a million x

I felt my stomach drop and my mouth filled with saliva. Of course I should have asked if I could have put up a photo of Juno. I didn't think too much about it because it was of her side profile and she wasn't looking at the camera – you wouldn't be able to recognise her unless you knew her. Still, I had truly let Evie down. When all I had been doing to date was trying to be a good friend to her. I felt foolish, embarrassed that she had sent the message.

I had taken tons of photos of the girls together before and not once had Evie said anything. But then I hadn't been active on social media when I first arrived. This new Instagram account was my first step back in that direction. Of course Evie didn't want Juno appearing on Instagram. I got that – once it's out there, there is no taking it back. And I had gathered from the snippets of information that Evie had given me that her relationship with Juno's father was troubled – perhaps that was linked to her not wanting Juno on social media? I now felt guilty for posting the photo, but I also felt the familiar swell of anger and frustration bubbling up inside me. It was as though things were spiralling out of control, because it could have only been one person who would have informed Evie about the photo of Juno on my grid. I deleted the photo and went to the message to reply to Evie. What would I say? How would I word it?

'Love?' David's voice filtered through. 'Your curry will get cold. Come and eat.'

I had no choice but to shelve the stress and humiliation, put my phone down and join my family for the meal I had prepared and had been looking forward to eating. I would think of what to say to Evie later.

I swung around, plastered a smile across my face – the way I had always seen my mother do – and sat down at the table. 'Yummy,' I said, gazing at the meal, but the words from the Instagram message were still swimming in front of my eyes.

'You can't say yummy when you made it, Mummy!' Anabel said.

'Yes, she can,' David said. Then he looked at me. 'It's delicious, darling.'

I tentatively spooned a little rice and a little tomato and onion salad onto my plate, then I added a spoonful of the curry.

'It's spicy, but not too spicy,' Anabel said. 'I like it.'

I couldn't help but smile at Anabel's comment, she was always so complimentary about my cooking, even when I got things a little wrong. I looked around at the spread and tried to see it through the eyes of David and Anabel, who were both hungry and now thoroughly enjoying the meal. I lifted a forkful of food to my mouth, but it was dry; I had well and truly lost my appetite.

31

BEFORE

The girl looked at her mother across the table. They had come out to a café to eat. The girl had chosen fish fingers and beans. The girl's mother had said they could go to a fancy restaurant if they wanted to, but the girl was perfectly happy eating at the pub they had found a mile down the road from the house.

Her mother had started to perk up little bit. That afternoon at the house, she had found some pebble-grey coloured paint under the stairs and had begun to redecorate the hallway. The girl had even heard her whistling and singing along to a song on the radio as she painted.

Her mother grinned at her, and the girl grinned back. She added more ketchup to her plate and eyed her mother to see if she would tell her off. She didn't. After their dinner, her mother ordered two ice-cream sundaes. It was coming up to eight o'clock. The girl often stayed up late these days – because she wasn't going to school any more, there was nothing to get up for. Her mother had ordered her some workbooks to help her practice her maths and writing. Each morning they spent an hour with the books, then they read together. Now the girl was helping her mother with the painting.

'Life skills,' her mother had said to her that afternoon as she showed her how to put tape along the skirting boards, so the paint didn't drip. The girl knew she would remember that tip for life.

The girl's mother asked the passing staff member if they could bring over the bill. A loud noise came from the front door. The girl's mother spun around as three men came spilling through the door, laughing and talking very loudly. The girl's mother seemed to visibly shrink into her seat. Her mother had admitted that she had grown quite sensitive to noises lately because of how much time they spent in the house alone. The girl thought maybe the men were drunk. Or maybe one of them reminded her mother of her father. And that was making her sad. Whatever it was, her mother didn't want to hang around and got up and went to the till and handed some notes to the staff member who had taken too long to get back to her with the bill. Then the girl's mother took their coats and hurried her and the girl out of the pub. It was almost dark outside, and her mother grabbed the girl's hand and hurried her to the car. She could strap her own seat belt on now, so her mother left her to it whilst she got into the driver's seat and started the engine.

The girl's mother drove home faster than she would normally have driven, the girl was sure of that. They got back to the house, and it was dark and cold. The girl's mother lit the fire and went into the kitchen. The girl went upstairs and changed into her pyjamas and went into the bathroom to brush her teeth. She knew how to do most things for herself, but she would want her mother to read to her tonight. The evening had ended too abruptly for her liking. And it had been such a good day as well. She had heard her mother and B and H talking about good days and bad days. This was a combination of both. She hoped tomorrow would be a better day. She took down the Chronicles of Narnia books to where her mother was sitting on the sofa with a cup of tea, staring at the television that wasn't on.

'I'm not sure I can go on much longer like this,' her mother whispered into her mug. The girl wasn't sure if her mother knew she was there and she was speaking directly to her or not.

'Something has to change.' This time, her mother looked at the girl and so she knew she was talking to her.

'What do you mean?' the girl asked.

'I don't know. But we need to do something different. I need to think of a plan.'

'I'm good at plans,' the girl said and her mother smiled, put her mug down on the coffee table – even though the table didn't belong to her, she still used a coaster and always had done – and she faced her daughter.

'Do you have a book for us to read?'

The girl nodded and handed *The Lion, the Witch and the Wardrobe* over to her mother.

'Thank you.'

The girl folded herself into the crook of her mother's waist and her mother held the book out in front of them both and read.

That night, the girl went to bed and dreamt of a huge wardrobe where she and her mother found themselves in a magical land, where no one could do them any harm.

The next morning, when the girl woke, her mother was up and had begun the painting again. There was no whistling or singing, but the girl guessed that they would be staying for a little while longer.

10 MAY 2019 – 3.09 P.M. – GLOUCESTER POLICE STATION

Interview with Beth Higgson

I liked them both very much from the minute I met them. I know that is not what you want me to say – you want me to have some information on either of them, to tell you something I had noted that I thought was suspicious. Nope. Sorry. I was super busy studying all spring when Verity moved here. I thought she was quiet when I met her, that was all. But I liked her – we had a few interesting chats. She asked me about my uni course and how I was finding it. We both babysat Juno, although obviously I was the babysitter before Verity came along, and then Evie began to share it out between us. Which suited me. I work in the shop as well. I don't need any more work really, I just do it to help Evie out, so when Verity moved here and Evie trusted her with looking after Juno as well, well, I was relieved.

I'm not sure why Evie asked me, actually – I don't think I'm that great with kids. I'm never really sure exactly what I should be saying to them. You know? Plus, there is all that worry of saying the wrong thing – 'inappropriate stuff'. I'm twenty-three so my life is basically studying or drinking. I can't really talk to kids about either of those things. But I did find myself in a conversation with Juno once that seemed a bit strange. I mean, not strange, exactly, but, well, I ended up feeling a bit sorry for her, I guess. I have a close relationship with my dad, and so that's also why I felt I couldn't connect with her. I mean, if my mum and dad had divorced, then I suppose I could have understood her a little bit more. Not that her parents had divorced. From what I knew, there was no father at all – he was off the scene right in the beginning. I don't think Juno ever knew him.

But anyway, this one evening, she and I got talking. How was school? Did she like her room? Who did she play with at school? What did she have for her tea...? You get it? I'm really not very good at small talk with kids. But that was okay, as Juno is a confident girl, and she always finds something to talk to me about, and I usually listen and go along with it. She can be quite entertaining when she wants to be, and she is also very intelligent. You would think she was ten or eleven, not eight.

Anyway, I digress. It was one night, a couple of weeks ago, Evie had to go out, and Verity, well, apparently, Verity had gone AWOL, although no one had officially said that. Bearing in mind this was a few weeks before it all happened. Maybe she had gone off to prepare herself for what was about to go down. Who knows? Anyway, sorry, I will get there. So, I get called in to babysit, because they know me, and Evie seemed quite stressed. I did actually have a date that night. I have been spending some time with our local vicar and we were going to go out for a drink. Did I say date? It wasn't a date like that. He's ten years older than me and a man of the church. It wouldn't be right. Anyway, I turned down 'the date' because I felt sorry for Evie. And Conner said it was the Christian thing to do. Not that I'm a Christian. But as I said, Evie seemed really out of sorts, and I had heard that her stepfather had been ill recently, so I stepped up. Would it sound callous if part of me did it because I knew it would please Conner? No, I shouldn't have said that, too much information.

So, there we were, me and Juno. She was waxing lyrical about God knows what, and I wasn't really paying much attention until I heard her say that she really hated her mum. Now I know that is normal for kids to hate their parents from time to time, but when I looked at her, she had tears in her eyes and she looked really sad. I put my arm around her, and she collapsed her whole body weight into me, like as if she hadn't hugged anyone for a long time. I felt a bit uncomfortable, but then I remembered she was just a little kid, and Evie was obviously going through some stuff and she was feeling left out.

I like to think of myself as an intelligent person – this time next year I could be starting a PhD or travelling the world, or working for Google – but even I didn't pick up on the clue, the sign that the goddamn kid was giving me or at least she was trying to give me. All this time, this whole thing had been blowing up between Evie, Verity and Miranda, and we were all spectators to it, waiting for the fireworks to go off, like a bunch of really sick voyeurs. But really, what we should have been doing was watching and listening to the kid. To Juno.

33

'Please don't move that,' I snapped at David for the fifteenth time that morning. It was the day of the picnic in the park and I had woken up determined that I was not going to get stressed, that I was going to stay perfectly calm and professional. I was going to be a bit more Hatty and a bit less Miranda. But that had all gone out the window when David had come down and insisted on making a full English breakfast after I had cleaned up the kitchen. Apparently, David needed to have bacon and eggs and mushrooms and a bloody hash brown for his breakfast, and so now the kitchen smelled like a greasy-spoon café. I was trying to make sure I had everything I needed with me. Hatty was first-aid trained but asked me to bring an extra packet of plasters and wet wipes, and I had the bunting all set out on the kitchen table. I had to pack our picnic food and now David was nudging the bunting aside so he could sit at the table with his stinking food.

'Sorry, love, but I need to eat.'

'Really, David? Right there in that spot? The table seats twelve for God's sake.'

He looked up at me like a wounded puppy, and I felt the guilt seep through me.

'It's my seat,' he said like a small child. And I shook my head and carried on packing the picnic bits.

I wasn't stressed about the practical elements of the day, even though I was also in charge of meeting and greeting the band. (For some reason, Hatty felt my metropolitan background qualified me for this role despite the fact they were all in their sixties and seventies and were playing folk music – they were as far from metropolitan as you could get!) But I was stressed over Evie, whom I hadn't seen or spoken to in over a week. I had meant to send the message explaining why I had posted the image and apologising the same night, but the more I thought about what to say, the more it became so jumbled in my brain. In the end, I didn't reply. It was the longest we'd gone without speaking. I knew I should have been over to see her the next day, or at least phoned her, but I had seized up. And then after that, I let the anger and the frustration seep in, and I began to convince myself that she was responsible for allowing the gap to widen in our friendship with everything she was keeping from me. Since Verity arrived, I had been playing second fiddle. I didn't want to feel like that any more. So, I signed Anabel up to breakfast club and dropped her at eight and put her into every after-school activity possible or I left her in after-school club. I told her it was just for this week as I had a lot on with the candles. Of course, that was a blatant lie, but she bought it and was happy; it was a novelty for her, and it was a lifesaver for me. I got to avoid Evie at drop off and pickups, meaning the awkwardness of us not speaking to one another wasn't there to stare either one of us in the face in the playground. I felt horribly guilty and extremely canny and clever all at once. It was a strange and uncomfortable sensation. But I knew I would need to speak to Evie soon, and it would probably happen today at the picnic. There was no way Evie was going to miss out on this event. She was always at the centre of all the happenings in the village, and besides, she was in charge of the raffle, the part of the picnic that the PTA and the whole of the village deemed the most important. Apparently, the villagers took it all very seriously, and they had to put a cap on how many two-pound strips could be bought. It didn't surprise me that Evie was at the forefront of this part of the event; her popularity around the village went hand in hand with such a prestigious prize-giving. How was it that she remained so popular when she was being so dishonest to me? It wasn't right, especially when someone like me had to try so hard.

David finally moved himself from the table and put his plate in the dishwasher. Even the sound of him moving around the kitchen was grating on me.

'First-time PTA-event nerves?' He turned to me as he closed the dishwasher.

'You say it like it's a thing,' I said flatly.

I saw he was trying to conceal a smirk. I bit the side of my lip – I couldn't cave now. I had carried the tense mood for too long. But then I felt David's hands on my shoulders, and I melted into his touch. It was his sure way of getting me every time.

'It's going to be fine,' he said, and I let him believe that it was the picnic that was stressing me out. I had also lied to David about the reason Anabel was in breakfast and after-school club all week. I would have to generate a few more hundred orders to compensate for that lie. I could feel my heart flutter and the need to take a few deeper breaths. I reminded myself that this wasn't like before. I would not let myself be carried away. I was a professional using social media purely for professional reasons. My lies were purely to protect David from worrying about me. I would navigate this on my own this time and keep myself in check.

I made myself my first coffee of the day, a decaf because I was so wired; my body wouldn't handle the caffeine with how much adrenaline was already rushing through my body. I was so nervous about seeing Evie. She was obviously disappointed with me and I had stupidly allowed a gap to open up into a huge, cavernous void. I should have fixed it immediately, but I was tired of feeling that everything I was doing was for nothing when Verity had clearly replaced me. It was Anabel who finally soothed me when she arrived downstairs, having picked out her own dress, a red and white spotted one with white patent sandals. She looked adorable.

'Oh, Anabel,' I gushed.

'Sweetheart, you look lovely,' David said.

'Are you ready?' I asked him. He had put on shorts, a shirt and boat shoes.

'I certainly am. Just need to get my deckchair.' He went off to the garage.

'You're such an old man!' I called after him.

* * *

I got us to the park half an hour before the villagers would be arriving, but it seemed that everyone had the same idea about getting there early to find the perfect spot; I was amazed to see that half the hay bales were already taken by families.

I waved at Hatty, who was under the gazebo I had dropped over to her house last week, which was serving as PTA HQ for the afternoon. There was another gazebo, and I saw that under it was the raffle stand and behind the table was Evie.

Oh Christ, I thought. I would have to say hello. I would have to say something, and I wasn't sure what exactly.

But before I had time to think about it, Hatty was waving manically at me and gesturing to look behind me. There were three heavily bearded men about to walk past me. I took them to be the band and so intercepted their route. They initially looked shocked and then I explained to them I had the very important job of making sure they had everything they needed and then showed them to the stage.

'Wow, it's better than Glastonbury,' one of the beards said.

'Oh, have you been?' I asked.

'He was the guitarist for Bowie in 2000,' the second beard said.

'Oh, wow!' I said, feeling very privileged and honoured. I turned around and gave Hatty the thumbs up – I couldn't wait to tell her later.

The field filled up with the villagers. Rugs were spread across the grass next to and around the hay bales. The band had warmed up and were about to start their first set. People were queuing up to buy raffle tickets, and there was a real sense of camaraderie in the air. Even though Evie and I had yet to say one word to one another, I felt a strange sense of satisfaction, joy even, that I was a part of this day, that I was a part of this community. It was such a simple idea – bring a picnic to a park – yet as I tried to look on from the outside, it looked like the most awesome thing ever, and I had been to some proper swanky gigs in London in my time. I took out my phone and took a quick photo so I could remember this moment when I looked back on it, and as I clicked the camera, I saw her. Verity was striding across the field. She was wearing denim shorts, cowboy boots and a white T-shirt. She looked as though she was carrying a bottle of lager in her hand and on her back was a bright red rucksack. I felt the dread hit my stomach as I thought about both Verity and Evie being in the vicinity. With the wonderful buzzing atmosphere of the picnic all around me, I had completely forgotten that there was a possibility that Verity might show up. But here she was, and if I wasn't mistaken, she seemed to have some sort of confident swagger about her that I had never seen on her before. Could it be that she was drunk? It was eleven thirty in the morning. Surely, she wouldn't show up to a family event drunk? I tried to push away the dread and fear of any potential confrontation that might come from crossing the path of an inebriated Verity and decided I would stay well away from her. This was a family day, and I was representing the PTA – I couldn't get into any more arguments with this woman.

I looked over at Evie, who was busy with the raffle. She hadn't seemed to notice that Verity had arrived. She had stopped to talk to Beth and Conner, who seemed to be everywhere together these days – a couple who weren't a couple. Beth must think we were all born yesterday. I noted the subtle looks and touches that each of them gave to the other, and it had been discussed by me and others around the village. It was clear the two of them had feelings for one another. But they seemed just as pleased to have Verity next to them for company, and they all chatted and laughed. I felt my anger spike and then drop again. Could no one see the side of Verity that I had encountered many times already? She seemed to have wooed the entire village from where I was standing. I wanted everything back to exactly how it was. But that would mean Verity no longer being here and that was something I had no control over. The more I thought about it, the more it felt as though she had always been here and my lovely relationship with Evie before had all been a dream. The life that felt more real was this chapter with Verity in it. She was a small woman, but I felt her presence in the village, even when I couldn't see her.

I had been listening to Anabel tell me how hungry she was for the last hour, but I wanted the food to last because I knew she would be starving again by three o'clock. However, with all my responsibilities taken care of, I began to lay out our picnic. David's eyes lit up as baguettes, hams, sun-dried tomatoes, olives, pickled onions, jam tarts and a punnet of strawber-ries accumulated on the picnic rug.

'Hello, David. Hello, Miranda,' came a sweet-sounding voice above me. I looked up and almost dropped the punnet of strawberries I was holding as I realised the saccharine voice belonged to Verity.

'Ahh, Verity, good to see you. How are you?' David chirped. I opened my mouth, as though I wanted to say something to stop him from being so polite to her, but of course, I hadn't mentioned our run-ins.

'I'm very well, thank you, David,' Verity said, a sly smile spreading over her face. David wouldn't have noticed, of course, he was just being polite – I could see he was edging to get stuck into the picnic.

'We're about to eat, Verity. Can I interest you in one of my wife's home-made sausage rolls?' David gestured to the spread on the picnic blanket.

'Home-made? My, my, what a gourmet you are, Miranda,' Verity said with such sincerity, I almost wished I could have believed her.

'We do like our food. We're what you might call *foodies*.' David laughed at himself. Verity laughed along too.

'Well, I like to see a man enjoying his lunch. I shan't hold you up. I have a few more people I'd like to say hello to.' Verity swept away as suddenly as she had arrived. I was poised, ready to say something about her to David, but he was already tucking into the picnic.

'Mummy, can Juno share our picnic?' Anabel asked, looking over to where Juno was sat all alone.

'Doesn't Juno have her own picnic?' I asked, glancing over at Juno, who was on a hay bale next to a picnic rug, which I presumed was Evie's.

'She's eaten hers and her mummy is busy with the raffle.'

'Oh gosh, yes, get her over here,' I said, feeling a pang of sadness for the little girl. Anabel ran over to her, and I watched Juno's face light up a little as she stood and followed Anabel back to us.

'Hey, Juno,' I said. 'Everything okay?' Juno was usually so full of life, but she seemed a little subdued today.

She shrugged. 'Yeah. Are those jam tarts?' I handed her the packet, and she took one. As I laid it back on the rug, I looked up above the girls' heads and saw Verity looking right at us. Every now and again, she would take a swig from her beer bottle, but her gaze stayed focused on us. Was she checking up on me, making sure I didn't take any more photos of Juno? I certainly wouldn't be doing that anytime soon, and not before I had spoken to Evie first. Maybe having the girls here together could be an icebreaker. Perhaps if I drank a nice cold glass of wine, I would have the confidence to address the elephant in the room.

'Mummy, I need a wee,' Anabel said.

'I need a wee too,' Juno said.

'Oh, okay.' I looked over at Evie, at her stall where the queue was still three people deep. 'David, if Evie comes looking for Juno, can you tell her that I took them to the toilet?'

'Will do. Don't be long – I'll have eaten the picnic.'

'You will not.' I slapped him lightly on his arm where he sat in his deckchair. 'Come on, girls.' Anabel and Juno stood up, and we set off to the village hall, who had given us access to their facilities for the day. The girls ran ahead, and by the time I got into the ladies, Juno was finishing up and washing her hands.

'Wow, that was quick,' I said. 'Wait for us outside – don't wander off anywhere.' I went into the spare cubicle. Juno nodded and walked outside. Anabel was singing to herself in her cubicle. She always took that much longer on the toilet than any other child I knew.

We both finished up at the same time and she grinned at me as we both went to the sinks and washed her hands. The paper towels had run out already, but it was a hot afternoon, so we shook our hands and went outside into the warm air to dry them. As we walked outside, Anabel gasped and bent down by a small privet bush.

'Oh, Mummy, look at that cat.' It was small with tortoiseshell-coloured fur. It looked like a kitten. 'Oh, do you think he lives around here, or is he lost?'

'I don't know, sweetie.' I bent down; I could see he was wearing a collar. Anabel was caught up stroking the cat, who I had to admit was very sweet. Maybe it was time to start thinking about a pet. A cat would be a good start.

Standing back up, I noticed that Juno wasn't standing right outside the door to the village hall, and thinking she must have wondered around the corner, I took a step around the building. As I did, I saw her, but Verity was there too, standing next to Juno. No, not just standing next to her. She had her hand gripped firmly on Juno's arm. Juno was pulling backwards, clearly trying to get away. Verity had the beer bottle in one hand and her rucksack balanced on her opposite shoulder.

'No, I told you, I don't want to!' Juno said firmly. Anger gripped me like a vice and instinctively, all my maternal protective forces went into overdrive, I stepped forward and shouted.

'What do you think you're doing? Get your hands off her immediately.'

Verity looked up at me, annoyance rather than shock was written across her face. But she did as I said and dropped Juno's arm. Juno ran over to me, past me and round the corner to where Anabel was still playing with the cat.

'What do you think you're doing? She's a child, for God's sake – you can't go around grabbing other people's children!' I hissed at her.

Verity wrinkled her nose, took a final swig of her beer, before throwing the bottle into the bin next to her. Then she adjusted her backpack on her shoulder. 'Just watch yourself, Miranda. And watch what you post on your stupid social media page. She isn't your child either, remember.'

'Oh yes, very clever, aren't you, Verity? Seeking me out on Instagram, stalking my grid. Reporting your findings back to Evie.'

'You can't stalk someone's grid if it's not set to private, Miranda.' Verity flicked her hair over her shoulder and batted a fly away. It made her look a little unhinged, like she had a tic.

'But you are trying to come between Evie and I, you are trying to split us up.'

'Oh, come on, what are you? Five? If you feel as if your friendship with Evie is under pressure, then maybe you need to take a good look at the foundations of your relationship.'

'It was perfectly stable before you arrived,' I spat.

I looked to my right and realised Juno was staring up at us and that Anabel had just walked around the corner.

'Anyway, good to talk to you as always, Verity.'

'Likewise.'

She turned and walked away with what was now an obvious stagger. But I was no longer interested in how much Verity had had to drink. Verity had confirmed that she *was* trying to drive a wedge between us by informing Evie of my photo on Instagram. And by not speaking to Evie for a week, I had made it easy for her. I felt my gut tighten. I wanted to fall to the ground, to groan and cry. I needed to speak to Evie as soon as possible.

I took a deep breath. It felt like a ray of sunshine penetrating my body and filling my lungs. I sighed as I released it. My heart was thudding in my chest and I tried to steady my voice.

'Come on then, girls, let's get back to the picnic.'

'All right?' David asked as the girls flopped down on the rug.

I nodded, although I wanted to blurt out what had happened.

'I managed to not eat all the picnic, as you can see.' David grinned, but then frowned when he saw through my reciprocating smile. 'What is it?' he asked quietly.

'Nothing, I just need to eat. Haven't had anything yet.' I sat down on the picnic blanket and popped an olive into my mouth. I wanted so badly to confide in David, to get his view on things, but it was all too petulant to an outsider. Already, I could hear the whininess of it as I considered retelling the story. I needed David to know I had got past all this silly nonsense.

'Well, at least fill your plate up a bit, love. There's half a baguette there.' David pointed out the obvious to me. *I did make the damn picnic*, I wanted to say, but remained tight-lipped. I had snapped enough times at him today already. It wasn't his fault that Verity and Evie were making me feel so frustrated.

The lack of contact with Evie was playing heavy on my mind now – I had some serious sucking up to do. I could blame it on work, say that I had a rush of orders and needed to work day and night to complete them, or I could tell her the truth. That I had been avoiding her since she had asked me to take down the photo of her daughter. We both knew it was the reason, and to try to dance around it any more would only make things worse.

But now there was the added concern of what I had witnessed outside the toilets. Verity had not acted appropriately towards Juno. And Evie had to be informed. There were so many elements to what I had just witnessed that were wrong. Verity must have followed us to the toilets and tried to take Juno away from my charge. Secondly, she was drunk. I knew I had seen something similar at the barbeque at our house, but I couldn't be sure because there were so many people around. But I had definitely seen Verity in the vicinity of Juno, and Juno looking distressed. And it had happened again. I couldn't ignore it this time. At least if I were to go to Evie and tell her about my recent experiences and observations of Verity's erratic behaviour, then it would take some of the heat off me and the photo of Juno. But also, I knew now was the time to tell Evie. Verity was a threat. Her behaviour towards Juno was causing me great concern, and Evie would have to listen to me.

If not as my friend, but for the safety of her own daughter.

34

The band played their second set, and as everyone had finished their picnic lunch, they were now up and dancing. I wished I felt like dancing, but my stomach was doing a dance all on its own. Partly because I knew I hadn't eaten enough, and partly because I knew I had to speak with Evie. I began to pack away our lunch bits to distract myself. Finally, the band played their final song, and then Evie's voice came over on another microphone as she introduced the raffle results.

Another painful half an hour later – where David won a luxury hamper and Evie and I had caught one another's eye as he received the prize and I had to feign a smile – the event was officially over. I had been watching Verity non-stop since the toilet incident. She didn't seem to be acting like someone who had behaved completely inappropriately; she was laughing and drinking and socialising and it riled me up even more.

I saw Evie was by herself, clearing down the raffle stand, so I made a beeline for her. But I was intercepted by Verity at the last second – it was as if she had been watching her out of the corner of her eye and had seized the moment in the same way as I had.

'Damn it,' I said under my breath. I watched the way Verity hung around Evie, saying something that Evie wasn't paying much attention to as she continued to clear up.

'What a triumph!' Hatty was suddenly next to me. 'Do you feel a real sense of accomplishment or what?'

I smiled and tried my best to sound enthusiastic. 'Oh, a triumph, indeed. No hiccups, a job well done by all. And look, everyone has had such a lovely time too.'

'Well, I am definitely signing you up for next year, Miranda. Thanks so much for your help. Especially with the band.'

Where I had been so keen earlier to mention to Hatty about one of the band members playing at Glastonbury, I didn't have the enthusiasm now to say anything. I kept watching Evie, waiting for Verity to leave, and then when she finally sloped away, Hatty was suddenly next to her.

'Oh, for God's sake,' I muttered.

'What a fantastic event.' I turned to see Conner, our local vicar. Had I just said *God's sake* out loud? If I did, he made no reference to it. He wasn't that kind of man – he was so subtle with his faith, and after that Mother's Day service, I would feel perfectly comfortable being in his company in the church again.

'Thank you, Conner. I am glad to see you were enjoying yourself.' I was referring to his time spent with Beth, but even if he understood my subtle reference, he didn't mention it.

'It's been a lovely afternoon, thank you so much for inviting me.'

He was so sweet – I could squeeze him. But I couldn't do that, and I wouldn't, not the way I was feeling today. The two emotions were just not compatible.

Finally, Hatty left Evie alone, and I saw another chance. 'Would you excuse me, Conner?'

'Absolutely,' he said. As I took one step forward, Juno launched herself from nowhere and was at Evie's side. Evie stopped her packing down and bent down to hug her. I noticed she didn't have to bend too far, not the way I did when I hugged Anabel, who was still so dinky for her age and looked small next to anyone, but I hadn't really noticed before how tall Juno was.

'Ready to go, love?' David was behind me. I half turned towards him.

'Yes,' I said reluctantly and bent down to pick up one of the bags. David and Anabel had kindly taken the bunting from the hay bales and put it in its box. David was carrying it now. I took one final glance over at Evie and Juno and realised what I had to say would have to wait until later.

* * *

That evening, David handed me a glass of wine and I took it gratefully. I took a long sip and sank onto the sofa. It was just gone eight. I had just finished packing away, giving Anabel a snack and getting her to bed, having read two chapters of the new David Walliams book to her.

'Here's to you, my darling wife, on your first successful PTA event.'

I smiled, even though I was sick of hearing people congratulate me. I had pointed three ageing musicians in the direction of the stage and bought some bunting online – I had hardly reinvented the wheel. But I knew David meant well. I just really wanted to speak to Evie.

I would now have to wait until David was settled in front of a TV programme and I knew that Evie would have put Juno to bed, then I would pop round and see her.

About an hour later, David had begun watching some crime thriller on Netflix and I stood up and put my cardigan on.

'I'm just popping over to see Evie – I didn't get a chance to speak much with her today and I don't fancy texting when we live so close.'

'Okay, love.' David kept his eyes on the screen.

I left the house and walked the few streets to Evie's. I took my time because I needed to go over what I was going to say. I wanted to get it right, not blurt it out. Evie must know that things had been strange and fraught between us this last week. I wanted to make things right, but I had to address the issues.

I walked down the driveway, and as it was almost dark, the security light came on. I paused at the doorstep before I knocked firmly.

A few seconds passed before Evie came to the door. I knew she had one of those spyholes, so she would have seen it was me. I listened to her take off all the latches and open all the locks. Although she had an open-door policy during the day, the woman was seriously safety conscious at night. I had to say I was the same, having come from living in London. Despite now living in such a quiet village, where nothing remotely dangerous or crime related ever happened, I still locked all the doors at night.

Evie's face finally appeared at the door, which she had only opened halfway.

'Hi,' she said quickly and quietly.

'Hi. Is Juno asleep?' I whispered.

'In bed, highly unlikely that she is asleep though.' I could hear the strain in her voice. She was trying hard to sound her usual friendly self.

'Okay, can we talk? I'll be quiet,' I assured her.

She opened the door fully and stepped back to let me through. When I was in the hallway, she went through the rigmarole of locking the door back up. Then we went through into the lounge. Evie listened at the door for a second, to check we hadn't disturbed Juno, before she closed it and we both sat down. I took the small sofa opposite. It really was a cosy little lounge, with a trendy blue sofa that faced the TV area and a chair and foot-stool that sat directly in front of the fireplace. It wasn't lit, but I could see that was where Evie had been sat, a paperback book was upturned on the arm of the chair and a half-full glass of red wine on the small table next to the chair.

'Would you like a glass of wine?' she asked. I didn't see a bottle anywhere and so I said no because I didn't want to inconvenience her. I had been drinking white at home and would probably need another glass of that after I left anyway, depending how the next half an hour went.

I took a deep breath. Evie sat back in the chair she had been in but kept herself leaning forward. I perched on the edge of the sofa.

'I thought I had better come on over and have a chat. I tried to grab you a few times at the end of the picnic, but it seems you were quite popular.' I let out a little nervous laugh. Evie did a half smile.

'It was a good event,' she said kindly.

'It was,' I said, but not wanting to say any more on the matter, because it was already distracting from what I needed to say, I got straight to the point. 'First of all, can we address the fact that we haven't spoken for a week?'

'Okay,' Evie said, with a hint of a question in her voice. 'I presumed you were busy, and, well, I have been too.'

'I know, I was, but you know as well as I do we would usually text one another, wouldn't we?'

Evie looked at me quizzically. 'Yes.'

'I should have messaged you straight away after you asked me to take the image off Instagram.'

Evie breathed in loud and long. 'Sorry. I should have messaged you again afterwards – I have just been really busy.'

I found my gaze fall upon the down-turned book on the armchair. 'No, it was me. I avoided you. It was churlish of me. I hate confrontation. I realise now I should have asked you first.'

'Well, it's done now, and thank you for taking the photo of the girls down. It's just I... I don't have a social media account – can't abide the thing. I don't like to expose Juno to it either, what with it being just us.'

'Oh gosh, Evie, I totally get it. I was just caught up in the moment and wasn't really thinking. The truth is, I haven't been on social media for a long time either. I just got back on it.' I realised the last part of the sentence came out rather triumphantly, and I noticed how Evie shifted uncomfortably in her chair. 'But then I suppose Verity also filled you in on that, did she?'

Evie brushed her hair away from her face. 'Look, what happened in your past is your past. It's no one's business, certainly not mine. I just didn't think it was a good idea to have Juno on your Instagram account. I haven't put her face on the internet, not once.'

'Okay, I understand that.' I shifted in my seat. 'All that stuff, from my past, like you said, that was then. This is now. I went through a terrible time, and I let it all get to me—'

'You really don't have to explain,' Evie said, and I felt a surge of annoyance.

'I do have to explain, Evie, because you're my friend. I hadn't meant for you to find out that way. I would have told you, at some point.'

'It's really fine,' she said, and I couldn't shift the feeling of annoyance. Why didn't she just ask me about it? Why was she so reluctant to talk about it? Why was she brushing it off? I was here, making an effort, ready to lay my soul bare if I had to and she was shirking away, as though she really didn't want to hear it.

For goodness' sake, Evie, just ask me about it, I thought. I would want to share in all her issues and her past that she keeps so well hidden from me. Friends are supposed to tell each other everything.

'But I want you to know about it,' I said. 'You're my friend, I feel as though I need to say it.'

'It will only bring you anxiety. From what I have heard, it sounds like a pretty messy time in your life. You don't need to dredge it all up for me.' Evie looked at me as if I were mad.

I took another deep breath and let it out too loudly, so it sounded like an aggravated sigh. 'I *need* to tell you, Evie. I want you to understand that this wasn't me. I am better than that. It was a blip.'

Evie let out a loud sigh. 'If it will make you feel any better, then sure. Tell me.'

I felt my mouth go dry. It had been such a long time since I had spoken to anyone about it, I wasn't sure how I could possibly articulate it. Whatever way I said it, it was going to sound bad. Very, very bad, indeed.

35

It had started off as a fun account on Instagram I had launched because I was terrified of hitting forty, to log my journey into the next phase of my life. I had a bit of money; I was married to the CEO of *Top Golfer* magazine and I didn't need to worry about working. So, I started dabbling around on Instagram. If I bought a new dress, I took a decent photo of myself in it and tagged the designer. If I ate at a fancy restaurant, I took a photo of the food and tagged the restaurant. Eventually, I got into stories and found they gained a lot of interest as well. Within three months, I had fourteen hundred followers. Within six months, I had forty thousand followers, and within a year, I had a hundred and eighty thousand followers.

Then I met Betty. It was a networking event I had been invited to through one of the sponsors who I had collaborated with. Betty made a beeline for me; said she admired my work. She had over five hundred thousand followers by that point with her menopause account. She knew a lot of people and she introduced me to all of them. By the end of that event, I had become part of a clan. We met up at weekends, went on mini breaks together, we went to all the gatherings hosted by the sponsors. And we posted it all over our grids. After another few months, I had gained another three hundred thousand followers, taking my audience to almost five hundred thousand, rivalling Betty's account. I was revelling in the glory, the freebies, the attention. The likes, the likes, the endless likes. People wanted to know things about me and even asked questions about Anabel. They wanted my style, my taste in food, my gifted holidays. Some even wanted David.

David laughed about it all to start with, but once my followers had exceeded five hundred thousand, I felt I was well on my way to a million.

'Just go easy, love,' David said one day as I raved about how successful the account had become, and I immediately brushed his comment off. At the time, I thought him ridiculous. Why would I need to go easy when this *was* easy? My life had changed radically within a year. I was forty-one, and the age I had worried about so much had come and gone and I had barely noticed I was so wrapped up in the Insta world. People gave me stuff all the time. There wasn't a day that went past when my inbox wasn't flooded with offers of this product or that product. I was flying higher than I had ever been before. I'd had jobs in the past that gave me a slight sense of satisfaction, marketing positions where I would get to sit in big meetings and have my ideas applauded by senior members of the company. But this was something else, people adored me. And I had never had that feeling before. Growing up with two parents who filled every hour of their waking day perfecting their hatred for one another meant that I was the trophy child; they lavished their attention on me. I loved it. I had never felt pure adoration like that before, the stuff you crave and live for, that sends your little developing synapses into overdrive. Of course, I had David. I knew he loved me and I him, but I craved that endless dopamine release that Instagram gave me. It was addictive, and I didn't want to give it up.

It was one of Betty's friends who started talking about the new site that had just gone up where people went to slag off minor celebs and influencers. A thread had just been uploaded about a recent ad I'd done as part of a collaboration with a new food-processor company. I had gone for the whole Nigella thing, dressed all in black and with a whole lot of cleavage, and I figured the audience would see it for what it was, a bit of tongue in cheek. To me, this forum sounded funny more than anything. I had managed to not engage myself with the trolls that came through on my Instagram comments or even into my inbox, so I knew that when I went and checked out the forum, I would be fine. I wouldn't be affected by the silliness of it all. For that was all it was.

But nothing could have prepared me for the horrific vulgarity of what I found. Betty's friend had been right. There was indeed a thread about me and the food-processor ad. But the content was a far cry from anything that had come through to my inbox before. At least with the stuff that came to me directly, I could control it. I could decide if I wanted to read it or delete it, and no one would ever need to see it again. But this was a public platform that anyone could go on at any point and write absolutely anything about me and each comment fuelled hatred in another reader.

I read the thread title:

Reprocessed sluttery

They were talking about how I was so desperate to be like Nigella the way I was dressed and the way I had tried to be seductive, but it looked *tacky* and *slutty*. Those were the words that kept cropping up regularly. And then of course, the 'Who does she think she is?' comments. Then as I scrolled more, I began to see how those were just the warm-up. Further down the page, the trolls had begun to say awful things about Anabel, about what a little slut she was going to grow up to be. She was six years old, for God's sake! I felt sick. Then they began to get derogatory and started discussing mine and David's sex life. It was appalling.

I didn't sleep that night, and then I messaged some of the girls from the Insta clan and casually asked how something like this forum was legal and surely someone needed to take it down. They all agreed it was terrible but made no suggestions of how we – as a strong collective – could make a stand. But it was their further response that really shocked me: this was part and parcel of being part of the Insta crew. You had to accept that some people enjoyed taking you to pieces, and the only way to deal with it was not to read it or get engaged with it. There was nothing else you could do.

If only I could have heeded their advice, as feeble as it was. Because I was not able to simply ignore it. I wanted to know exactly what these trolls were saying about me. So I went on the forum the next day and the following day, and everything I said and did was splattered across the forum. Each time I posted something, they came up with some snidey twist on the content of the post and began their school-girl gossip. Except it was worse than any school-girl gossip I remember. It was women going to the absolute depths of their rotten souls to dredge up all their anger and frustrations and turn that into hateful, spiteful comments about me and my family. I absolutely knew this, of course I did, but the words were so strong and so hurtful it was hard to try to look past them, to remember that they themselves were desperately unhappy. Because this was my life they were discussing, my family. Sure, it was me who had put it all out there for them to see and rip apart, and I could have stopped looking at the forum at any point, but it became an addiction. And I had to look every day. I began to neglect Anabel, because if my job as an influencer wasn't taking up enough of my time, then the amount of time I was checking the troll forum was eating into any other spare time I should have been spending with her. I became snappy and irritable. I barely made any effort for her seventh birthday party, which was unlike me, as I loved to make a fuss of her. David couldn't work out why I wouldn't just let it be. 'Ignore them,' he told me, just like everyone else. But I couldn't. It became my obsession.

Then one day, I was looking at a new thread someone had posted the day before, when it suddenly occurred to me that I needed to tell these people that they had it all wrong, that I was a good person, that I fell into the Instagram world and that I did it because I enjoyed it, and if they had been offered free products and sponsorship in return for content, they would jump at the chance. It was pure jealousy; couldn't they just see that they needed to stop the things they were saying because it was bullying? But I knew that would make me seem desperate and pathetic.

Then it came to me. I would go undercover, create myself a name on this forum and become involved in the conversations. I would then be able to convince them from the inside that they needed to look at me and my family differently.

So that was what I did. Once I was inside the forum, I felt an immense feeling of relief, but I was also nervous. I was suddenly going to be amongst these people, writing comments. It was scary, like being thrown to the lions. I began by saying hi and tried a very neutral comment.

I really liked her top on that post – I wonder where she got it from?

The torrent of abuse that came from my one comment was unbelievable. It was as though I had egged them on even more.

Total slut, if you ask me. I mean, could she be gagging for it any more?

You'd think she got enough attention from that hot husband of hers, but some people are just never satisfied. Sad.

It was probably another damn freebie. Seriously, do these people ever think about paying for anything themselves.

I tried again a few days later, adding my positive comment to their negativity to try and balance it out, but the same response came back. On my third attempt, someone piped up.

Are you working for her or something?

I panicked. I didn't know how else to get out of the situation I had put myself in. I ignored the comment, but the next time someone posted something about me, I decided I needed to even out my positivity with a few negative comments. I started out by saying a few pointless things like:

What was she thinking?
Why did she do that?

Which fuelled so much more hatred, as they all came back with their backlog of reasons as to what they thought they knew about me and my family. I began to mix it up more but found that no matter how many positive comments I wrote to their negativity, someone always shot me straight back down again.

Then one day someone picked up on my inconsistencies and said that I was me, only undercover. I panicked again. I didn't want to be found out and be exposed. They already hated me. What would they have to say if they knew it was me undercover? So I upped the negativity and before I knew it, I was joining in with their slanging matches. I can't even think about some of the things I mentioned and how many of my loved ones I talked about with such disrespect. I made crass comments about women I had recently considered friends. I talked about David in such a derogatory way, I can't even bear to think of the things I said about him. I slagged off myself to the point I didn't even know who I was any more. I drew the line at Anabel – she was still a little girl.

But somewhere, behind the scenes, someone had not given up and had managed to piece together the order of my inconsistencies with certain posts and how when that someone had tried to out me the first time, I quickly changed my tune. I had been found out. And they destroyed me. But not as much as I destroyed myself. The stuff that I had written, every word of it, was suddenly out there all over the internet, all over Instagram and even showed up on online news sites.

I was a mess. I took myself off Instagram. I rarely used the internet if I could help it, I was so fearful of coming across anything about myself. I was losing sleep. David began to spend more nights away in hotels for work, even though we were still living in London and he was a short drive away.

I retreated from Anabel and her affections. A few people came around and tried to spur me on, but mainly it was just Anabel and me spending day after day in the house. I didn't know what to do with her, I couldn't lift myself out of the black hole. Anabel came to me daily to try to coax me out of myself, but it was taking too long. Something needed to be done, something I had been considering for such a long time, and it seemed like exactly the right time for it to happen.

A few months after the troll site drama, we moved to Helesbury.

* * *

'And so here I am,' I said, feeling the energy drain out of me. Dredging up the past was exhausting.

'It's a really mad crazy story. I mean, not story. I know it's your life. *Was* your life. But you explained yourself articulately enough. I understand how these things work,' Evie said.

'So, so you don't hate me?'

'Miranda, I could never hate you.'

I sucked in a huge breath and expelled it. 'Okay. Well, now I have got that out in the open, and you understand it was a past mistake and I have grown so incredibly as a person since then, do you mind if I talk to you about something else? Something a little more delicate?'

Evie frowned. 'Okay.'

'Today at the picnic, I took Juno to the toilet with me. She finished up quickly and waited for us outside. Only, when I came out with Anabel, I saw Verity with her. Juno looked visibly distressed. Verity had her hand around Juno's arm and was trying to get her to do something, to go with her, and Juno was clearly telling her no, and Verity wasn't listening.' I waited a beat for a reaction from Evie. But nothing came. 'I confronted her and asked her what she was doing. She let go of Juno, but she was very rude to me. And that wasn't the first time she's been rude to me. She was rude when she saw me with my friend Betty, and she worked out who she was. She'd been following all that stuff on social media apparently and knew the whole story inside out.'

I waited again to see if Evie would say anything. She was now looking forward at the fireplace, only occasionally flitting her eyes to me. She remained silent.

'And,' I added, trying for a third time to make the words sink in. 'That was not the first time I saw Verity and Juno together, with Juno looking and sounding uncomfortable.' I was getting nothing back from Evie, but I continued. 'At my barbeque, she said something to Juno out in the hallway, and Juno again sounded distressed, and when I looked into the hallway, Verity was walking away, and Juno was just standing there looking... I don't know... unhappy.'

The silence in the room was palpable.

'And, she told Juno off for running around at the barbeque,' I contin-ued. 'Which was weird, don't you think?' I knew I sounded desperate now. I waited several seconds and finally Evie spoke.

'I don't know what you want me to say, Miranda.'

That was one of my pet hates, as if my whole being there was just to get some sort of reaction from her. I wanted her to know because Juno was her daughter, and I felt her safety was being jeopardised by Verity.

'I don't *want* you to say anything, but surely you must have something to say on the matter, on any of the matters?'

Evie seemed to think for a moment.

'Okay, Miranda, I can see how this may all seem to you. You haven't really quite taken to Verity—'

'Has anyone?' I snorted.

'I admit, yes, she is a different sort of character. But the whole Juno thing... Juno is a complicated girl. She hasn't always had it easy, and I don't want to go into it, but sometimes, she is prone to overreacting. Being a bit whingy even.'

'But, Evie, Verity had her hand on Juno's arm and Juno was asking her to stop!'

Evie screwed her face up. 'She was probably acting up. And Verity is the sort of person who felt it appropriate to say or do something. She wasn't hitting her or dragging her. You said she had her hand on her arm.'

I cleared my throat. 'Yes.'

'On or around? Because before you said around her arm.'

I looked at Evie, stunned. Was she trying to protect Verity's actions? I thought back to the toilet incident and tried to remember if Verity's hand was on or around Juno's arm. Was she pulling her, or guiding her? Suddenly, it all seemed a little fuzzy. I didn't know what to say. Had I imagined it all? Was my mind constructing Verity as a bad character because of the way I felt about her moving in on Evie? I knew I hadn't imagined the venom in her voice when she spoke to me outside my car and outside the village hall.

'Verity is a complex character, I'll give you that,' Evie continued. 'She also likes to keep herself to herself. So maybe she became a little offended when she found out about the whole Instagram past thing and that she thought it inappropriate that Juno should be featured on your, whatever you call it—'

'Grid,' I said.

'Right. Grid.'

I shook my head. 'Can I ask, Evie, what is it about Verity that draws you two together? I know you are allowed more than one friend, but you have been – from my perspective – spending a considerable amount of time with her over me since she moved here.'

'I like to spend time with lots of people, Miranda. I think you may have just interpreted it that way.' Evie sounded exhausted, as though this conversation was now draining the life out of her.

I shook my head. 'I don't... I don't know.' Again, she had bamboozled me. Had I misinterpreted it?

'But you were with her that day when you went to see Frank?' I pushed on.

Evie shifted in her seat. 'Did I say that?'

'You said in your text to me "On *our* way back". I wondered who you were referring to, as I presumed you went alone. To see Frank.'

'I did,' she said firmly. 'I spend all my time with Juno. I must have put "our" by mistake. I am so used to it always being the two of us.'

'Oh,' I said. That did make sense. I had no proof that Evie had been with Verity that day. But I did have proof of one thing. That there was no Frank Pollard staying at the John Radcliffe Hospital. But I was reluctant to say it because it was clear from every one of my statements that Evie had batted away that she thought I was imagining the whole thing. But she did say the John Radcliffe Hospital and I did check. But to tell her would make me seem quite needy, creepy even. But I had nothing left.

'You said Frank was staying at the John Radcliffe. But I called and checked and there was no Frank Pollard there.'

Evie let out a loud sigh this time. 'Jesus, Miranda. Are you stalking me now?'

Panic rose in my chest. This was the last thing I had intended or expected. I was not one of those mad, needy women. I just wanted Evie to understand how all this was making me feel.

'I was never a stalker, Evie! I thought because you said "our" in your text, I presumed you had chosen to take Verity with you to support you that day. So, I don't know why, but yes, I checked.' I felt the heat rising through my chest into my face.

'If I remember, it was you who asked me was he staying at the John

Radcliffe,' Evie snapped back. 'And I had just had a shock that day and I wasn't thinking straight, so I must have just said yes. He was actually at the Nuffield. It's private. I had forgotten. It was a long day, with the drive and the shock.'

'Okay.' A wave of guilt rushed over me like a tsunami. 'I'm sorry, Evie, I really am. I just—'

'I think, Miranda, you need to take a step back,' Evie said firmly.

I sat up straight as though she had struck me.

'You obviously have some sort of bee in your bonnet about Verity,' she continued, 'which I think stems from your trauma over the Instagram thing, which wasn't that long ago, and I would imagine that level of exposure would affect anyone's well-being, and I think Verity has triggered something in you. Whatever it is, I don't want or need my family's lives under a microscope and for you to be constantly watching and analysing our every move.'

'It's not that. I'm not doing that to you. It's Verity, she has been rude to me and—'

'Just stop, Miranda. Please!' Evie bellowed. 'You don't know what you're talking about.' She dropped her voice to a whisper, knowing any shouting would wake Juno, and turned away from me as her voice broke on the last word.

I took a deep breath and sat back and waited. Too shocked to say anything, too scared that these might be our final words to one another.

'Just go and chill out and enjoy your life in the countryside. That was what you came here to do, wasn't it? Not get caught up in worrying about what everyone else is up to.' Evie spoke more reservedly.

I looked down into my lap. I had a sudden urge to wretch as my throat tightened and my mouth became watery. 'Okay, you're right. I'm sorry,' I said hurriedly. I needed to fix the situation, there and then. I didn't want to lose Evie. I *couldn't* lose Evie. But she spoke first.

'It's fine, Miranda. I just... I just think we shouldn't see as much of one another for a while. I haven't seen or heard from you for a week, and actually, I was fine with it.'

I felt the panic rising in me. 'Our kids, the girls, they love spending time with each other. We can't drag them into this, it's not fair.'

'They can still see one another at school, and if they want to have play dates, they can. I wouldn't deny the girls their time.'

I screwed my face in frustration. I felt like a helpless child. 'You make it sound like you're breaking up with me.' I almost laughed the words, but the anxiety was rising high in my chest. I couldn't control what was happening here. I didn't want to hear the words, but still they came at me.

'I just, I don't know what it is. Just please, Miranda, would you mind if you left me alone? I've had a really long, tiring day. I need to go to bed.'

She wanted me to go? Evie had never asked me to go in the whole time I had known her. Usually, we would be chatting long into the night and forget what the time was, the next day laughing about how tired or hungover we were. Was this it? Was I losing her for good? I was a complete failure. I couldn't hang on to one decent friendship.

I sat still for a moment, then when Evie didn't say anything else, I stood up and walked to the door and opened it. She stayed in her seat, looking straight ahead into the empty fireplace.

'Okay, well, goodnight then. I'll see you around.' I felt my insides go weak, as though I needed to sit down again, but I wanted to leave with some dignity.

I saw Evie nod, but she said nothing else. I closed the lounge door behind me and went through the hallway towards the front door. As I did, I heard a sound. I turned and saw a flash of white nightgown on the stairs. Juno. Had she been listening?

I let myself out of the front door and closed it quietly behind me. I stood on the other side of the door, oblivious to anyone or anything, and let out a loud sob.

36

10 MAY 2019 – 4.13 P.M. – GLOUCESTER POLICE STATION

Interview with Hatty Whilloby (continued)

Miranda and I had many conversations prior to that night at the pub. We talked a bit about Verity, and we both came to the conclusion that she was quite lost and that maybe there was some trauma there. But we couldn't fathom why she would come to a village like Helesbury and want to keep herself to herself. But then I don't know any other writers – if that's how they all act, I'm not sure I want to know any more.

A lot of people don't notice things about other people – too into their own worlds, you see. But I do. But I didn't ever mention to Miranda that I knew how frustrated she had become since Verity arrived in the village. I didn't want to rile her up. There was a rumour that she had been involved in some sort of social media scandal. Poor thing. No wonder she became so affected by what was going on around her. She had no control over any of it. I didn't know in the beginning why Evie and Verity became so close so quickly. Of course, I understand now. But the attention that Evie gave Verity really took its toll on Miranda. And to be honest, it wasn't really a lot of attention. From what I saw in the beginning, it was their single status that drew them together. I could tell that Miranda was slowly starting to go mad with it. I could see the way she looked at Verity and Evie – she was always checking them out. Especially at the picnic in the park. I think that was when she really seemed to get affected. She was so distant all day. I guessed there was some sort of rift between her and Evie that day, because those two had been joined at the hip, but at the picnic they didn't go anywhere near each other. I have a sort of sixth sense for this sort of thing. Miranda always struck me as the sort of person to not take things lying down. And well, she didn't, did she? Not in the end.

37

I woke the next morning feeling as though my heart had been ripped out of my chest. Losing a real friend hurt so much that I realised that any of the friendships that came before were worth nothing. What I had with Evie was the real thing. The pain was just as intense as from any first-love break-up. Luckily, it was a Sunday, and so I didn't have to be anywhere or organise anything. Except I remembered with sudden panic that David was going to play golf today, which meant I would be on my own with Anabel and she would want to be entertained. How could I entertain an eight-year-old girl when my heart was shattered into tiny pieces? I could barely lift my head off the pillow, let alone bring a smile to my lips or make the day fun for her. I remembered how hard it was when everything kicked off on the troll site and I was exposed for the liar I had been. I had neglected Anabel back then, too. I couldn't do that to her again. I had to find a way to pause the pain during the day. I could let it smother me in the evening when she couldn't witness it, but when she was awake, I needed to be there for her.

I decided there was only one thing for it. I would take her into town, take her to Claire's Accessories for some new hair stuff, stop at Pizza Express for lunch and then head to the cinema. That way, I wouldn't need to put on a fake smile – retail therapy and a funny film would do the job for me.

David was already up and getting himself ready for the day, so I got up and showered and slowly dressed so that I would look half-decent and not like someone who was crumbling away on the inside. I had managed to bypass David last night, as he had fallen asleep on the sofa when I got home, and went straight up to bed. He didn't come up until about three in the morning, and I hadn't really slept a wink.

I arrived downstairs in tight white jeans and a pink T-shirt. David was packing the car with his clubs. The kitchen reeked of bacon, and I thought I might puke.

'Where's Anabel?' I asked as he came back into the house to collect his phone and the rest of his sandwich.

'Oh, morning, love. She's in the garden. It's such a beautiful day, she wanted to have her breakfast with nature.' David smiled. I felt my cold, broken heart warm a little at the thought of Anabel sat outside, eating her breakfast, and so I said goodbye to David – making sure I plastered on my best smile, assuring him all was well and I was only a little tired this morning – made myself a cup of tea and went outside and joined her. I found her at the bottom of the garden where we had put a small table and a couple of chairs there, mainly for Anabel and her friends. It was surrounded by low-hanging trees and the birds were singing such a loud sweet song that the sight of Anabel in her dressing gown with her bowl of Cheerios was quite enough to make me feel a little more whole again. After all, she and David were my world. Friends made everything rosier, but I had my daughter and my husband, and I needed to be thankful for that.

Anabel looked up and grinned when she saw me. 'Hello, Mummy. Have you come to join me?'

'I have,' I said. I listened to the birds. I knew I should be feeling incredibly lucky to be sitting here right now, after the drama of my life a year ago. David could have been one of those husbands who didn't understand, but he had dealt with it with real dignity. And he had listened to my needs. He saw through my colossal blunder; he knew I was trying to protect my family, and so he did the same by taking us out of that situation and bringing us here. And so I had to do what was best for him and Anabel. I had to take control. I had to put on a brave face. Evie agreed we didn't need to let the girls know there was anything wrong and they could continue to have their relationship. I just needed some time to myself to get my head around everything Evie had said last night. I needed a few hours alone so I could dissect her every word and then put them back together, wondering what I could have done differently. Then I would feel a bit better. But I wasn't going to get that today, today I had to be strong.

* * *

As it turned out, the film Anabel wanted to see was only showing at eleven, so she dressed quickly and we shot into town, where I sat through a sickly American comedy about a family going on a road trip. And there was a love interest, which made Anabel squirm in her seat and hide behind her popcorn. It was quite sweet, really.

By one o'clock, we were hungry, and I needed to eat as I had skipped breakfast. We settled ourselves into a booth at Pizza Express and I listened to Anabel talk about everything and nothing. It was amazing how an eight-year-old kid had so much to say, and she never seemed to be short on topics. I sat and listened, but my mind would occasionally wander away from her monologuing and I would try to look at my phone without her noticing. Perhaps I had missed a text message from Evie. There was quite a lot of clattering from the kitchen and my phone volume was turned down low. But there was nothing. And the disappointment burnt.

Anabel asked if she could go to the toilet, and as it was just next to where we were sitting, I let her go alone.

I took the moment to bash out a text message to Evie.

I'm so sorry again about all the upset between us. I hope we can move on from this. I miss you x

I hit send before I could change my mind. Then instantly regretted the 'I miss you' part. She might read that as emotional blackmail. Damn it, why did I have to be so rash? It would sound so needy, but I wanted Evie to feel she could rely on me to be there for her.

Anabel came back to the table.

'You okay, darling?'

'Yes,' she said and picked at her pizza crusts.

'Dessert?' I asked her.

She grinned and nodded, and I caught the eye of our waitress, who minutes later brought over a bowl of ice cream with sauces. I watched as Anabel devoured the whole bowl, and I waited in anticipation for my phone to ping a message. I had purposely sent it on WhatsApp so I could check that Evie had read it.

What had that whole conversation been about last night, anyway? I had wracked my brains all night trying to think how Evie had ended up asking me to leave and saying that we should not see each other any more. I was so confused. I was sure I had sussed Verity out and that I was simply passing on important information to Evie about her daughter's welfare. I had been sure that once I told Evie how I had seen Verity act towards Juno, she would thank me for noticing and being there for her and Juno. I did not expect the opposite to happen.

I thought I was the sort of person who was well in tune with what was going on around me. That was why I was enticed to go onto the troll site in the first place – I wanted to protect my family. I look back now and realise there was no way I could have changed the opinion of those kinds of people. I wish I had stayed well away. Had that one unfortunate incident in my life been the reason my relationship was now marred with Evie?

Anabel had finished her dessert, so I took us to the till, paid the bill and we left. I had my head in the zone of getting home when Anabel asked about Claire's Accessories. And I thought I had managed to bypass that. It was all so bright and the shops were always so small. But I put myself through it for my daughter – this was her day after all. My stress was still on hold, but I could feel it building, like a balloon tightening. I didn't want it to pop.

We left Claire's with a bag of hair accessories, three lip balms and some studded earrings, and I was finally able to go home and feel like crap without offending anyone. I was just getting into the car when my phoned pinged. My heart leapt! It would be Evie – she was sorry for what she had said and was going to suggest a coffee for old times. But of course it wasn't from Evie. When I looked at my phone, it was a message from David, asking if we were having a roast for dinner. My heart sank. That was his way of suggesting I pick up a leg of lamb from the farm shop on the way back into the village. Had he not had enough bacon bloody sandwiches today? That was all they ate on these golfing days.

I text back to say I would do a roast, even though I didn't have much appetite. Then I drove us home, stopping at the farm store on the way.

* * *

An hour after arriving home, I had everything prepped, and the lamb was about to go in for a slow roast. I took a photo of the roast all prepped on the kitchen side and posted it on the account. My heart wasn't really in it, but it felt as though it might bring me some joy when I received a few likes. I sat down at the table and waited for David to come home. I lay my head in my arms on the table and all of the thoughts of Evie were running through my head. Why would she just push me away like that? Then I remembered standing outside Anabel's bedroom door and overhearing the conversation between her and Juno. Of course, that was it. Juno had just told Anabel something and had asked her not to say anything to me. The girls were at that age where their lives began to have a little more meaning to them; they were that much more aware of themselves and the world around them. It wasn't just dollies and fairies any more, although Anabel was still a big fan of both. Whatever Anabel had been told it could have some significance to Evie's behaviour. I needed Anabel to tell me what it was. Maybe, just maybe, it would be the answer I was looking for.

I sought her out in her bedroom, sat on her bed, where she was trying on all the different hairbands she had bought.

'Anabel, can I have a moment?' I asked, then I realised how formal I sounded. 'I just need a quick word,' I added.

Anabel stopped doing her hair and looked at me.

'Do you remember when Juno came here that day and we went to the farm and she fell in the cowpat?'

Anabel smirked and sniggered. 'Yes, I will remember it forever.'

'Oh good. Well, the thing is, when you two were in the bathroom together, I happened to be walking past and I overheard Juno say that she had told you something and that you weren't to tell anyone.'

Anabel looked sheepish and looked down. 'Are you going to make me tell? Because she said I would tell you and I promised her I wouldn't and if I tell you that makes me a terrible friend.'

I cleared my throat and perched myself on the edge of the bed.

'Sweetie. I appreciate that you are a big now, I really do, and I know you and Juno and any of your other friends will have secrets and there will be things that you won't want to tell me. But sometimes and only sometimes, I might need to ask you to tell me something, but not because I want to pry and want to know all your secrets, but because I am worried about something. Or someone in this case.'

'Are you worried about Juno?' Anabel asked.

'Yes, sweetie, yes, I am. But I don't want you to worry. Because if you tell me what it was that Juno told you, I promise it will be just as if you didn't tell me – if it is just a small thing. If I think it is something that means she might need help, then it will be a big thing, and then you would have done the right thing by telling me. I won't tell anyone that you told me. You are allowed to break the secret code when it's your mum asking you to.'

'In case it's important?'

'Yes, sweetie, in case it's important.'

'*Hello!*' came David's voice from downstairs. Anabel's face lit up.

'Daddy!' she said excitedly.

'Down in a minute!' I shouted to the open door. I waited a beat to see if David would come upstairs, but he didn't. I turned back to Anabel. 'So, do we have a deal?'

Anabel looked at the collection of hair things scattered around her.

'I want to show Daddy my new hairbands,' she said forlornly.

'And you will. I just need to know this little thing first, and then you can go off and show Daddy, okay?'

Anabel looked down at her hands and began squeezing them. I felt sorry for her, I really did. She wanted to be a good friend to Juno in the same way I wanted to be to Evie. But I had failed Evie. Or so it seemed to her. Now I was trying to get Anabel to do the same. I felt like the worst mother today.

'Okay,' Anabel said and looked at me. 'I will tell you.' I felt relief flood through me, but then I braced myself for whatever it was Anabel was about to say.

38

BEFORE

The girl wanted to shout at the men, to tell them to stop. Why wasn't her mother telling them to stop?

She was just sitting there on the sofa, letting them take everything and put it in the back of a car. The girl didn't want to leave. Not this time. She wouldn't have minded this time last week, but something had changed. The girl had made a friend. She was a funny friend too. The girl's mother had warned her that making friends wasn't supposed to happen for this very reason. They never knew when they might be leaving again.

'Why, Mama, why?' The girl knelt down in front of her mother as she sat looking out of the window.

'Please, stop mithering,' her mother said to her. She didn't know what that word meant. She had never heard her mother use it before. Her mother had become less and less fun over the last few weeks. She had been spending all her time looking at her phone, looking at photos of people that the girl didn't know. When she asked her mother who they were, the mother said it was called social media, and it was a good distraction. That was why the girl had found the friend. Her mother had taken to staring at her phone most of the day, so the girl had decided to explore outside on a few occasions. Her mother had told her not to – she had said she should stay indoors and play with the sewing that she been given by B and H – but it was boring doing it on her own. Her mother had done some with her initially, and then she stopped and picked up her phone again. She didn't want to do sewing alone. So she had gone for a walk along the street. Not far, she wasn't silly – she knew that it was wrong to walk along streets by herself at her age. But the boredom was killing her. Plus, she had heard the sound of children playing in the street below her window.

She found a group of them a few yards along the road. They were playing with a ball. The road was quiet and the aim of the game was to hit the kerb and have it bounce back to you. The girl got really good at it and wanted to play more. The children said she could come back tomorrow, and so she did. She started talking more and more to a girl who was about her age called Nora. Nora asked the girl if she liked living here, and the girl said yes, she did. She hadn't up until a day ago, and then she had met Nora and everything changed. She thought what it would be like to stay here and have a friend like Nora to play with every day, and then she started to feel better. She began to realise the importance of having one solid friend in your life. Everyone should have a friend. That was something she just knew. She didn't need to learn it or be told it; it was something she felt inside her.

She spoke to her mother the next day and said that she was happy here and she thought her mother could be too. Maybe if she got a friend, then she might feel a bit better about living here, and the smell that came from the sink every time she put the washing on wouldn't seem so bad, or the loud cranking sound that came from the pipes when air got caught in there and they had to race to the tap to turn it on to release it wouldn't seem like it was the worst thing in the world – even when it did it in the middle of the night and woke them both up.

But obviously her mother hadn't listened to her, otherwise she wouldn't be watching these men coming and taking their stuff and putting it into a car. A car, that was all it took to pack their stuff. They were travelling light and had been for some time now. The girl wondered if they would ever be able to have a sofa of their own, or a lampshade that was theirs. But she needed to stop thinking and hoping about things like that, because none of it mattered. Her mother was getting worse. With every move, another little piece of the light seemed to disappear from her eyes. Maybe, the girl thought, that was why her mother wanted to keep them closed so much during the day.

The girl watched the men take the last box and the last suitcase, and then they stood in the doorway and gestured to the girl to get into the car. She looked at her mother, who stirred from the sofa, and then stood and took her hand. Together, they walked out of the house for the last time, closing the door behind them. The girl didn't know how you were supposed to tell someone that you were leaving. She wasn't sure what she would say either, as she didn't know where she was going. But she wished more than anything that she would be able to see Nora again. As the car drove them away down the street, the girl looked out of her window as they passed the group of children playing. The girl lifted her hand and gave a small wave, and as she did, Nora lifted hers too. The girl wasn't sure she liked moving house any more. She knew the next time she moved, she wanted to stay for a very long time, find the perfect friend and never, ever move again.

39

'Okay, sweetie, in your own time. Tell me what it was that Juno told you in the bathroom that day.'

'Well, it is quite weird, and I feel a teeny bit weird speaking about it, but the thing is, Mummy, Juno is not like me. She is different. She's become a woman. Juno gets her monthlies.' The words tumbled out of Anabel's mouth.

'What!' I said, astounded. 'Juno? How...' I stopped myself from saying any more. This was what Juno had told Anabel and asked her not to relay to me? I could understand why, because the girls had reached an age where they wanted privacy. But still, eight years old? That was seriously young. Poor Juno. I couldn't imagine Anabel having to deal with periods every month. Only a slight feeling of doubt washed over me. Could Juno have made it up, to get attention, to make Anabel feel jealous? Without a dad on the scene, it was only Evie and Juno – maybe there were some attention issues at play. How could an eight-year-old have her period? I mean, I had heard of children even younger, but still, it felt so wrong. And why hadn't Evie told me, for goodness' sake? Especially when Juno was staying over at my house?

'Okay, Anabel, thank you for telling me this information. I will keep your secret. You have nothing to worry about. At least now I know and I can be a bit more understanding when Juno is here. I will leave some ladies' things in the bottom drawer in the bathroom and you can show her where they are, okay?'

'Okay,' Anabel said, not sounding in the least bit interested. 'Can I go and show Daddy what I bought from Claire's now?'

I sighed. 'Yes... Off you go.' She stuffed all the accessories back into the bag, hopped off the bed and trotted downstairs. I heard the sound of David's voice lift up as he greeted Anabel and then the sound of Anabel getting more and more animated as she told her dad about her day.

I had to admit, I was in shock, that little – well, not so little Juno – was on her way to becoming a woman. It was the sort of thing that I had expected Evie to want to share with me. I wondered if Verity knew; if it was the sort of thing she would have shared with her.

I straightened up Anabel's room and went downstairs. I greeted David with a kiss on his cheek, which smelt of a day spent outdoors, before I began putting the vegetables and meat into the different parts of the oven on different temperatures and told David it would be about an hour and a half.

Finally, I would have some time to myself to wallow in my own self-pity. I told David and Anabel I had a bit of headache and was going to lie down upstairs. Then I opened the door to my bedroom and sank into the duvet.

* * *

I woke to David standing over me. He must have shaken me gently, as I could still feel the vibration of where his hand had just been.

'Love, time to wake up. The roast is ready.'

I sat up and rubbed my head. 'Shit. The lamb.' I looked at my phone, I'd been asleep for almost two hours. 'It'll be ruined.'

'I think I saved it. I pulled it out about half an hour ago.'

'Oh.' I groaned. 'You lifesaver.'

'I'll go and set the table.' David touched my leg and left the room. Shit. I hadn't felt this stressed about a friendship since the whole Instagram thing. I had been adamant that I wouldn't let it get to me. But what could I do? Evie had clearly made her mind up. She didn't want me around her. I looked at my phone just in case she had replied to my message. I saw she had read it and the last time she had looked at her WhatsApp was hours ago. But she hadn't replied. I felt my stomach tighten. I had to respect her wishes. I just had to accept that our friendship was over.

* * *

The lamb was perfectly done – David had rescued it in good time. Anabel was excused from the table having not eaten very much at all, but I knew she would be full after all the dough balls, pizza and ice cream. I shoved the food around my plate and eventually David asked, 'Are you going to tell me what's wrong?'

I looked up at him and our eyes met. I didn't have the words. I knew I would disappoint him. Why couldn't my friendships be easy, like his were? Go and play some golf with a few chums, come home and carry on with my life. I felt as though women were so much more complex, we needed to feel one another. We couldn't just come home and switch off from the friendship. It became part of us.

'It's nothing, really,' I lied.

'Okay.' His tone said he didn't believe me.

'I don't want to bog you down. It's something and nothing, and it will soon blow over.'

'Okay,' he said again, clearly not satisfied with that. 'Is this to do with social media?'

'No, God no.' I looked straight at him. 'No, absolutely not.' I assured him. But I knew that if Evie hadn't found out from Verity about my past, then we would still be tight. My past had followed me here. I was never going to be free from those mistakes. 'I'm just a bit tired, to be honest. I think I'm letting everything get on top of me. I just need a few early nights. A nice bath tonight will sort me out.'

'Okay,' he said for the third time.

'In fact, I'll go and have that bath now. Are you okay with clearing this up?'

'I think I can handle it.' He pushed his plate away and picked up the Sunday supplement and began flicking through it. I went upstairs and began running the bath. The water ran heavy and loud, and so I allowed a few tears to fall and a few minor sobs to escape my mouth. I was safe in our en suite bathroom – no one could hear me over the running water. But then the sobs began heavier and louder and before long I was on my knees, my hands clutching the side of the bath, my stomach muscles clenching as I heaved out the sorrow and frustration.

40

10 MAY 2019 – 5.55 P.M. – GLOUCESTER POLICE STATION

Interview with Jerry Styles, manager of The Old Goat, Helesbury.

It had been really busy that night, to be fair. Thursdays are one of our busiest nights of the week. It was a warm evening and I had a band on. There were people spilling outside. There was a really good atmosphere. I was feeling good, cos, you know, I made it happen. I like to see a happy punter, and a hundred happy punters, well, that's not just money in my pocket, but it makes for a happier community, doesn't it? I pay quite a bit of attention to the comings and goings of the pub. I keep my eye on who's had too much to drink, as well as any newbies. This pub does attract a lot of out-of-towners, but I usually know who's who, where they've come from.

I knew Miranda, because, well, who doesn't know Miranda? Since she came to the village, let's just say, she brightened up my world. I know she's married, and very happily from what I can gather, but a man can look, can't he? She has that certain way about her. I can't describe it, but she brings a certain quality to the village. She's a special kind of sort. So the thing is, what I'm trying to say to you is that when Miranda comes into the pub, which isn't as often as I would like, I tend to notice. But I respect her husband too – he's a decent, hard-working fellow.

So there was Miranda that night, looking – can I say, pretty hot? Well, she was, so there we go. I said it, so bloody sue me. I had seen her in there on the few occasions she had frequented with Evie. I knew those two were friends, but I had also seen her in with Hatty. I know Hatty really well, she's a good lass. So it was a bit strange I suppose that both Evie and Miranda were in the pub that night, but they weren't together. In fact, they seemed to stay as far apart from one another as they could. Like I say, I notice these things. It wasn't because I was gawping at Miranda all night, as I said it was pretty busy. I had plenty of help, so I was able to go out onto the floor, which is what I like to do, so I chat to the punters, you know. And yes, I did get chatting to Miranda that night. I just happened to walk past her and noticed she was on her own, and that she seemed a bit, how can I say, on edge? I had seen her chatting with someone beforehand though, a woman. Very garish-looking, stood out like a sore thumb. Not the sort of woman you saw around these parts. I wondered why she wasn't with her husband. Cos if she were my wife, I would want to be out with her in the pub.

Anyway, when I stopped to chat to her, I noticed two things about her. One, she was drunk – she slurred her words a lot, and so she didn't have much to say to me. Which was a shame, cos I did like to chat with Miranda. I gave up after a few minutes and left her to it, but I kept my eye on her, cos that's my job. Then she just put her drink down, turned and practically ran out of the pub. I presumed she was going to be sick or something, so I ran outside to check on her. But she was walking very fast – albeit a little unsteadily – in the direction of Evie's house. Which I thought was strange as Evie was in the pub. If I had known what she was going to do, I would have stopped her, then I would have intercepted what came next. I would have been there for the whole thing. I could have helped. Done something, I suppose. But I had a pub to run – a busy, full pub. I wasn't to know. I was just doing my job. I wasn't to know!

41

I turned the corner, and she was there. I wanted to get into the village shop, but it was almost as if she was purposely blocking my way. I edged to the right, and so did Verity. I edged to the left, and she followed, as though she were my mirror image.

'Excuse me,' I said in a tense whisper.

'I noticed your Instagram account is flourishing,' she said, deadpan. I looked into her stony eyes, the ones she seemed to only reserve for me. 'I do like the funky new brand name, Cushy. Very on trend. I presume you'll just be using it for marketing your candle business from now on, and not putting up images of everyone else's children?'

I felt my blood begin to boil.

'It was one person's child. Evie's. She is the only person I am close to in this village. I apologised to her and the photo has gone.'

'Good, I'm glad to hear it.' Verity looked away along the street.

'You know, if I'm keeping you from something...?' I said, and Verity looked at me again and then stepped to the side.

'Right, yes,' she said, and I barged forward, my arm brushing hers as I stepped into the shop. I turned just as I was across the threshold and watched Verity walking away, her hands stuffed into her coat pocket, her shoulders hunched over.

Thoughts of Evie raced through my mind as I perused the shelves, no longer sure what it was I was there for. As usual I felt shaken by another prickly conversation with Verity and it only reminded me just how far Evie and I had slipped away from one another.

There were good days and there were bad days. On the good days, I would look across the playground at Evie and try to smile, but it would feel fake and forced. She would acknowledge me, for the sake of the playground politics, but, of course, people knew. How could they not? This was a small village – standing in the school playground, someone may as well have put a microscope over us and said, 'Hey, look at these two – they used to be joined at the hip, now they don't go anywhere near one another.'

It was painful to see Evie on the other side of the playground with the other mums who, even though they were desperately trying not to, would glance over in my direction and shift uncomfortably, maybe whisper something to the woman they were standing next to and then my whole world would shrink further and I'd long for a giant hand to scoop me up and take me away. Instead, I would say goodbye to Anabel – who skipped over to Juno without any care – then I would walk solemnly back out of the gate and go home.

On the bad days I would crave that easy friendship we had struck up so quickly, as though it were a drug I was being denied. I would type out message after message on my phone and then delete them. I would take a piece of paper and pen and write out a long letter, then screw it up and throw it in the bin. I would then look back over our previous text messages to try to see if there were any signs I had missed, then maybe I could understand why such a simple act as me trying to warn her away from someone I saw as a threat would cause her to recoil and put up all her defence mechanisms. But I just drove myself mad trying to read between the lines and analysing every bit of text. I hid my feelings from David as much as I could, but by now, of course, he knew that Evie and I were no longer as close as we once were. He didn't really try to dig too deep into it, and I was thankful for it. Besides, I knew he would try to understand, and he would agree with me that I had done the right thing, but that would be as far as it went. What I needed was empathy, someone who would really understand.

A woman.

A woman like Evie.

* * *

'I'm worried about book club next week,' I said to Hatty over a cup of English breakfast at hers after the school run one morning.

'It's at Olivia's, isn't it?' Hatty slurped her tea and pushed the plate of home-made oat biscuits towards me. I was tempted; they smelt delicious.

'Yes. But will Evie come, and if she does, will she ignore me?'

'Oh, I don't think she will ignore you – she really isn't that way at all,' Hatty said, topping up my teacup instead as the biscuits sat neglected. I felt a wave of annoyance at her comment. Why did people have to say things like, 'Oh she's not like that', when she clearly was; to me, at least. I was sure that on a day-to-day basis Evie was being pleasant enough to everyone else. But it had been two weeks of a barely-there smile whenever we were in the playground. I had planned trips out in the village to the shop and the post office based on what I could remember about her schedule so I wouldn't bump into her, and even then I would hover around outside the shop first, making sure she wasn't arriving at the same time, and I would be hyper alert the whole time I was browsing.

'Well, maybe she won't come then. Because it's not as if she can avoid talking to me at book club, can she? And if she has made her decision that she really doesn't want to be around me, why would she go out of her way to come?'

Hatty shook her head. 'I just don't know. In all my years living here, I have never known anyone to fall out like this. Sure, people have their disagreements, but this, this feels so... personal.'

I looked at Hatty. What did she mean? What was she trying to say? My back prickled and my palms went damp, so I surreptitiously wiped them on my jeans.

'Personal?' I eventually said, questioningly.

'Yes, like some sort of vendetta,' Hatty said, absently looking away into the distance.

Another shiver ran down my spine.

'Hatty, what are you saying?' I said, trying to keep the panic from my voice and almost laughing.

Hatty looked at me. 'Oh, sorry, my love.' She laughed. 'I didn't mean anything.' She grabbed my hand across the table. 'I was just being silly, got a bit carried away. It's all those Swedish thrillers I've been watching on the telly.'

I took a deep breath and let it out slowly out. It didn't help. Hatty's words were stuck in my mind. A vendetta? For goodness' sake, I know I had done a few people wrong in the past, but the idea that my past was somehow linked to this situation with Verity and Evie was ludicrous. I immediately sought to remove the idea from my mind and went about the rest of my day trying not to think about it. But every now and then, Hatty's words would creep back into my mind and I would find myself reliving my own past, to see if it had somehow impacted my life now.

* * *

'Can Juno come for tea?' Anabel asked with her pleading eyes. I had found myself trying to avoid eye contact with Evie on the school run again later that day. Anabel had come running out to greet me. I was ready to grab her and run the way I had been doing for weeks now. I'd known this day would come soon enough. I couldn't keep fobbing Anabel off.

'Pleeeease, Mummy.' Anabel even put her hands in prayer fashion.

'Anabel, please don't be so dramatic.' I pushed her clasped hands down. I didn't need any more attention on myself.

'I haven't had a play date with her for ages. Pleeeease, Mummy.'

'All right, Anabel, all right,' I said, to keep her quiet. 'I just have to...' I looked over at Evie. She was standing with one other mum in the corner of the playground. I felt my stomach tighten. Did I really have to do this? 'Okay, come with me then,' I said to Anabel; I would use her as moral support.

Evie was chatting away to the other mum quite animatedly as I approached, so I cleared my throat loudly. The mum stopped laughing hysterically, looked at me, then said goodbye to Evie and walked away with her son in tow.

'Hi,' I said, instantly looking down at Anabel. Anywhere that wasn't Evie's face.

'Hi,' she said.

'Anabel was wondering if Juno would like to come to our house for a play date? I can make them some tea. Probably pesto pasta,' I said quite specifically and removing as much emotion and feeling from my voice as possible.

'Yes, I'm sure she would love that,' Evie said, stroking Juno's head.

'Oh.' I looked up at Evie. Somehow I had envisioned her saying no, because even though she had said our break-up wouldn't affect the girls, I somehow imagined it would. 'Right, well, we'll... What time would you like to pick her up, or I can walk her—'

'I can collect her just after six, if that's okay?'

'Perfect,' I said, and I was surprised to see that Evie was smiling. Not just because the girls were there, but because it seemed she wanted to. It seemed natural. I smiled back and in that moment I wanted to pull her into me and tell her I was sorry again and for everything to go back to normal.

'Okay then,' I said, not knowing what else to say, but not wanting the moment to end. Then a loud trill echoed around us. Evie looked down at her phone, which was in her hand. It was impossible not to see it was Verity's name on the screen, even though I was reading it upside down. I felt my heart sink at the same time as Evie's face morphed into a perturbed expression.

'Right, sweetie, be good.' Evie patted Juno's head and without looking at me again, she turned her back on us and answered her phone. 'Hi,' she said, and I was sure I hadn't imagined the agitation, the tension that caught in her throat. I stood there watching her walk away, noticing how her shoulders hunched down as she did, exactly how I had seen Verity's shrink down as she walked away from me outside the shop earlier. They both seemed to be carrying a heavy weight.

The girls were already wandering towards the gates. I followed them, my mind awash with thoughts. Perhaps it wasn't Evie who was calling the shots, but Verity. Verity must have some sort of control over Evie. Perhaps whatever weight Verity was carrying, she was placing some of that strain on

Evie. I watched Evie wander out of the school gates. *What is it, Evie? I thought to myself. What is it you cannot tell me?*

* * *

I opened the door to Evie at ten past six. I had been hovering in the hallway waiting for her. The girls were in the garden.

'Hi.'

'Hi,' she said quickly. 'Is Juno there? I won't come in.' Her demeanour had changed since I had spoken with her in the playground. Since she had taken that call from Verity.

I stepped out into the driveway and pulled the door to behind me.

'Evie,' I began. I saw the look of horror etch itself across her face. She did not want to hear it. 'If there is something you need to talk about, that you want to say, please, please, Evie, for the love of God, talk to me. I am here. I am your friend. You can't just push me away. Please, talk to me!' I spoke urgently but quietly.

'Miranda, I just came here to get Juno,' Evie said flatly, trying to stare past me.

'I know, and I will call her in a moment. I just want to know if there is something you feel you need to say, but maybe you can't, I am here to help. I can help you.'

Evie let out a soft snort. Then she seemed to be shaking her head. 'Just let me get Juno and go. I knew this was a bad idea.' She had pushed past me, opened the door and was calling out to Juno.

'Evie, please stop.' I grabbed her arm. I hadn't meant to do it as firmly as I had. She stopped and looked at my hand, shrugged me off and then walked into the house. 'Juno!' she shouted again.

'They're in the garden,' I said behind her. She swung around and looked at me.

'Miranda. Just... Whatever it is you think you know about me, just stop, stop all this. Think about you and your own family. Believe me. It's not worth it,' she whispered with urgency. It sounded like a firm warning.

I narrowed my eyes at her. What had happened in such a short space of time to make her this way?

Juno appeared in the hallway, with Anabel behind her.

'Mum, can we have a drink?' Anabel asked.

'No,' I snapped. I saw the look on Anabel's face, confusion, and she looked crushed. Juno didn't appear fazed. 'I mean, sweetie,' I said more quietly. 'Juno has to go.'

Juno walked over to the door, picking up her school bag and water bottle. 'Bye, thank you for having me,' she said, and Anabel looked even more upset.

'Bye,' Evie muttered, and I closed the door behind her.

'I wanted Juno to stay for longer. Can she stay for longer next time? Can she come for a sleepover, Mummy?' I felt as though my head were about to explode. I could feel the frustration creeping through my body and seizing me.

'For goodness' sake, Anabel, would you give it a rest?' I walked past her as she remained frozen in the hallway, looking bewildered, and marched into the garden and stood in the middle of the lawn, my hands on my hips. I stretched backwards and looked up to the sky. So big and blue and vast. How had it all become so complicated?

42

BEFORE.

The girl's mother brought out a cake after dinner to celebrate being at the new house for one year. Her mother seemed happy now, the girl thought, and she was happy too. She had started at school, just two days a week for now. The rest of the time, she stayed at home with her mother, who didn't want her away too often. It was too much for her, she had said. Little baby steps. But the girl knew she didn't need to go to school, that one day she would be an actor like the ones she watched on TV. She practised all the time in her room when her mother was resting on the sofa. She had heard what the people said on those reality TV shows: *if you want something enough, it will come to you*. So that was what the girl was aiming for. She thought about it every day, and she was sure that one day, it would come to her.

She had allowed the year at this new house to settle her. Her mother had painted her room. They had even got a goldfish – won at the local fair a few months ago. Her mother had named her Claudia, and the girl was happy with that. Little knick-knacks had appeared here and there – things her mother had picked up from the local town – cushions, a magazine rack, a few books and some bookends, some new lamps and a pretty red rug. The mother seemed content. That was a word the girl had learnt at school recently and she liked the way it sounded. She had begun to like her room and the way the heating clinked through the pipes in the winter and the way they sang a low humming tune whenever they used the toilet. She had begun to recognise the smell of her own house when they came through the door. It wasn't too bad.

She still thought of Nora, but she was making a plan. When all this was over, when she and her mother finally got their forever home, she would try to find Nora and write to her. Maybe one day she could invite her to stay for the weekend, because that was what friends did with one another. The girl really wanted a friend for life, someone she could really rely on.

So it all came as a bit of shock when her mother told her one afternoon that things would be changing again. A little flutter of fear pelted through the little girl's tummy. She would continue to have those pangs for the rest of her life in uncertain circumstances. Sometimes, even when things were fine and she was perfectly safe, she was doomed to have them; only she did not yet know that.

The pang hit her stomach, and she let the wave of sadness wash over her. It wasn't so much the moving that had derailed her, just the uncertainty of not knowing where she was going, how long she would be there and if she would be happy.

'Can't you change things, Mum? Can't you make it different?' the girl asked.

'I wish I could, but things are completely out of my hands. This time, things will be even more different, so I need you to be really strong and brave. You might not like it at first – in fact, I know you will hate it. But in the long term, it will all make sense and you will be really happy.'

The girl looked at her mother and without thinking she said, 'But what about you, Mum? When do you get to be happy?'

'I don't know, my darling, but I hope it will be soon. I am putting your happiness before my own – you are the most important one of the two of us. I know one day, not long from now, things will be better. I just know they will.' And they put their arms around one another and stayed that way for a long while. Until it was time.

43

'David, Anabel wants you to read her a goodnight story.'

David was lying on the sofa, watching the TV.

'Why are you watching the news? You never watch the news,' I asked.

'Bedtime story, did you say?' David flicked off the television and sat up. 'How can I refuse that request?' He stood up and stretched. 'I was catching up on that Tate Jones story – it's made the major news channels now. Released, insufficient evidence apparently. Everyone is in uproar.'

I shook my head. Thoughts of Evie had been plaguing me all day and now David was speaking but it wasn't making any sense. 'What?' I snapped.

'Tate, the guy who used to live near us. Anyway, I don't know him, but I know *of* him.'

'The gangster?' I asked.

David walked past me and ruffled my hair like I was a child. 'That's the one. Good girl, you were listening.'

I pushed his hand away. 'Well, let's add that to another reason why we moved to the countryside.'

'Oh, he won't be going back to our neck of the woods. No, he'll be off somewhere, hiding. That's what these types do – very heavily protected. That's how he'll have got out in the first place. There's no way he was innocent of killing that man. That was no road rage incident.'

'Well, I'm glad you've taken such an avid interest in the local gangsters, but you might want to tone it down to *Diary of a Wimpy Kid* level for the next half an hour.'

'*Diary of a Wimpy Kid*? Yes! My favourite,' David said, sounding just like an eight-year-old kid himself. He did a funny little skip out of the lounge. I allowed myself a small smile, even though I was feeling utterly miserable. I had thought from the way Evie had smiled at me the other day that things would slowly start getting back to normal, but things had gone back to how they were, if not worse now that I had seen with my own eyes that it was Verity who had triggered the change in her behaviour. But there was nothing I could do except sit back and look on. And it was torture.

I was starting to feel uneasy, restless; a strange fear would creep through me at random moments of the day. I had been tired for days now, and was finding it hard to concentrate on little else, which was why I hadn't been running lately. Even though I was so tired I could have fallen asleep on the sofa in the dip where David had just been lying, I knew I needed to get myself out and move. I went upstairs, passing Anabel's room on the way where I could hear David doing his best voice for the characters in her book and occasionally Anabel's laughter. I pulled on my running gear, which felt like so much of an effort that I doubted I would even make it to the end of the road.

I left a note on the kitchen table – *Gone running* – which felt so old school when I could just text David, but I thought he could have his phone in his pocket, and I didn't want to disturb his storytelling time.

I did a warm-up in the driveway and then set off. A light jog to get myself back into the flow that I had slipped away from the last few weeks. It was silly of me, because I knew more than anyone that running or any form of exercise was the way out of the hole that I had put myself in with all the stress over Evie and Verity, but it was so very hard to climb out once you were in. I tried to remind myself that within half an hour, I would feel so much better. It was only just starting to get dark – I probably had another twenty minutes of good light, which was just enough for my workout.

I got myself into a stride, clicked my ear pods on and began running in time to the beat. I soon began to think of nothing other than moving forward and trying to make my feet hit the tarmac to the beat. I was well into my own world, and I hadn't even thought about the possibility of bumping into Evie at this time of night – she would be at home putting Juno to bed – so it was quite a shock when I ran around the corner, and almost collided with her.

'What the—' I pulled my earbud out. 'Evie?' I said, shocked that I hadn't prepared myself for this eventuality and also that she was here at all. 'What are you doing?' She was crying. No, she looked traumatised. 'Are you okay?'

Evie gulped back tears and looked at me, then she looked away up the street behind me. 'Have you seen her?'

'Who?' I said, looking around.

Evie looked the other way up the street. 'She was just here, I didn't think...'

She was rambling, but the only thing I could think of was that Juno was missing. 'Is it Juno?' I asked.

Evie nodded with her hand over her mouth, as though she didn't dare say it.

'Okay, why don't I go that way and you go the other and we'll meet in the middle. If we haven't found her, we call the police.'

Evie nodded and ran off past me. I began jogging again, back past my house, past the field, and then round the corner to Evie's house. The door was open as it always was in the daylight and I stepped into the hallway and called Juno's name. I ran upstairs to her bedroom, just in case she had come home and was hiding in her room, but there was no sign of her. Back downstairs, I looked outside into the small garden, but she wasn't there either. I ran back out of the house, pulling the door to behind me, and ran around the corner. I stopped dead in my tracks as I saw Verity and Juno outside Potter's Earth. I watched the two of them from a distance. I observed the strange way Verity was wringing her hands. Then I saw Juno place her hand on Verity's clenched fists, as though she were calming her, then the two of them disappeared into Verity's house without either of them seeing me on the corner.

I pulled my mobile out from my phone strap on my arm and called Evie.

She answered breathlessly after two rings.

'I have just seen her, Verity was taking her into her house.'

'Okay, thank you.'

'Do you want me to call the police, Evie?'

'No, don't be silly,' Evie said, suddenly sounding anything but the anxious mess she had been five minutes ago. 'Verity was probably about to ring me.'

'Oh, Evie,' I said, and as I did, she rounded the corner and we came face to face. I ended the call and looked at her.

'You really believe that?' I asked, dropping my phone to my side. Just then, Evie's phone rang. She looked down at it in her hand, then lifted the phone to show me Verity's name on the screen. She answered the call.

'Verity?' she said.

I shook my head in dismay.

'Great, she's with you. I'll see you in a sec.' Evie rang off. 'Look, Miranda, I'm sorry for alarming you and distracting you from your run. You know what it's like – when they disappear for a second, your heart is in your mouth.'

I knew that feeling. Anabel had wandered metres away from me on more than one occasion and it had utterly terrified me for those mere seconds she was out of my sight, every thought running through my head as I searched for her. But the look that had been on Evie's face before had been so much more than that; it had been pure dread and fear, as though that something terrible had already happened. Yet here she was now, standing in front of me as though everything was fine.

I let out a long sigh. 'I'm glad Juno has been found.'

'Thank you for stopping and helping. I'm sorry I startled you. We live in a safe village, and I should have known that there is always someone around to help. Verity must have been out walking and bumped into Juno.'

I hoped that was the case. I truly did. But somehow, I didn't believe any of it.

'Goodnight, Evie.' I walked on. Part of me wanted to stop and look back and watch Evie go into Verity's but I didn't. I needed to stop obsessing over them all now. Whatever weird thing they had going on between them, I was going to leave them to it.

I arrived home and bumped into David coming down the stairs.

'Oh, are you going for a run,' he said. Obviously, he hadn't seen my note.

'I've been.' I knew I didn't look very hot or sweaty and David may or may not have noticed, but he said nothing and so I went upstairs and took a shower.

* * *

'She's not coming,' Hatty said to me as I sat down in the lounge at Olivia's on book club the next night.

'That doesn't surprise me,' I said as I slipped my shoes off and dropped my handbag to the floor. Olivia appeared and handed me a glass of Prosecco. 'Oh wow! Thank you,' I said.

'I say, why not!' Olivia hooted and went off to answer the doorbell, which had just rung.

'She said she felt unwell. Juno was off today as well,' Hatty continued.

'Was she?' I said, surprised. Whatever had happened last night with Juno running off had spilled into today. But I tried not to consider why because I was trying not to make it any of my business.

'So just five of us tonight. I never thought Verity would come back, did you?' Hatty said.

'Oh no,' I said. 'I don't think I would have let her.' I chuckled, trying to make light of it, but knowing full well that woman was not welcome anywhere I was.

'How did you know Juno was off school?' I asked. Damn it, I *was* interested.

'Well, I had to take Bruno's hay fever medicine in and I saw the receptionist had written down Juno's name on the absent list. Perhaps they had a mummy-and-daughter day. I would absolutely do that if I had a daughter. My boys have never been interested in that sort of thing. They can't wait to get through those school gates and start causing havoc,' Hatty said. 'I say, Olivia, I am so looking forward to your birthday next week.' Hatty huddled up to Olivia and Olivia began filling her in on all the plans for the pub gathering.

Beth and Tash came through into the lounge, laughing. Tash brought with her a cloud of perfume. We all stood and greeted one another, then sat down and instantly started discussing the book. Amongst all the chatter, I looked around and felt Evie's absence desperately, but I pulled a smile onto my face, said something funny about one of the characters in the book and allowed their laughter to dissolve my thoughts.

44

Interview with David Wallace

We moved here for peace and quiet, you see, and well, it seems we brought some of the drama of the city life with us.

I had been worried about Miranda for some time, she won't mind me saying that. We've been married long enough that I know her inside out and upside down. She was really happy when we first moved here. I knew it was the right step.

Things had been... difficult for us, but we were over the worst of it. This was like a clean break. Miranda made some good friends – Hatty, Olivia and Evie. Evie was her main friend, her best friend, if you like. I was happy for her – I know how much Miranda values her friends. But earlier this year, things started to turn sour when Verity moved into town.

Miranda is such a sensitive thing really, she may come across quite confident, but she had to work at that. But she is really intuitive as well, and she knew that something wasn't right. She didn't tell me all of this originally, because, well, because of the Instagram thing that happened before when we lived in London. It affected her and lots of other people, and me, as well. So I think she was scared to talk to me about it. To be honest, the thought of going through something like that with Miranda again after the fresh start, I just couldn't. I think she knew that. So I was being a bit of a coward, I suppose, by not broaching the subject with her, you know, really making her talk. I guess it's a man thing. I hate to divide the sexes in such a way. It's such a cliché, isn't it, but it is true. I am a man and I don't like to overcomplicate things if I don't have to. I just hoped and presumed it would all blow over. What happened before was sad and unfortunate, but I thought there was no way something like that would ever happen again. Not here, in this small village. And of course, I was right about that. It didn't happen again. It was something so much worse, wasn't it? And I... her own husband... Excuse me, sorry... I couldn't even get my head out of my own arse to look into what was happening.

I nearly went out with her that night. I nearly did, but we couldn't get a babysitter – they were all at the pub as well. But to be honest, I was glad when I knew I would be the one to stay at home with Anabel. I didn't fancy the pub – Thursdays are always busy, and I was happy to just be at home on the sofa. I don't know, it all seems so surreal, so unbelievable. It's a male ego thing, I suppose. I wanted to be the one to rescue her. She shouldn't have had to go through that alone. I suppose I will have to just live with that for the rest of my life.

45

'Beth can't babysit. She's coming to the pub as well,' I called from the bedroom.

'Oh right,' David called back from our bathroom. I heard the relief in his voice.

'It's Olivia's birthday, so well, everyone will be going out. Sorry.' I waited for David's response. I knew he was glad he didn't have to come. When I had mentioned drinks for Olivia's birthday, his response was, 'On a Thursday night?' He was a bit of an old man in that respect. He liked his comforts. His idea of the pub was somewhere quiet, where he can hear himself talk. I'm the opposite, I love all that shouting over the bar to the staff and making yourself hoarse trying to have a conversation with your mates. I had wanted David to be there; Evie had been invited and I had been reliably informed that she had accepted, so I could have done with the moral support. I didn't want to feel awkward the whole evening. Of course, Hatty, Tash and Beth were going to be there, but it was Evie I felt – had felt – the most comfortable with.

'So you'll be okay on your own then?' I called. He appeared at the door to the bathroom.

'Of course. Don't worry about me. Go and have a good time.'

I looked at him for a moment. He wasn't doing a very good job of hiding how pleased he was that he'd have to stay in with Anabel. He had been banging on about a new crime series on Netflix, so no doubt he would be bingeing on that until the early hours.

'Okay. I will try. I can't promise I won't be rip-roaring drunk though.'

'Oh no, is it a night in the spare room for me then? The snoring, babes, I love you, but you and drunk snoring.'

'All right, all right. Don't go on. The spare room is made up,' I said.

'Right. Time for a quick steak and salad before you go?'

'Sounds fab.'

Because it was highly probable that I would drink several glasses of Prosecco and gin and tonic this evening, I made sure I ate plenty of the ciabatta bread with oil and balsamic vinegar that David had laid out on the table.

Then I slipped into my dress and heels, threw a pashmina around my shoulders and kissed David and Anabel goodnight.

I trotted over the road, round the corner and towards Hatty's, who lived just around the corner from the pub.

'I feel like a kid again, calling for my friend to come out to play.' I laughed as she closed the front door on the chaos and commotion.

'Ahh, silence,' she said.

'Shall we?' I held my arm out and Hatty slipped hers through it. We walked the hundred yards to the pub, where the punters were already spilling outside onto the benches.

Inside the front entrance, I scanned the room for any sign of Evie, but before I could look properly, Olivia had practically bundled us together.

'So glad you came!' The smell of her perfume was all over me.

'Oh,' I said, righting myself. 'Happy birthday!' I handed her a small paper bag; inside was a small online purchase from Oliver Bonas.

'Oh, darling Miranda. You shouldn't have,' she said, taking a sneaky peek.

'I absolutely should have.'

'You're right. I totally deserve it! Come, Jerry reserved us seats – I feel like a proper VIP!'

'As opposed to an OAP?' Hatty laughed, and Olivia slapped her arm.

'I have a few more years until I collect my pension, thank you very much.' Olivia took my hand and pulled me towards a small, raised area at the back of the pub with a few *Reserved* signs on the table.

'Blimey, Olivia, where's the bouncer?' Hatty laughed again.

'My goodness, you are full of comedy today. Where's my present?' Olivia said to Hatty.

Hatty pulled out an envelope from her handbag and handed it to the birthday girl. Olivia ripped it open and squealed. Hatty had told me she had booked her and Olivia into the exclusive spa just on the outskirts of the village.

As Hatty and Olivia embraced, I took a moment to look around the pub again. Jerry, the manager, was at the bar; he smiled and winked at me. He was a proper flirt, that one, but I didn't mind, it was all harmless enough. Plus it was nice to get that little bit of attention. It had been suffocating at times in the city, but here, I welcomed the compliments and small amount of attention.

I returned a smile to Jerry and then I saw Evie. She was walking over to us. Olivia and Hatty were still cooing over Olivia's gift, and everyone else was in the cordoned-off area, blocked in by Hatty and Olivia, leaving me at the front, the first person she came to.

'Hi,' I said, feeling my mouth get dry and my palms get sweaty.

'Hi,' Evie said, looking anywhere but at me.

'How's Juno?' I asked. It had been over a week since I had bumped into Evie the night Juno had run away from her.

'She's fine,' Evie said causally. Then she looked at me. 'She's really good.'

'Right, well I'm glad to hear it.' Our small talk would not convince anyone who happened to be listening in. 'Anyway, I need a drink,' and never had any word spoken been more true. I moved past Evie and heard the squeals of Olivia again as she greeted her. I rolled my eyes, wishing I had not made the effort to come out at all, but reminded myself I was here for Olivia, who was really basking in all the attention.

The bar was fairly busy, but after Jerry had finished with his customer, he came straight over to me.

'Hey, Miranda, how are you?' He had that cheeky grin on his face and I instantly felt better.

'I'm good thanks, Jerry.' And I did, for that moment.

'What will it be tonight?' he asked.

'Erm, I think, a glass… No, make it a bottle of Prosecco, for me, Hatty and the birthday girl. Three glasses, please.'

'Coming up.' He pulled out a bottle of Prosecco from the fridge and put it in an ice bucket. He handed me the glasses and gave me another wink before moving swiftly on to the next customer.

'It's on the tab,' he called back to me.

'Oh, okay. Great,' I said and went back over to Olivia's area. A few more people had arrived since I had been gone and also Olivia's husband, Jack, had appeared. He came down the step and stooped to give me a kiss – he was a tall man. We exchanged some pleasantries, mainly about how fabulous Olivia was, and then I took the Prosecco up to where Olivia was sitting. Her eyes widened when she saw me and the bubbles.

'Oh, Miranda, you're spoiling me – thank you for the necklace and earrings, such a thoughtful and tasteful gift. I am truly honoured to have you as a friend.' She squeezed my arm. 'I hope everything is okay between you and Evie, and things won't be too awkward tonight,' Olivia said more quietly. 'I do believe that Verity is her babysitter tonight, so maybe you and Evie might get a chance to have a chat, try and smooth things over.'

I hadn't spoken to anyone about exactly what had happened to make Evie so upset with me – I was still trying to work it all out myself – but it didn't surprise me that most people knew. I looked over to where Evie was sitting amongst everyone, looking the height of sociability. How could she appear so happy when everything was so wrong between us? I wanted to die, but she was carrying on as though nothing was happening.

I poured two glasses of the Prosecco and handed one to Olivia. Hatty was off using the ladies. Olivia and I clinked glasses.

'Happy birthday,' I said. I looked past Olivia and saw Evie looking at me. She wasn't smiling, just staring, so I looked away and took a long drink of the Prosecco.

* * *

Within an hour, I was savouring the sweet sensation of three glasses of Prosecco in my system. I was a hardy drinker, having grown up in a house overflowing with alcohol. My parents would buy far too much in for the dinner parties and there was always so much leftover the next day. I was seven years old when I first tasted wine. It was a sweet dessert wine left over from one of Mum and Dad's gatherings the night before. I took one small sip. I couldn't say I enjoyed it, but there was something quite special about the taste, and that was the beginning of my relationship with alcohol.

As I looked around at the pub getting busier, I knew I was ready to move on to a spirit – I couldn't keep drinking Prosecco all night, it would make me too gassy. There was talk of shots. I declined. That was one thing I couldn't handle. It would only take one or two and I'd be so drunk that I wouldn't know what I was doing.

Jerry brushed past me, collecting glasses.

'Did the Prosecco go down well?' he called over the music as he leant in towards me.

'Too well!' I called back, and he grinned at me.

Some of the party were dancing – Jerry had the music turned right up. Hatty had been first up. She seemed to have an abundance of energy. The alcohol was doing its job and numbing some of my emotions. I didn't feel as anxious as I had been when I first arrived. I considered going over to Evie in our little cordoned-off area and starting a chat. But even in my inebriated state, I knew that there was only so much rejection I could handle.

Through the hazy film the alcohol had produced, I was sure I had just seen a woman who looked exactly like Betty arrive though the door, but the couple of glasses of Prosecco I had drunk so quickly must have tainted my vision. Why would Betty be here in the pub? The figure grew closer. As she did, Betty's face came into full focus.

'What the hell are you doing here?' I took a step towards her, unable to work out why or how she was here in this context.

'Well, that's a nice way to welcome your old friend.' Betty pulled me into a full, firm embrace.

I pushed my way out of her grip. 'Seriously, Betty, why are you here?'

'I came to see you. I went along last minute to this conference in Gloucester, an Instagram thing. Truth be told, I was sat there amongst all the influencers and all I could think of was how lovely your life was here. I have to say, Miranda, I am a little jealous of you right now. You did the right thing, getting away from it all.'

'But how did you know I was here?' We started to navigate our way through the crowd to the bar.

'Your phone, silly. You posted a picture an hour ago of a bottle of Prosecco. It told me exactly where you were. I thought, well, I'm in the area – I'll drive and see you. There's an Instagram brunch thing tomorrow, you should come too!'

Of course, I had just posted a photo. It had become second nature to me, almost like I had done it almost unconsciously. I was surprised by how quickly I had been able to fall back into the swing of social media. I hadn't neglected my child or fallen prey to any trolls. I was doing well.

We ordered gins and tonics and propped ourselves up at the bar.

'So, you'll come, to the Insta brunch tomorrow?' Betty clinked my glass.

'Wow, yes, I mean, who will be there?' I sipped my drink, knowing what I had really wanted to ask was, will all the women I slagged off on the troll site be there?

'The usual suspects, but you know what, Miranda, I know what you're thinking, and people have moved on – it's been over a year. That's like seven years in the Insta world.' She laughed and I smiled. 'I mean, they barely even remember the details, which is great, right? It was horrible for all of us.'

I took another long sip of gin and let her words sink in.

'How was it horrible for you, Betty?'

Betty cleared her throat and tried to look nonchalant, but I could see beneath her veil for the first time. She looked uncomfortable.

'Oh, you know, I had no idea that woman was a reporter when I started talking to her at that event not long after you were exposed on the site. You knew that, right?' She looked at me for second then back at the bar. 'I look back at it and see how I had allowed myself to get just as caught up in it as you. How naïve we were. It was an awful time, for all of us. I'm just so glad it's behind us now. Everyone is. That's what I mean when I say people have moved on. They really don't want to dwell on the past. They all – we all – have a job to do.' Betty took a long drink and glanced apprehensively around the pub.

I shook my head. The alcohol hadn't completely knocked me sideways yet, but Betty's comments had. She spoke as though it were all just a bit of a misunderstanding, when it was she who had added fuel to the fire – and worse – that we had both suffered together. I'd had my suspicions at the time, because Betty had made many references to my rapidly growing status and followers. I had thought that odd at the time. But I had never thought she would see us as competition. We were a family. That was what she told me time and time again; we were all there to help one another's accounts grow and flourish. But it was clear to me now that Betty had seen me as a threat and so when I showed I was weak with the troll sites, she had used that opportunity to expose to me to as many people as possible, including a journalist.

'I'm sorry, what? It was you? You who brought that tsunami of hatred my way by spreading the news that poor Miranda had lost the plot.' My voice had gone up in volume considerably as I remembered the headline on the internet. Jerry who was wiping the bar just a few metres away, looked our way for a second.

Betty swung around on her stool and glared at me. 'Hold on a sec, Miranda. It was me who got you out of that shit show – I went around and explained to everyone afterwards what a misunderstanding it was, and it was me who inspired you to get back on the grid and I believe you are well into your thousands on the followers again. Plus, I am inviting you to this brunch tomorrow, which will be filled with all the people you need to know to get yourself right back up there again.'

I shook my head in complete disbelief. 'How could I have been so bloody stupid?' I scraped my stool backwards. This time, Jerry looked more concerned. I shook my head at him to indicate I was fine. 'It was you who fuelled the fire. Yes, it was me who made the silly mistake in the first place, but you, you were supposed to be my friend, my mentor, but you were always jealous of me. You've even admitted it again now. That's why you're here, isn't it? To try and coax me from my cosy nest, where I am finally starting to feel connected, where I am worth something to my community and my own family, and you just want to see me mess it all up again. Pure bloody schadenfreude.' I tipped my drink back in one. 'I think you need to go, Betty. This is my village. Run back to your Insta family. I am staying here, where I am finally making a real life for myself.'

Betty threw her own drink down her throat. 'There was a point when I thought you might become interesting, but you really are just very, very boring,' she snarled, and slammed her glass down, picked up her bag and strode out of the pub.

I instantly grabbed the attention of one of the bar staff and ordered myself another gin and tonic. What the hell had just happened? I felt as though my heart might pump straight out of my chest. I had no one I could process it with, so I would have to sit there at the bar until I had calmed enough to go back to the party.

I looked over to the group and I could see that Jerry had brought over a platter of food, which suddenly looked very appetising, even though I had eaten the huge steak and salad before I came out. I edged my way over to what had now become a buffet table and picked up a prawn in a light, almost translucent batter and dipped it in some sweet chilli sauce. I chewed with intention, staring into oblivion, Betty's words swimming through my mind.

* * *

Eventually, I began chatting with Olivia's sister, who had flown in from Scotland to be with Olivia this weekend. She was telling me a funny anecdote about when she and Olivia were small, when I noticed Evie pressing her phone to one ear and blocking her other ear with her finger. She was trying to block out more external noise by moving her head towards her legs. Then she stood up, shoved the phone in her handbag, went past me, out of the VIP area and through the front door. Without thinking too much about it, I knew I needed to follow her, so I quickly excused myself and walked out of the pub. There were a few smokers sat outside on benches, making the most of the warm evening air and the light, but I couldn't see Evie anywhere. I moved around the side of the building until I was almost at the bins. Then I heard a male voice.

'I've told you, you have absolutely nothing to worry about. I have spoken to all the relevant departments. I have checked and double checked, contacted everyone I know who is in the know and the chances are slim. Very slim.'

I dared to move my head an inch so I could peer around the corner. There was Evie talking to who looked like the same guy she had been arguing and shouting with outside her house that night I came to return her phone to her. Graham, I think she had called him.

'Slim, but not entirely impossible,' Evie said in a staged whisper.

'Evie, nothing is impossible, is it? I can only do as much as I can. Which, believe me, is more than you will ever realise.'

'I just want to know, that's all. I can't stand all this waiting, not bloody knowing. I came out tonight to relax. I feel so on edge.'

'Well, like I say, I've covered everything. Just enjoy your evening. Go back to the pub, try to relax. I'm heading back now.'

'Tonight?'

'Yes.'

'But, can't you stay? Just tonight?' Evie whispered, and there was suddenly a softer, needier tone to her voice.

I edged forward another inch, so I could see what was happening. Graham moved forward and took Evie's hands in his. She looked up at him as though in anticipation.

'I can't, Evie. I want to, so badly. But you know we can't. Not yet. I have to do what I have to do first and then, when things are different, better, then.'

'I feel so safe when you're around.' I thought I heard Evie say, but it was hard to tell as she had muttered it. From behind me came a loud wail and mass laughter as a group of people spilled out of the front door. I took two steps back, then turned and headed back into the pub. I couldn't let Evie see me spying on her.

The change in atmosphere hit me as I walked through the door. The heat mixed with the smells of people and the loud music. I was so buzzing with thoughts of what I had just witnessed, it almost washed away the echo of the harsh words I had spat at Betty before she had left. Before, I had presumed Graham was Juno's father, but now it seemed he was a boyfriend, maybe? Definitely someone close to her, someone she spent a lot of time with. Someone she wanted to be closer to, but for whatever reason, they couldn't be. It was so frustrating because I desperately wanted to know what was going on in her world. We had been so close once, and these were the sort of things we should be discussing now. I could help her, be her confidant. But she had pushed me away.

A sudden rush of anger rose through me as I headed back to the bar. I could see Jerry eyeing me, as he was with another customer, but one of his staff got to me first. I ordered a double vodka lime and lemonade, and as I was walking back to our party, Evie came back through the front door. Our eyes met for a second and then she went back to where she had been sitting, right in the middle of the party guests.

I had been trying to play down the relationship between Evie and Verity as I had been so fixated on Verity's aloofness, but now it was clearer to me than ever before that there was some correlation between Evie's change in behaviour and Verity's arrival. I no longer felt completely rejected, I could see beyond my own needs and emotions, and all I wanted was for Evie to open up, to unburden herself, and tell me what was going on in her life and reveal the secrets she seemed to be harbouring so resentfully.

I still had Hatty and Olivia and even Tash and Beth, but it was Evie who I wanted back, problems and all. I wanted to weather the storm with her.

I took a long drink of the vodka and felt the strength of it warm through me. Hatty waved me over to join her, and so I did. But I quickly became restless; the conversations weren't going anywhere. If I was talking to Evie, I knew we would be having the time of our lives. Under normal circumstances.

I slipped away from the group and headed to the bar. For my third spirit. I would make it my last. One for the road. This party wasn't doing anything for me. Jerry served me this time.

'How's the party going?'

'It's going,' I said.

He looked at me with a bemused expression.

'I mean, yes, it's fine. It's good.'

'Okay. Here's the vodka. Nice combo that. Enjoy.' He walked away to serve another customer. I pulled myself onto a bar stool and found that it was quite comfortable. I could keep an eye on the party, but also see everything that was happening around the pub.

I took a long drink and found, yet again, it was going down very well. I looked over at Evie. She was surrounded by Hatty and Olivia and Beth, who had now arrived, and there was Conner – one of them never seemed to be without the other these days. I felt that pang shoot through me. What was that? Was it pure anger, frustration? Jealousy? I did not know. I pulled my phone out of my handbag. There was a message from David.

Hope you're having a lovely night. I'm shattered. I might be asleep when you get back. X

It was coming up for ten o'clock. I drank down the rest of the vodka and placed it on the bar. I swung myself back round on the stool, so I was facing outwards towards the party. Olivia was having a great time by the looks of things. There was Evie in the middle of them all still, laughing. Actually laughing. I felt the anger rising through me. I watched Evie, the way her whole mouth opened so wide as she laughed and she threw her head back. Why did she get to be so happy and I got to sit on the sidelines? It was never meant to be like this. It was all Verity's fault. All her fault. Why did she get to waltz into this village and turn Evie into someone I barely recognised? I could hear Evie's laugh from where I was sitting. I looked to the bar. It was still so busy. My head was woozy; everything around me felt soft, like a big fluffy cloud. I thought about the prospect of falling off the stool and how it probably wouldn't hurt initially, but come tomorrow, there would be bruises and pain.

I could hear Evie's laugh. I could still see Betty's face, her mouth forming the word *boring*. Then her face morphed into Verity's face. Evie's laugh penetrated the room.

Verity. The very name made me want to spit it out of my mouth as though it were poison.

Verity.

Verity.

Verity, who would be all alone at Evie's. Juno would be fast asleep now. I could walk over there. I knew where Evie kept the spare key. I could let myself in and speak to her. Have it out, as they say in the soap operas. If Evie refused to tell me what the hell was going on, then I would go straight to the source. I realised I was already standing up and walking towards the door. The decision had been made. I took one final glance towards the party, heard the loud laugh of Evie reverberating around the room, and then left the pub.

46

'You will be fine here, okay?' the mother said to the girl. The girl looked doubtfully at her mother. Why would she leave her here? Alone. Well, she wasn't alone – there was that woman standing in the corner, but the girl thought she had a silly smile on her face.

'I am going to go and sort everything out, and then I will come back and make everything right for us. We will be happy together one day. Just not today. Or tomorrow. Or for a little while.'

'But you'll come back?'

'I will,' her mother said. And the girl thought of all the other promises her mother had made and then broken. Should she trust her this time?

The mother kissed her and then she left.

Days went by, weeks came and went. And eventually months. But she didn't come back like she had promised. Occasionally, the other woman would take her somewhere to see her mother for an hour or two, then they would come home. For that was what she had started to call it now.

Then one day, her mother came back. 'I live here now,' her mother said to her. 'But you will stay living here, and I will live in that house, just behind you.' Her mother pointed out of the kitchen window. 'Imagine it as though you have two people who both love you very much, one on each side, giving you a very big hug, always protecting you. Always watching out for you.'

47

All the lights were off at Evie's house. Perhaps Verity had gone to bed. Maybe she slept there some nights. Or maybe – I hadn't considered it before now – Juno was sleeping at Verity's house.

I walked around the side of the house. I couldn't see a thing. Was it usually this dark? Then I realised the security light hadn't come on. I took my phone out and put the torch on. I shone the light along the side of the house and towards the garden. Along the wall, it lit up the kitchen window. I gasped – one of the panes was out. That was unlike Evie to let something like that happen and leave it. She usually brought someone in or dealt with herself – even though she was renting, she never bothered the landlords. That was the sort of person Evie was. Caring, considerate. Yes, I thought, of course she was kind and considerate, that was who Evie was. She wasn't the sort of person to just dismiss someone the way she had done to me. It wasn't her who was doing this, it was Verity. My instincts had been right about her all long. She was the wrong one. I navigated my way back to the front of the house with only the light from my phone. I used my phone to look for the fake rock that had a compartment in the bottom that held the spare front-door key. I took it out, replaced the rock and went to put the key in the door. The last double vodka had hit me now, and I was shocked at how inept I had suddenly become as I tried to get the key to stay in a straight line and into the tiny gap. Eventually, it clicked in and I turned the lock. The door opened, and I stumbled into the hallway. It was dark and painfully quiet. There was whooshing in my ears as I tried to listen out for anything; anyone.

I closed the door quietly behind me. Juno would be well and truly asleep now; even though I knew she was a late sleeper, it was gone ten o'clock. I wondered if Evie might make a sudden appearance, decide she'd had enough. But when I had left; she didn't look ready to go anywhere. In a way, the drunk me wished that Evie would show up, so I could make my speech to both. But it was Verity I had come to see.

I could sense life in the house. That feeling as though someone had just arrived or just left. There was some sort of energy lingering in the air. I popped the key in my jeans pocket and walked through the hallway to the kitchen directly ahead of me, still using my phone for the light. The lights were all off, although I could smell the remnants of a dinner. There were a few used plates on the side, alongside an open bag of marshmallows and two candles and a bag of kebab sticks. I walked around to the other side of the kitchen and let out a small wail as my leg slipped beneath me. I looked down and could just about see a mass of something on the floor. I pointed my phone light downwards and saw there was a big puddle of orange juice, and an overturned carton on the kitchen side. Who goes to bed and leaves that kind of mess everywhere?

I took one last look around the kitchen. The almost-fall had somehow sobered me up a little. What was I doing? What was I thinking walking into Evie's house? There was no way I would have done something like this sober. I put my phone away in my pocket as my eyes were beginning to adjust to the dark. A little panicky feeling began to flutter in my chest. This was a bad idea. It was time to go. I would go home, be with David. He had gone to bed. That was where I should be, then I would have half a chance at a fresh head for taking Anabel to school tomorrow.

I turned and walked out of the kitchen, heading for the door. I hadn't meant to detour, to look anywhere else. I had set my sights on leaving. But something made me turn before I reached the front door. The lounge door on my left was open. I had sensed an energy as I walked past when I came in, as though there was someone there, or perhaps had been. I stopped and looked through the dark. Then, just like one of those magic drawings where you suddenly see the other picture within the picture, two pairs of eyes, low down on the floor, emerged before me. I couldn't make out why, then I remembered that was where the sofa was. A stylish blue one with tall legs, meaning there was quite a gap underneath it. I couldn't see the sofa; I could just about make out the outline. But the eyes, two pairs of them were looking at me from underneath and after a few moments of staring, and my eyes adjusting to the dark, two faces started to appear. The face of a small child. Juno. And next to her, Verity.

48

I stumbled backwards. My efforts to concentrate had made my head spin. Were they playing some strange game of hide-and-seek, in the dark at night-time? All sorts of possibilities were flying through my head. But it was disturbing how wide both of their eyes were. Verity's especially as they both looked out at me. Neither of them spoke, but as I began to edge forward, I could see that Verity looked as though she wanted to say something to me. I bent down so I was almost at the level that Verity was. It was Verity, wasn't it? My mind wasn't playing tricks on me? I had drunk quite a lot in a short space of time.

I stuck my neck out so I could peer closer. Verity was mouthing something to me, but I couldn't make it out in the darkness.

'What?' I half whispered. If it was a game, I found I was instinctually playing along. 'What are you saying?' The darkness and the quiet made me feel I needed to keep up the whispering charade.

Verity mouthed the words again. I looked to my left, to where Juno was. I needed to get a better look at her, to make sure she was okay.

'Juno, sweetie, it's Miranda. Are you okay?' I whispered. Juno said nothing. Okay, this wasn't right. All my instincts fell in line with one another. I needed to intervene. Verity had been getting away with this for far too long, as far as I was concerned. Whatever weird game she was trying to inflict upon poor Juno at this time of night was about to come to an end. I moved forward, this time on my knees. I reached out my hand.

'Come on, Juno, come out, I've got you.' I reached out my hand even further, then I saw Juno's hand creep out to meet mine.

'Miranda, no!' came Verity's voice, so loudly and suddenly it all seemed so wrong and out of sync with the situation.

Instinctually, I looked behind me. My reflexes were quite slow due to the drink, but my eyes tried to focus on a dark figure looming behind me. Then everything went black.

49

Interview with Evie Pollard

I wished things had been different. That's what I wish. But it was a very tricky situation, and certainly not one I could explain to just anyone. Let alone someone like Miranda. She was so... insistent. She was always the sort of woman who wasn't going to take no for an answer, that was why I had to break it off with her in the end. She was getting too close. She would have revealed it all. She would have exposed us. I had to do it. I had no choice.

She left me with no choice.

50

My head. My head. That was all I could think. Had I hit it? Had I fallen? Had I drunk so much I had passed out and this was the hangover from hell? I opened my eyes, but everything was dark. I remembered where I was and why. I was in Evie's house. All the lights had been off, and they still were. I needed to get up, I was trying to help Juno. Time to get up. I had obviously fallen. But when I tried to move, I couldn't. My legs wouldn't move. And my arms. They were stuck. I looked down and tried to feel with one of my shoes. Where were my shoes? My feet were bare. I tried to feel around with my feet to see where I was. I was certain I was in Evie's lounge. Yes, that was where I had been when... There had been someone behind me. I wanted to reach up and touch my head, but my hands were bound.

'Miranda,' a wobbly voice came at me. I looked around. I could see no one.

'Miranda.' The voice again. 'It's me, Verity. Don't scream or they'll hurt Juno.'

'What?' I said. I was hearing things. Imagining it. This couldn't be happening. That wasn't Verity. She sounded different. I couldn't see her. I tried to work out where I was in relation to when I first arrived in the lounge. The sofa had been on the right and that was where Verity's voice was coming from now, which meant I was on the floor next to the sofa I had sat on when I last came to see Evie.

'You must keep quiet. If we scream, they will hurt Juno. Do you understand? Please don't try anything. Just stay very still.'

'What? Verity, is that you? Can you stop pissing around and get me untied, please? Everyone will be wondering where I am.'

'Miranda, I'm serious,' Verity hissed. 'You have to trust me.'

'Trust you?' I said.

'Shh. Please, Miranda.'

Was that? Was Verity... crying?

'Are you crying?' All I heard were snorts and sniffles.

'No. No, I'm not,' Verity said quickly.

'Can you just tell whoever is doing this, to stop it right now? My husband will be here any minute. Everyone at the pub knew I was coming here – Evie will be here in a minute.'

'Miranda, there's no point speaking. I know you came alone. You wouldn't have told your husband or anyone what you were doing here tonight.' Verity was sobbing. I felt my blood run cold. This no longer felt like a joke. This was something, and it was serious.

'Where is Juno?' I asked.

'She's... she's here. We were told to be quiet and wait. That's what they said.'

'They? Verity, who are they?'

'The damn people I have been trying to hide from for five years. They have found us, Miranda. They have found us.' Verity wept. 'Me and my daughter. Me and Juno.'

51

Everything I thought I had known about Verity had now been replaced with something completely new and alien and I was still trying to get my head around it from the snippets of information Verity was able to coherently give me. But most importantly I now knew everything that Evie hadn't been able to tell me all this time. Verity was Juno's mother. It was hard to process it because all I could think about was that we were here, trapped, the three of us. Verity told me she and Juno were bound. She spoke in hurried whispers, not able to finish a sentence.

'There's been a hold-up... An interception. Someone must be on to them... I don't know for sure. Please pray for us, pray we will be okay,' Verity whispered.

'Mummy,' I heard Juno whisper for the first time.

'It's okay, it's okay,' Verity whispered.

I cleared my throat. 'Verity,' I whispered. It was the first time I had ever had to reassure her, but then it was the first time I'd ever seen her vulnerable, for that matter. Was this the Verity that had been hiding behind a veil of lies all this time? Just an ordinary woman. A mother. A terrified mother, trying to protect her child? 'We'll be okay,' I said quietly. 'It's all going to be okay.'

Verity let out a sob, then I heard her trying to control her breathing.

I didn't know what to say. I had been stupid, ignorant. But now I was a part of this. I had judged Verity on what I thought I knew about her. But none of it had been right. I knew more than anyone that making those sorts of judgements before knowing all the facts about someone was very wrong. Whatever this was. Now was not the time to dwell on what had been, I just needed to pray to someone that I would come out of this alive. I thought of my time in the church on Mother's Day. I had gone for the flowers and the chocolate, but now I began chanting quietly and slowly to myself. 'Please, keep me safe, for my daughter's sake.' I didn't know if I was praying to a god, it just felt like the right thing to do. 'I went to the church on Mother's Day because I had run out of ways to help my daughter. I knew they would be onto us when I read about Tate getting out of prison. I'm not a religious person, but I think now is as good a time as any to pray.' Verity lost control of her voice on the last word.

She let out a loud sob and my heart wrenched for her, for Juno. For Anabel.

There was nothing else to say.

At least, I thought, it was dark. If I was going to go, I would want it to be in the dark.

And I couldn't see Verity.

All we could do was wait. The anticipation was enough to almost end me as my heart thumped hard and fast against my ribcage. Should I say something else to Verity? Let her know I was wrong, that I was sorry. My head tilted to one side, and I felt a solo tear slip down my cheek. I closed my eyes, listening to the muffled sounds of Verity and Juno shuffling under the sofa, Juno's tiny voice trying to comfort her mother. Verity's sobs.

Suddenly, a loud crash. The front door, kicked open? This was it.

Then a lot of shouting, and two gunshots.

Verity screamed, hysterical screams that didn't stop but echoed all around the room, so loudly I thought, it can only be me. I had been shot.

52

I felt hands on mine, a voice talking to me, but my heart was racing so fast I was sure this was what hyperventilating was. Verity had stopped screaming, but she was sobbing and muttering. The room was still dark. My legs were being untied. I was lifted from the floor and carried outside to the driveway.

It was bright outside, brighter than it had been when I arrived here. Was it morning? But as I opened my eyes just enough to see, there were two cars parked, and their headlights illuminated the gravel.

Someone placed a blanket around me and then Juno was in my arms.

I looked around for Verity. Where was she? Then the sound of sirens. So many of them, echoing loudly through the usually so silent village. Then a voice telling me it was all okay. I was safe, everyone was safe. I turned as I saw someone coming out of the door. It was the man, Graham, the man that Evie had been talking to tonight and before arguing in this very driveway. He was carrying Verity.

'Mummy!' Juno jumped from my lap and ran towards Graham, who was placing Verity on the ground. Verity was wringing her hands, her mouth wobbling as she tried to hold back the tears for the sake of her daughter. Juno carefully wrapped herself in her mother's arms. It occurred to me right then, that I had never actually heard Juno call Evie *Mummy*. Not once. I remembered hearing her call out *Mummy* the day I dropped her home.

We had walked through the hallway with Anabel in tow, only to discover that Verity was in the lounge with Evie. She must have been speaking to her real mum.

Watching the mother and daughter embrace now, my heart panged for my own family.

53

Dear Anabel,

A lot has happened over the last few days, and some of it may be very difficult to understand. Mum thought it best if I wrote this letter to you so you had it all written down. Me and my mum are in Norfolk for a few weeks. We have been given a big house here by the beach to help us recover and be close to one another again.

There is so much to tell you, so I will start at the beginning.

My real name is Rachel. I am ten years old. I have been living with Evie, who is a friend of my grandparents. Everyone knows me as Juno. Five years ago, my dad was killed by a man who worked for Tate Jones. Tate Jones is a not a nice man – he is what is called a gangster. My dad was killed because he had been doing some business with Tate and things went wrong between them. The police said it was a road-rage killing and Tate went to prison. But then he got released early because they didn't believe he had done anything wrong after all. My mum had been in the car with my dad when it happened, and ever since then, my mum and I have been under police protection, because the man who killed my dad said they were coming for her and me too. Mum was so scared and terrified that she hid me in a beach hut after it had happened. A kind lady found me, but soon I got to be with my mum again. We had to move around a lot because the police were worried that the bad guys might find us. And then I moved here so I could be super safe, and Mum moved here a little bit afterwards because she missed me so much. I never got to make any real friends. Except when I came to stay with Evie. Sometimes, my mum would get very upset and run down and would sit looking at her phone all day instead of playing with me, but I understood why. When I came to live with Evie, I wanted to go back to my mum straight away, but then I got to go to school and I made friends, like you, Anabel. I went into the class below what I should have been in, so I could catch up, but also it was part of the plan to keep me safe. I had to pretend that I was younger than I really was. I didn't mind lying, because my mum said it wasn't really lying, it was just acting and that was okay. It was a just a bit tricky, but you were always super kind and understanding.

Mum missed me so much that she decided to go against what the police told her to do and she came to live in the village. But we all had to keep pretending for a little bit longer. Everyone was really worried that Tate Jones was going to be let out of prison and come and find us, and then he did. Mum and Evie had to go and have an emergency meeting that day I came to stay with you and your mum and I fell in that cowpat that absolutely stunk. Miranda – your mum – is really nice. She was Evie's best friend when she moved to the village, but my mum said that Evie should probably not have had such a close relationship with her because Miranda did a lot of stuff on social media and she put a photo of me on her Instagram account. And when you do that, it means lots of people can see you, and I was supposed to be in hiding. Your mum didn't mean to do any harm, she was just doing her job, but Mum was really freaking out in case someone recognised me and they traced the photo to the village.

The best bit to come out of this situation has been living in this village. I would never have come to Helesbury if I wasn't in hiding. And now I get to stay. I will officially move into Potter's Earth with my mum. But now Tate and his accomplice are in prison – for good, this time – it means me and Mum are really safe now. And I still get to see Evie and you and your mum and all my other school friends. They all like calling *me Juno, so they will still call me that. Would you still like to call me that? Mum asked me what I would really like to do, now we are truly safe, and I said I'd like to go and find Nora. She lived on one the streets we lived in. Mum remembers which one and is going to have a letter sent to her house. I wonder if she will come and stay. I hope you like her too – I want all three of us to be best friends.*

54

The doorbell rang and I had to stop myself from running to answer it. Anabel was there before me, and she swung the door open and pulled Juno through the threshold and into a firm embrace. They began laughing straight away, as if four weeks hadn't passed by without them seeing one another. Evie moved past Juno and Anabel, and we embraced for what felt like a long time. It was needed. Evie had been away too, staying with her mum in France. She looked vibrant, her face was relaxed and she was hugging me in a way that meant everything was back on track again.

It had been a stressful month whilst we all gave statements to the police and Verity, Juno and Evie went away to recuperate. It had given me time to reflect on everything too. David had been on a better track than I had been with his fascination with the very man who sent those two guys to Evie's house to... Well, to do whatever they might have done to Juno and Verity. It was Graham, who was part of the police protection scheme, who had been in the village that night and who'd had a hunch something wasn't right. He and Evie had become close since he came to the team, but they couldn't cement their relationship whilst he was doing his job. Evie had tried to get him to stick around that night, but he was trying to remain professional.

Once he left the village, he saw who he thought to be one of Jones' crew, at a petrol station about thirty miles outside Helesbury. He thought it was too coincidental. They tracked the vehicle and by the time Graham and his crew had got the go-ahead, I was already on my way to Evie's. I almost messed things up for them – me and my stupid drunken decisions.

I felt it in Evie's hug that I had my friend back again, and I now understood that she had tried to push me away for my own safety, and for Juno's too. Things began to get scary for them once Tate had been released from prison. I had no idea the pressure they were all under. I was looking forward to getting to know Verity too. I could see how much pain she had been in, how much she had been hiding herself in order to protect her daughter. I could cry whenever I thought about it, because I too was in pain. I had been hiding so much about myself from Evie and Verity, but Verity had been hiding everything about who she really was and had been for five years. She was taking it easy since she had come back from Norfolk. She had declined my invitation here today but promised to come another day.

Evie and I released one another and we laughed as we clutched each other's hands. A figure moved in the doorway, and Evie let go of my hand.

'Come in, come in,' I said.

Evie ushered in a small girl, about Anabel's height and stature.

Juno moved away from Anabel and took the girl's hand.

'Anabel, I want you to meet my friend. Anabel, this is Nora. Nora, this is Anabel.'

Anabel looked up at me, a flicker of uncertainty. And was that jealousy across her face? I nodded firmly at her. 'It's okay, sweetie,' I said as Anabel tentatively stepped forward and lifted her hand to wave at Nora. Because I knew it would be from now on.

ACKNOWLEDGMENTS

Thanks to all you wonderful readers for supporting me by buying my books. It means the world because I love to write.

Once again thank you to all of the Boldwood team for being such a brilliant Publisher and congratulations on achieving such massive success in such a short time.

Thank you to Claire Fenby who does a fabulous job with marketing.

Thank you Nia Beynon for always being there at the end of an email.

A big shout out to all the Boldwood authors for their continued support on the forums and next year is definitely the year we will finally all meet in person.

A heartfelt thank you to Emily Ruston on this, our first full project together. Here's to many more. Your input is highly valued.

Rebecca Millar, I feel proud to be one of the authors you work with. Thank you for all your suggestions and your eagle eye.

Finally, a shout out to my wonderful family who have supported no end through this writing process which happened during a big move from Dorset to the Oxfordshire border. I am looking forward to seeing what inspiration the countryside brings for my next book.

BOOK CLUB QUESTIONS

1. Do you think there is a tendency for tensions to develop between residents in small villages? And is this something you have ever experienced before?
2. Can you put yourself in Miranda's shoes when she sees and meets Verity for the first time at the book club that she launched?
3. How does Miranda's life compare now to how it was when she was living in London and making a living through social media? What struggles is she facing to fit in?
4. In what ways are Miranda and Verity similar in the end?
5. How does Miranda's own upbringing and what she observed through her own parents' behaviour affect her in the present day?
6. In what ways did Evie try and protect Miranda from everything that was going on?
7. How easy do you think it is to get affected by the comments people make on social media accounts and do you think hatred forums should be banned?
8. Who was your favourite character and why?
9. What surprised you most about the novel?

MORE FROM NINA MANNING

We hope you enjoyed reading *Queen Bee*. If you did, please leave a review.

If you'd like to gift a copy, this book is also available as an ebook, digital audio download and audiobook CD.

Sign up to Nina Manning's mailing list for news, competitions and updates on future books.

http://bit.ly/NinaManningNewsletter

Explore more gripping psychological thrillers from Nina Manning.

ABOUT THE AUTHOR

Nina Manning studied psychology and was a restaurant-owner and private chef (including to members of the royal family). She is the founder and co-host of Sniffing The Pages, a book review podcast.

Visit Nina's website:
https://www.ninamanningauthor.com/

Follow Nina on social media:

 twitter.com/ninamanning78

 instagram.com/ninamanning_author

facebook.com/ninamanningauthor1

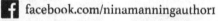 bookbub.com/authors/nina-manning

ABOUT BOLDWOOD BOOKS

Boldwood Books is a fiction publishing company seeking out the best stories from around the world.

Find out more at www.boldwoodbooks.com

Sign up to the Book and Tonic newsletter for news, offers and competitions from Boldwood Books!

http://www.bit.ly/bookandtonic

We'd love to hear from you, follow us on social media:

facebook.com/BookandTonic

twitter.com/BoldwoodBooks

instagram.com/BookandTonic

Ingram Content Group UK Ltd.
Milton Keynes UK
UKHW011507260623
424052UK00002B/10